"Lilly." He gaspe

She tightened her ~~legs around his waist.~~ "No."

"Lilly," he said again, burying his forehead under her chin. "Not here. Not now." He was but a hair's breadth from coming completely undone.

As a hint of sanity began to niggle its way back into Lilly's passion-clouded thoughts, she dropped her legs from around his waist.

They sat quietly, holding each other as their breathing slowed. Michael turned his head and pressed his ear against her chest. The beat of her heart squeezed at his own.

"I will speak to your father." He finally found his voice. "When will he arrive in London? If not soon, then I will journey to Plymouth myself."

"He should be here when we return from your house party." There was a smile in her voice. She was everything he ever wanted.

Remembering he was leaving tomorrow, he pulled her closer once again.

"I wish I could go with you." It was as though she read his mind.

Michael laughed and moaned a little, both at the same time. "I'd have to take you to Gretna Green first, my love." He then lifted his face to gaze into her golden eyes. "Be patient, Lilly. We have the rest of our lives."

Praise for Annabelle Anders

"Annabelle Anders has a wonderful way of bringing the glamour and romance of Regency to life. As a reader, you are swept into a rich, historical world that you'll never want to leave."

~Nadine Millard, bestselling author

Nobody's Lady

by

Annabelle Anders

Lord Love a Lady Series

Nobody's Lady

Cover Art by *Debbie Taylor*

The Wild Rose Press, Inc.
PO Box 708
Adams Basin, NY 14410-0708
Visit us at www.thewildrosepress.com

Publishing History
First Tea Rose Edition, 2018
Print ISBN 978-1-5092-2043-4
Digital ISBN 978-1-5092-2044-1

Lord Love a Lady Series
Published in the United States of America

Dedication

To my daughter Amanda Lei (Manny),
who helps me with edits
even though she hates romances…

Chapter One
An Inauspicious Beginning

An isolated road southwest of London, March 1824

Michael Redmond, the eighth Duke of Cortland (with several other titles to boot), tipped his flask upside down and scowled when nothing came out.

The day had begun with so much promise!

En route to London, he and his dedicated man of business, Mr. Martin, had been dozing peacefully. They'd just finalized the details amassed within the mountain of paperwork they carried with them— hundreds of pages the duke was to present to Parliament in support of his amendment. They'd spent the entire winter gathering the evidence.

And now it was gone.

As was his carriage. As were his horses, his jacket. And his boots! *Hic.* A man ought never to be without his favorite boots!

"Damn bloody highway bobbers." Thick and slow, Michael's tongue refused to cooperate. "Highway mobbers—rob—bers. Robbers."

They'd stolen everything. And, *Devil take it*, Michael had failed to carry his pistols today!

The robbers had dangled from branches hanging over the road, dropped onto the carriage, and without a single shot fired, overpowered his outriders.

1

What good was an outrider who could be disabled so easily? Michael had been tempted to deliver a tongue-lashing and sack every last one of them on the spot, but in hindsight, foiling such an attack would have been nearly impossible.

In addition to that, Michael was a fair-minded employer.

Arty and…What was the other one called? Cam, that's right. Decent fellows, really. If not for Arty, there would have been no whiskey! In fact, both outriders, as well as his driver, had just so happened to have flasks of spirits hidden in their clothing. Clever fellows…And Arty had withdrawn not one, but two, from his breeches. Lucky for him.

Catching up from behind, Arty fell into step beside him. He must have astutely realized his employer was out of drink for he took the empty flask from Michael's hand and replaced it with another. Then, putting a heavy arm around him, he urged them forward. Hiking for hours now, Michael no longer noticed the mud and sludge oozing between his toes. He leaned into his servant as they proceeded along the highway. Stumbling and swaying, they would likely cover the width of the road as well as the length of it, but this was of no matter. Surely, the inn was around the next bend!

"A leg shackle at the end of the season, eh, Your Grace? How about some advice for the wedding night?" Arty slapped Michael on the back in a jovial manner. He was apparently beyond comprehensible thought at this point. As was Michael. For under normal circumstances, no servant would have broached such a subject with the duke—ever. Michael, by necessity and inclination, was a private man. He never discussed personal matters with anybody, including his fiancée. What was her name? Oh, yes, Lady Natalie.

All but Martin broke into uproarious laughter. Of course, as his personal servants, they were well aware he'd not led a celibate life. Many a night, they'd waited for him down the street from the home of a high-priced courtesan or a beautiful and lonely widow, while he'd found pleasure inside. They'd known not to gossip about his activities, however, as he demanded discretion from those he employed. Damned if he would provide fodder for the busybodies of the *ton*.

But ah, no, his bride need not worry.

Except that…

Michael shook his head in a vain attempt to clear his thoughts. He'd kissed her, hadn't he? Oh, yes, upon her acceptance of his proposal.

And he'd danced with her often, as would be expected throughout the upcoming season. At the end of May, they would marry. It would be the wedding of the year. The highlight and grand finale. None of it could be avoided. He'd signed the contracts. He would not disappoint her father.

Surely she wasn't frigid! He hoped not anyhow. But, a niggling voice reminded him, whenever he was with her, he never felt any…sizzle.

Likely, she was coy, shy—too innocent to know the mechanics of it, even. He'd have to teach her. Hopefully she would be willing.

With Lilly, there had been plenty of sizzle.

Lightning struck nearby, and thunder boomed closely in its wake. A few sprinkles began to fall. Rain? But of course, it would rain! Why ever would it not?

That was what he got for thinking her name. He

knew better than to allow his thoughts to drift in that direction. More thunder grumbled in the distance.

Must be the drink. He hadn't allowed himself to think of her for years, nearly a decade in fact. Or so he tried to convince himself.

Michael refused to allow his thoughts to linger on…her.

He was a different man now, betrothed to…whatshername.

Lady Natalie! Yes—everything a duchess ought to be. Poised, elegant, of noble birth, and beautiful. She was the daughter of one of the most powerful men in all England. But he could not picture her face. Instead he remembered golden eyes. Oh, hell, now he was becoming maudlin. Tipping back his head, he took another long draw of the whiskey. Very good stuff, really, quite excellent.

In a deliberate attempt to steer his thoughts away from his upcoming nuptials, Michael broke into verse. Recognizing the old tune, Arty, Cam, and John joined in with ribald enthusiasm.

Oh say, gentle maiden, may I be your lover
Condemn me no longer to moan and to weep
Struck down like a hawk, I lie wounded and bleeding
Oh, let down your drawbridge, I'll enter your keep
Enter your keep, nonnie nonnie, enter your keep,
nonnie nonnie
Let down your drawbridge, I'll enter your keep.

Stumbling along as they sang, John broke into falsetto voice to sing the maiden's part. Stepping in front of Michael, he dipped into an exaggerated curtsy.

Alas, gentle errant, I am not a maiden
I'm married to Sir Oswald, that cunning old Celt

4

He's gone to war for twelve months or longer
And he's taken the key to my chastity belt!

They sang the raunchy ditty as the sprinkles turned into large drops, which in turn grew to a torrential deluge.

Warmed from the inside, the men marched onward.

Ducking his head to shield his eyes from water streaming down his face, Michael caught sight of his feet. How very odd! Toes he rarely paid heed now peeked through his torn and bloodied stockings.

"Halt!" he ordered drunkenly, holding out one ducal hand. His comrades staggered to a stop, and Michael stripped off his stockings. Gawking at a few gruesome lacerations, he was amazed he hadn't noticed any pain. "Damned bloody pansy-ass holes—hose." The other men's more serviceable stockings offered their feet far greater protection. Michael removed his stockings and threw them into the woods. With a flourish, he then swept his hand forward, indicating they resume where they had left off.

As the miles passed, each took a turn composing his own lyrics while the others sang the nonnie nonnie part repeatedly. And, as men were wont to do whilst drinking and separated from genteel company, they invented lyrics unfit for anyone's ears but their own.

Their hearty laughter echoed off the trees around them.

Michael hadn't participated in such uninhibited raucousness in years, and all in all, found the day to be rather refreshing—except for the losing of his coach and boots and years' worth of work, that was.

A sign up ahead! Thank God! Michael had never been so happy to come upon an inn as he was in that moment. A petrified-looking wooden sign directed them off the road to a small clearing in the trees to the Forty Winks Inn and Tavern. They had been trudging through the mud for nearly six hours.

Six bloody hours!

Hoping to see his other coaches, the ones which carried his trunks and other servants, Michael peered into a long carriage house that lined the drive. Only a few smaller buggies, a small cart, and an unfamiliar carriage were parked inside. Hmm...A rather inauspicious sign. Nothing to worry over, however. Michael was a duke.

Dukes were never turned away.

Donning his noble demeanor, Michael shook off the remaining effects of the liquor, brushed at his shirt, and ran his fingers through his hair. What the hell? He glanced at his hand in confusion. It had come away with bits of grass and dirt. His valet was going to have conniptions over this.

If he could find him, that was.

Before departing from the Three-Legged Dog Inn earlier that morning, his valet, Duncan, had ascertained Michael was appropriately attired in his necessary ducal finery. In addition to preparing His Grace's unmentionables, Duncan had skillfully tied Michael's ivory linen cravat, carefully brushed the perfectly fitted wool jacket and breeches, and polished Michael's timeworn favorite hessians to a high shine. There was an image to be maintained, and Duncan's reputation as a gentleman's gentleman was at stake.

Michael didn't feel very ducal now.

With the arrogance acquired by one in such a position, however, he surmised his very manner, his bearing, would alleviate any doubts as to his identity. He opened the door to the open sitting area, identified the innkeeper behind a wooden bar, and strode forward with his normal self-assurance.

The innkeeper eyed him warily. "What can I be doing for you?" he asked suspiciously.

Michael didn't hesitate. "I am Cortland." He barely slurred his words at all. "The Duke of Cortland. My servants and myself require five rooms. A private suite for myself, of course." It wasn't a question, but a command. Rather, a statement of fact. Martin stood beside him, in pleasant agreement, while John, Arty, and Cam swayed unsteadily near the door.

The innkeeper, a robust older gentleman, looked from Michael to Martin and the men across the room, and then after a short pause, burst forth in uncontrollable laughter. Bending over, the provoking man slapped his leg several times. After finally catching his breath between chortles of mirth, he wiped a few tears from his eyes.

"That's a good one, mate!" he announced when he'd finally recovered. "And just for that, I'll allow you fellows to take refuge in the barn. There's some blankets in the back, and you can clean up at the stream." Wiping his eyes, he shook his head and laughed again. "A bloody duke! Now that's a good one! But for now, you're getting mud all over my floor. Take yourselves outside now..." He shooed them away.

Michael very slowly wiped the spittle that had been sprayed on his face from the innkeeper's laughter and summoned his haughtiest tone. The innkeeper's reaction had been strangely sobering.

"We've been besieged by highway robbers and

forced to hike nearly twenty miles. It is in your best interests—*hic*—sir, for you to show us to our rooms—without further delay. I am in no mood for jokes and cannot appreciate your attempt at humor." Michael tried to glare but was having difficulty focusing. A serious but good-humored man, he was never addressed with such rudeness and disrespect. Ever.

The innkeeper straightened and looked him in the eye. As the dozen or so occupants went silent, tension mounted within the taproom. "Listen here, mister. I was going to let you bunk in the stables, but I'm taking back that offer. I don't allow vagrants and drunks to loiter in my inn, and I'll not be *telling* you again. Take yourself off my property. Now!"

Just then, a rustling on the stairs suggested the drama was about to be interrupted by the arrival of, God save them all, a pair of women of quality. Lowering the lorgnette she had been observing the altercation through, the smallest of the women approached him.

Glancing at her dismissively, he turned back to the innkeeper. This entire day had been infuriatingly unproductive. Although the situation was only temporary, Michael found it horrifying, really, that such a calamity could befall him. Closing his eyes, he calmed himself.

He must speak coherently. "I—"

But his words never formed. For when he opened his mouth to speak, a disturbingly familiar voice cut him off.

"Mr. Jackson"—the woman's cultured voice addressed the innkeeper—"I fear you had best hold your tongue. This filthy, barefooted, and foul-smelling drunk is, in fact, telling the truth. Standing before you, dear sir, is none other than Michael Redmond, the eighth Duke of Cortland."

Michael pivoted in disbelief. Had he conjured her up with his drunken musings? Surely not. But there she stood, staring at him with those same golden eyes. His breath swooshed out of him, as though he'd taken a blow to the gut, as he watched Lilly execute a deep and elegant curtsy. She lacked any humility, however, and met his gaze defiantly upon rising.

"It has been a long time, Your Grace. Nonetheless, I am honored to make your acquaintance once again. I am now Lady Beauchamp. Perhaps I may be of some assistance this evening." Her voice echoed inside his head, formal and cool.

Michael knew exactly who she was. He'd dreamt of that voice for months. And those golden eyes—not to mention her silky platinum-blonde hair. But she had been Miss Lilly Bridge then, and the moment he'd been called away from London, she'd moved on to another suitor. Oh, yes, he knew exactly who she was.

Regardless of who she'd been to him in the past, it appeared today she was to be his savior. He sobered considerably at the thought. "Indeed, it has been a long time." Nearly a decade. "I beg your pardon, *my lady.* Do forgive my 'filthy, foul-smelling' condition. We've suffered considerable...er...hardships today." Bowing, he took her gloved hand in his. Before he could raise it to his lips, however, a small dog (longer than it was tall) took up her defense. Baring sharp teeth, it growled a low warning.

Michael dropped her hand quickly. He didn't need to add a dog bite to the day's calamities. Especially from a dog resembling a large rat.

The innkeeper burst out laughing again but quickly checked himself when Michael glared in his direction. With his brows wrinkling, the feisty old man took a moment to assess him more thoroughly. And what did the innkeeper see? Mud covered him from head to toe, but Michael's garments were expertly tailored, made of the finest linen and wool. Gold buttons fastened his shirt, and, ah yes, now the innkeeper saw it: the ducal posture and deportment. He might have saved them both some embarrassment if he'd only looked closer upon his first inspection. Mr. Jackson turned to Lilly and asked, "It is true, my lady? He is really a duke?" Concern laced his voice.

Kneeling beside her protective pet, Lilly peered up at Michael with a hint of sadness. "I'm afraid so, Mr. Jackson. I'm afraid so."

Chapter Two
Saved by a Belle

Life wasn't fair.

Although smeared liberally with sweat and dirt,
half his hair standing on end, and befuddled with drink,
Michael Redmond was more handsome now than when
he'd first captured her heart. His current attire, or lack
thereof, hid nothing of the powerful musculature on his
frame, nor the pride of his bearing. He had been tall and
fit at the age of one-and-twenty. At thirty, he pulsed
with a vitality which nearly took her breath away. Even
standing in a taproom barefoot, his demeanor was noble
and arrogant. He'd been full of confidence before, but
this was different. He was the same, and yet not. Much
like herself.

Lilly reached up to touch the hair bound at the nape
of her neck.

She was a widow, a matron, a chaperone to her
stepdaughter—whereas he appeared a prime specimen
for the marriage mart, drat the man. She knew he hadn't
married. Such a wedding would have been announced.
As a duke, he likely was one of England's most sought-
after bachelors.

Well, they could have him.

Scooping Miss Fussy into her arms, she rose
warily. She touched her lips to the soft fur on top of the
dog's head and looked at him from under her lashes.

11

For a moment, their eyes held. His had mesmerized her from the very beginning. Like sunshine reflecting through cobalt glass, they glimmered. He was once again just Michael, and she was merely Lilly. But only for a moment.

Glenda stepped forward and elbowed Lilly. Returning herself to the moment at hand, Lilly gestured toward her. "May I present to you my daughter, Miss Glenda Beauchamp? Glenda, His Grace, the Duke of Cortland." Glenda performed a sweet short curtsy, all the while keeping her eyes downward.

Lilly glanced sideways at Glenda and watched as romantic daydreams dawned behind her gaze. After seeing Glenda in such melancholy for the full year after her father's death, it was a relief to see some excitement cross her youthful features. Glenda was taller than Lilly with layers of chestnut curls and warm brown eyes. Fair skinned and slim, she was nearly the spitting image of her deceased mother, Lilly's older sister, Rose.

Lilly would make certain Glenda found a good match, somebody kind. She hoped for a gentleman with a sweet temperament and a tolerant spirit. Glenda wanted a love match, but Lilly had been compelled to warn her of the perils attached to such a messy emotion.

Lilly had known love and the resulting anguish of its aftermath.

Michael—the duke now, Cortland—bowed and addressed Glenda. "A pleasure, Miss Beauchamp. I assume you are traveling to town for the season?" He looked to Lilly questioningly.

It was Glenda who answered, however. "We are, Your Grace. I am to have my coming out. My stepmother is to sponsor me." By now Glenda had found the courage to look him in the eyes. In fact, she fluttered her lashes as she spoke. "Were you truly attacked by highwaymen? How very brave to continue your travels on foot. We must assist the duke, Lilly! Especially after his harrowing experience!"

Lilly nearly rolled her eyes at Glenda's words. But of course, Glenda considered Michael the epitome of everything a husband-hunting debutante desired.

Which was perfectly fine…or ought to be anyhow. What Lilly had felt for Michael, what she'd thought he'd felt for her, had all been an illusion. Best to leave such nonsense in the past.

Michael lived in a different world now.

As did she.

He did, however, appear to be in something of a pickle. Perhaps they *could* be of some assistance. But should she? She was torn. She had once felt very close to him. They had held each other in great affection.

Until he abandoned her.

A part of her wanted to leave him to walk the remainder of the distance to London. Barefooted even. Good manners however, won out.

"You were traveling with only one carriage?" she asked. Surely a man of his stature would have an entire entourage?

Instead of answering her question, Michael glanced around. Several of the inn's guests, keen to know his response, listened to their conversation shamelessly. His arrival had certainly livened things up around here. "Please allow me to clean up, my lady." And then he surprised her. "Will you and your stepdaughter join me for dinner?" He turned to the innkeeper. "You do have a private dining room available, do you not?"

13

Having come to terms with the fact that he had insulted an actual duke, the innkeeper launched into a series of bows and bobs. "Of course! Of course! And a suite for His Grace as well." He waved toward the stairs for Michael and his men to follow him. "There was a gentleman here earlier, must have been your valet then, a Mr. Dunkin. He departed along with your other servants but left a portmanteau in my keeping for you, for Your Grace, sir. Because of the rain, we are short on rooms. He asked that we relay to His Grace, er, to you that is, that they would go ahead and meet up with you in London. I'm sorry for not knowing you were His Grace, er, Your Grace...heh, heh...But truly, I was expecting something of a fancier...not that you aren't fancy, it's just that...er..." He trailed off uncomfortably.

Best stop now, Lilly thought. Poor man! Michael did look rather vagrant-like. Mr. Jackson turned to lead the duke and his men toward the back stairs.

Michael bowed once again toward Lilly. "I'll see you at dinner then, madam." He'd scowled upon hearing the news regarding his baggage coaches. His shoulders slumped, and he rubbed a hand across his face wearily. He must be exhausted!

After they disappeared, Lilly sighed.

He'd called her *madam*.

How was it possible to feel so old when one was a mere six-and-twenty? She pinched her lips together and pivoted in the opposite direction. "We'd better get Miss Fussy outside, or there will be more than mud on this floor."

Glenda trailed after her excitedly. "Is he really a duke, Lilly?" And "How is it that you know a duke?

You've never mentioned knowing a duke before! Oh, Lilly, how delicious! Tonight, we dine with a real live duke! And we haven't even arrived in London yet!"

Leading Miss Fussy outside onto a somewhat soggy, grassy area, Lilly ignored Glenda's questions for the moment. The ground was saturated but not entirely muddied. Lilly untied the leading string and allowed her pet to explore. Miss Fussy would go to a great deal of trouble discovering the perfect location to do her business. She nosed around in somewhat of a figure eight, then circled back diligently and squatted. The familiar ritual was accomplished with a great deal of dignity.

"Lilly—" Glenda implored her. "You must tell me more about him. Is he married? Is he in search of a wife? Oh, I know a duke is far above me, and he is very old, but, oh, he is so handsome!"

"Take a breath, Glenda." Lilly finally spoke. "If you would but give me a moment, I will endeavor to answer some of your questions." And then she paused. "I met the duke before he was titled. He was a second son and had been on leave from the military. His father and brother died within a very short time of each other, shortly after Mich—shortly after the duke and I met. Just before I married your father, in fact."

****

April 1815

"But why would you need a season?" Lilly's father, Mr. George Bridge, had reasoned with her when she reminded him of the promise he'd made when she was but twelve years old. "I've a perfectly sound match for you here."

A landed gentleman, Mr. Bridge enjoyed a small

income, but Lilly and her mother could not depend upon it to secure their distant future. For their home, their estate, most everything the family owned of any value, were entailed through the male line.

They didn't speak of the precariousness of their situation often, but Lilly knew her father worried. Her parents had not been blessed with any sons. A distant nephew stood to inherit everything.

So concerned with financials as of late, Lilly's father was now attempting to retract his promise for the London season. He'd asserted it wasn't necessary.

Lilly's sister, Rose, dead for three years, had left a grieving husband and a motherless eight-year-old. Everyone declared a marriage between seventeen-year-old Lilly and Rose's widower to be the perfect solution. Everyone but Lilly, that was.

"You promised me a season, Father. I will find my own husband." She'd held her ground fiercely. She would never marry Lord Beauchamp!

Her brother-in-law had been obsessed with Rose and had gone into full mourning upon her death. Three years later, he continued to wear all black, going so far, even, as to carry black handkerchiefs. Although he'd always treated her politely, he came across as...pompous and somewhat eccentric. Marrying him was incomprehensible. Lilly found the entire suggestion repulsive.

She would find her own prince.

And so, her father had relented. One season, he'd said. If she failed to land a suitable and well-heeled husband by the end of it, she'd marry the baron.

Lilly was not worried. London abounded with eligible bachelors! And although not the beauty that her sister was, Lilly possessed reasonably good looks. And she would have the help of her aunt, Lady Eleanor Sheffield. Having marched with the *ton* for decades, Aunt would have received invitations to all the balls, garden parties, and recitals necessary for Lilly to find her prince.

She was to sponsor Lilly.

Hardly a week passed in London before the whirlwind began.

Nearly as excited as Lilly, Aunt Eleanor embraced her role as sponsor wholeheartedly. She had even engaged her favorite modiste to design a gown for her niece—special for tonight—for Lilly's debut in society.

The dress, fit for a princess, consisted of white chiffon with a silver lace overlay. Aunt Eleanor had insisted it enhanced Lilly's unusual platinum hair. Cut high at the waist, and the bodice demure, the dress flattered Lilly's status as a debutante.

Not to be left out, Lilly's mother purchased additional lace and threaded it through Lilly's upswept hair. A string of pearls completed the ensemble.

The night promised magic!

Before she knew it, the three of them had stepped out of the carriage and then climbed the steps to the Willoughby Mansion. Her first ball ever!

Guests milled everywhere! It was most certainly going to be a squeeze.

Lilly stood silently as her mother and Aunt Eleanor chatted with a few other matrons as they all waited in the reception line to greet their hosts. Already, there was so much to see!

The giant foyer beckoned inhabitants with its marbled floor, but the ceiling, majestically painted with cherubs, angels, and heavenly clouds, nearly had Lilly falling over backward as she gazed up at the artwork. Could this really be the Willoughby's *home?*

Statues balanced upon alabaster pedestals in out-of-the-way places, and gilded paintings hung along the full length of the corridor. In awe, Lilly's curiosity did not allow her to ignore any of her surroundings. She would remember every second of this extraordinary night.

And then, she spotted *him.*

She was first caught by the beauty of his eyes. Like a lake reflecting a perfect summer sky, they mesmerized. Watching her, he appeared amused at her wonder, at her awe. She would have felt foolish except for something else in his regard. It lacked any mockery whatsoever. And when their gazes locked, he didn't look away.

Neither did she.

He presented himself in military regimentals, which alone could make any girl's heart flutter. But Lilly saw more than that. His face was friendly and handsome. At least a foot taller than she, he filled out his uniform nicely. His nearly black hair was tied back, but one wayward lock fell across his eyes. He didn't use a pomade, so it appeared to be soft to the touch. Lilly held his gaze until he sheepishly dropped his lashes to stare at his feet. He hesitated a moment.

Then, running a hand through his hair, he slanted his eyes back toward her almost sleepily.

Lilly's breath caught. She knew such boldness was not appropriate. She oughtn't to allow him to eye her so, and yet paralyzed, she could not look away if her life depended on it.

And then he sent her a slow, lazy smile.

Barely aware of herself, Lilly's countenance broke, and she grinned back. An unusual joy swept through her. They held each other's eyes for only a few seconds, but it might as well have been a lifetime. Unable to bear the intensity a moment longer, she forced herself to turn away from him. She felt as though she had been burned. She was terrified to look at him again, and yet she knew it was not the end.

How could it be?

"You're holding the line up, dear." Taking her arm, Aunt Eleanor pulled her along the receiving line. Lord Whosit? Of Whatsit? A pleasure to meet this lord and that lady…In a daze, Lilly responded with practiced curtsies and, apparently, the proper greetings.

But she could not shake the effects of her earlier encounter…with him.

Dazed, she floated along beside her aunt and mother as the major-domo announced them. She'd been dreadfully nervous for this moment all day, and now that her name rang out in the ballroom, the buzzing inside her drowned it out.

Once inside, her aunt steered them to a carpeted area away from the orchestra and began introducing her to her oh-so-dearest friends, and her oh-so-dearest friend's nephew, or son, or grandson, etc. Lilly's dance card filled quickly, but her thoughts refused to stray from the gentleman she had seen in the foyer. Where was he? Would he find her? She wanted to dance with *him*!

As if conjuring his presence with her very thoughts, he appeared at her side in the company of another, older gentleman. She had already been introduced to the older gentleman, a friend of her aunt's, but could not remember his name.

"Miss Lilly Bridge, it is my honor to present to you the younger son of my old friend, the Duke of Cortland, Captain Michael Redmond. Captain Redmond, this is Miss Lilly Bridge, the niece of Lady Eleanor Sheffield."

Lilly dipped into a precise curtsy, tipping her head in reverence, for she was certain the man who stood before her would one day be her husband. The moment assumed a crisp clarity. Suddenly, everything in her life made perfect sense. Fate's mission had been to bring her to *him*. He took hold of her fingertips and bowed. Even though they both wore gloves, warmth spread through her at his touch. He hadn't been so bold as to touch his lips to her hand, but he'd thought about it. She could tell by the gleam in his eye.

"Miss Bridge, it is my pleasure to make your acquaintance. Are you new to London this season?" He spoke in low gravelly tones. Lilly wondered if he, too, understood the momentousness of the occasion.

"I am entering society for the first time tonight, Captain Redmond." And then her mind went blank. It was as though she'd forgotten how to speak for all of fifteen seconds. But she must make some attempt at conversation! For he had already caught her gawking like a child in the Willoughby foyer. "I've never seen so many candles aflame in one room," she finally commented, indicating the chandelier and sconces all around them. She gently waved her fan below her face. "It's no wonder the room is so warm." It *was* heating up in here.

"May I escort you to the refreshment table? I

wouldn't mind a drink, myself." With a nod of permission from her mother, Lilly accepted. Turning, he winged an arm, and she tentatively wrapped her hand around it, just below his elbow.

His jacket was a soft wool. She absorbed his strength and essence as they crossed the room.

"I've pondered the duplicitous nature of candles myself." He glanced down with a dashing smile. "Hostesses in London trust the flames to bow to their wishes and remain safely upon the wick. They have been lucky so far."

As they reached the refreshment room, Captain Redmond drew her closer, protecting her from the jostling crowd. And then, instead of procuring lemonade as Lilly expected, he scooped up two flutes of champagne from a nearby waiter's tray.

Handing one to her, he steered them to a granite bench near the terrace doors. Without relinquishing his arm, Lilly sat on the cool bench sipping the intoxicating drink. What did one say when conversing with the man of her dreams? Well, she must say something, that was for certain.

Anything!

"Are you just returned from the continent?" Her voice came out sounding breathless. She fluttered her fan again. It was frightening, really, to imagine the future father of her children fighting in some distant land.

The specter of a shadow crossed his face. "I am. I have been attending matters in Brussels until a few weeks past. With the battles won, I found myself yearning for England."

"How long were you there?" She hoped she wasn't

treading into a distressing subject. Many families had lost young men to the effort. It could be a touchy subject.

He grimaced. "Just over a year. I left Oxford before completing my studies." Before she could ask if he intended to return to Oxford, he spoke again. "Where do you hail from, Miss Bridge?"

Oh, but this was something she would have no difficulty talking about. "The south, a small village near Plymouth. My father's property is a day's drive from the sea. I had never been far from there until a few weeks ago. And it is all so very different. London overwhelms me at times! So much humanity in one place! I'm still not certain how I feel, having so many people all around me. The sensation can be...unnerving at times." Was she rambling? "I'm not finding fault though. Please forgive me if I sound ungrateful to be here."

She *was* rambling now! First tongue-tied and then a nattering ninny!

He laughed as though she'd said something clever. Her hand still rested upon his arm.

"And yet you are here. You aren't afraid of experiencing new things?" he asked.

"Oh, no!" She considered her words a moment. "I would have died if Father hadn't allowed me to come! How can a person grow up if he or she has never been to London? By simply being here, I realize there is so much more to the world than I could ever imagine." She was a little homesick though. "I was so happy to leave home, but now that I am here, I feel a greater appreciation for all that is familiar to me. I think, perhaps, home will mean more to me for having left it."

She paused and took another sip of the bubbling liquid in her glass. Tilting her head, she met his gaze boldly. "What about you?" She wanted to know more about *him*. "Are you looking forward to going home after your time away?"

His jaw clenched a few times before he spoke. "My father's home, where I grew up, will one day belong to my brother. He is soon to be betrothed, and I won't want to intrude..." The captain seemed to look off into nowhere for a moment. "My father will stay there, of course, but I no longer consider Summers Park my home. I do have a property of my own...south, but closer to London. I've only been a few times to check in with the steward. I hadn't thought about settling down there yet."

Lilly looked at him from beneath her lashes. "Well, you hadn't met me, so why would you have?" She laughed. It must be the champagne! She was only partly joking. She didn't know how she could say something so bold, but in that moment felt as though they'd known each other a lifetime. She expected him to laugh as well, but instead, he looked deeply into her eyes. He glanced at her lips and then back to her eyes again.

"Quite true, Miss Bridge, quite true."

Chapter Three
A Well-Needed Bath

1824

Michael let out a slow sigh of relief as the door closed behind the last of the inn's servants who had filled his bath. The harried maids had unpacked the bags left by his valet, turned down his bed, and placed towels and soaps within reach of the tub. Having been an army man earlier in life, he was more than capable of handling his own toilette.

God, what a day it had been!

Enjoying the privacy, Michael shed his filthy garments and stepped carefully into hot, fragrant water. His entire body ached, causing him to wince while lowering into the copper tub. Not since first returning from the war had a bath felt so heavenly. As the water eased his muscles, he began to feel human. Perhaps later, he'd even feel like a duke again.

She'd changed.

With his eyes closed, and his head tilted back, he could not shake himself of her image.

This disturbed him.

He slid down and immersed his head beneath the steaming water. Perhaps it would wash away the torrent of memories assaulting him. Perhaps it would distract him from rehashing her betrayal.

With tightly closed eyes, he held his breath and allowed the water to embrace him.

Why now? Why after all these years? He'd known she'd married. He'd even known where she lived. She'd made her choice. She'd made the choice for both of them.

When he could hold his breath not a second longer, he burst out of the water and then shook his head like a dog. The droplets flew away from him, onto the floor and privacy screen.

She and her stepdaughter were to join him for dinner.

Michael rubbed his face and groaned. It had taken him years to forget. Of course, she would turn up in his life again now! Her timing couldn't be worse!

He had finally set his mind on a woman to marry and—of course!—he ran into Lilly again.

He'd put it off for years, frankly unconvinced another woman existed who could hold his interest long enough to merit entering the institution. He'd persuaded himself his efforts and time were better spent improving his estates. Hundreds depended upon the ducal lands for a living, and Michael took this very much to heart.

But this past year he had also decided, for that very same reason, he needed an heir. He needed to ensure the future as well as the present. And so, in a rational and calculated manner he had chosen his future duchess.

Closing his eyes, Michael endeavored to bring Lady Natalie Spencer's image to mind.

The girl had turned one-and-twenty this past winter. She was pretty and pleasant. Her father's lands abutted one of Michael's larger estates and combined they could increase efficiencies by thirty percent. And then there was her astoundingly large dowry. Not that he needed the funds, but if one is to marry, one might as well make an excellent business transaction out of it.

But what did she *look* like, for heaven's sake!

Blond hair, yes, but it was yellower than Lilly's. Natalie was taller, slimmer. He'd glimpsed her ankles on a few occasions and decided she must have fabulous legs. They had danced together several times, and Michael had enjoyed the feel of her in his arms. She was very graceful but a bit aloof.

Her face was…Dammit, what was the color of her eyes? He tried to picture her lips, but images of Lilly intruded. Suddenly, his mind's eye pictured golden eyes.

Had she been too young to realize what they had had together? She'd come to London and easily acquired a devoted, lovesick beau. He'd happily followed her from one social event to another throughout the entire season. Had she not experienced love as he had?

And then he recalled how she had yielded to him both physically and emotionally. She'd held back nothing. She'd been his, completely: heart, mind, and soul. Or so he had thought.

When he'd first met Lilly, she had been a vivacious, gorgeous girl.

She'd grown into a hauntingly beautiful woman.

Dressed as a matron, she'd not fooled him with her shapeless gown and severely styled hair. In fact, the utter lack of frivolity about Lilly's person merely pronounced her delicate features all the more.

Rosebud lips which had once opened so generously

for him, and only him, couldn't help but stir his desire. He tortured himself further with the memory of how those golden eyes had stared into his very soul.

Michael opened his eyes as a servant entered the room.

"Would you care for some brandy, Your Grace?"

"Scotch," he answered. "Might as well bring the decanter."

What a fool he'd been! He couldn't help remembering the first time they'd met.

****

Spring 1815

If the white dress hadn't given her away as a debutante, then her wonder and excitement would have. So open in her appreciation of her surroundings, she sparkled. Everything about her sparkled—her dress, her hair, even her skin.

This girl failed miserably at feigning even the slightest ennui.

Michael couldn't help smiling as he observed her.

She was going to tug one of the pearls off the back of her gloves if she continued fidgeting with them. She was either restless or nervous, likely a little of both.

Tipping her head back to examine the artwork on the rounded ceiling, she dislodged a few ringlets from her coiffure. The graceful arc of her neck had him unconsciously licking his lips. Her hair shimmered like silk, nearly the color of her pearls. She was utterly delightful.

And then, after dragging her attention away from the ceiling, her gaze drifted around the room and she caught him watching her.

The color of her eyes surprised him. They were

such a light brown as to be golden. Michael's heart jumped as though coming to life after a long slumber. In some way, a connection already existed between them. Surprising himself, he turned away.

She had somehow stolen his equilibrium. Besides her fragile beauty, she possessed an intangible allure he could not identify.

Casting his gaze downwards, he took a deep breath. He'd fancied himself a bit of a rake, not a complete degenerate, like some of his acquaintances, but somewhat of a ladies' man. He'd never failed to maintain his composure where a woman was concerned. And so, when he looked a second time, he openly admired her. This time it was she who quickly turned away.

Her chaperones chose that moment to pull her along the line, and she disappeared into the throngs of guests.

Occasionally, while in France and especially during his years at Oxford, Michael had flirted and even dallied with alluring young ladies—regardless of class. It had been the exotic actresses and dancers though, who appealed to him almost exclusively. They were safer by far than ladies of gentle birth. Having seen a few gentlemen caught in parson's traps, Michael had learned to take care with his attentions when among the *beau monde*. Regardless of a lady's charm, he never let it appear he had singled any one of them out.

None had compelled him into pursuit so much as this one.

He would require an introduction. He needed to discover if that intense spark was real or if it had only been an illusion.

By the time he maneuvered into the ballroom, it was already stifling and crowded. Candles flickered everywhere, in sconces and on the huge chandeliers dangling overhead. His eyes searched with a deceptively lazy intent. She was not alone, of course. She attended with two matrons, a mother and aunt perhaps, as they had some physical similarities. Ah, yes, the smaller woman must be her mother. An older, muted version of her daughter—without the golden eyes. The taller of her chaperones was encouraging his angel to fill her dance card as quickly as possible, introducing the poor girl to every dandy in the room.

Luckily, the dragon was also acquainted with an old friend of his father's. Perfect! Just what he needed. He sidled over to Lord Gifford and greeted him cheerfully, striking up some casual conversation. "My lord, I'm surprised to see you in town this season. I'd heard you were permanently rusticating in the country these days."

Lord James Gifford shook Michael's hand and smiled. "Good to see you, Redmond! Even better to see you made it back in one piece. Your father mentioned you had joined up. His Grace was proud to boast his younger son had joined the effort against old Boney! Are you home for long?"

Michael was momentarily distracted at the mention of his father's praise but quickly recovered and answered vaguely. Questions like this were always difficult when he didn't know the answer himself. He exchanged a few more platitudes with Lord Gifford, all the while keeping the blond girl in his sights.

Lord Gifford took notice of the direction of Michael's gaze and changed the subject accordingly.

"Beautiful little gel, isn't she? The niece of Lady Sheffield. I imagine you'd like an introduction?" He laughed. "I was once a young buck myself. Think I wouldn't notice? Well, come along then."

As Michael moved closer to her, that spark, whatever it was, flared up inside of him again.

Lord Gifford moved aside and allowed Michael to step forward. "Miss Lilly Bridge, it is my honor to present to you the younger son of my good friend, the Duke of Cortland, Captain Michael Redmond. Captain Redmond, this is Miss Lilly Bridge, the niece of Lady Eleanor Sheffield."

Graceful and poised, she curtsied low before him. Michael took her hand briefly. He wanted to place a kiss upon the inside of her wrist, but he dared not.

Next time.

Her name was Lilly, like the flower of innocence. It was perfect for her. She smiled at him as if they shared a secret. Then she commented on the candles and the warmth of the room. Michael leapt on the opportunity to offer to escort her away from her chaperones.

She would not refuse. There was a pull between the two of them. Neither of them would resist it.

Winging his arm to escort her to the other end of the ballroom, he was acutely aware of her delicate hand as she slid it into the crook of his elbow. He had escorted ladies thusly hundreds of times before, but never had he felt the rightness of the noble gesture as he did then. When he thought they might be jostled by the crowd, he reached across with his other hand to protectively cover hers.

This brought them closer together. Her perfume

was a mixture of citrus and something warm, something subtle that he couldn't identify. The scent of her made him think of sunshine.

Michael garnered two glasses of champagne and then located a quiet place to sit. He wanted to keep her to himself—he wanted to know her.

She, apparently, was perfectly fine with this.

The rest of the world disappeared while they sat together. All that existed in those moments were her eyes, her voice, her lips. Intent upon this woman alone, he managed to mute the chattering of the other guests in the ballroom, the sounds of the dancers, and even the full orchestra as they played their lively tunes.

Surprisingly, they talked, almost like old friends. But they also flirted like future lovers.

Could it have been fate that brought them together? Did he even believe in such a thing?

He learned she was adventurous and kind-hearted. She loved her family but wasn't afraid to meet new people. When he spoke of the war, she listened with compassion and understanding, not pressing him for details. She was graceful, warm, and beautiful. She possessed a sense of humor.

They spent an unfashionable, if not scandalous amount of time in each other's company that night.

He spoke of his estate, Edgewater Heights. "I do have a property of my own...south, but closer to London. I hadn't thought about settling down there yet." The second the words left his mouth, a different perspective of Edgewater Heights began to evolve in his mind. As a young bachelor, he'd only considered the property as a source of income, a financial asset. He had a duty to visit and ensure it was cared for properly.

But in this moment, he could picture it as a home, a future home for himself and his family. Until now, he'd kept the concept a distant probability. But meeting this particular woman, looking into her eyes, and listening to her sweet voice, an image began unfolding in his mind.

He suddenly could envision very blond children running about the grounds. He could picture Lilly nurturing the garden, decorating for Christmas.

Warming his bed.

Throughout the evening, he managed to claim three dances (scandalous!) and take a few turns about the room.

Eventually, they slipped out to the garden for a stroll in the cooling air. And again, she tucked her tiny hand through his right arm.

She *belonged* at his side.

They walked quietly, enjoying the fragrant breeze and moonlit gardens. The energy sizzling between them rendered moot the need for polite conversation. Finally, he halted and turned her so they stood face to face. Keeping one hand on her arm, he let his other drift to her waist. The smooth silk of her dress was light and flimsy; he could feel the ridges of her corset beneath it.

The hour had grown late.

"I know you are excited for the season...I know there are all these new people in London you are dying to meet." He looked off into the darkness before continuing. "Every man you meet will be eager to put his name upon your dance card. Your home will overflow with flowers and gifts." He reached up to play with the tendrils of hair that curled around her ear. Such tender skin invited his touch. "But I am giving you notice tonight: I intend to court you. And when you are ready, I will speak with your father."

He spoke with absolute certainty. His words, a vow.

She stared solemnly into his eyes. "As a debutante, I am supposed to be demure...but..." She seemed to hold her breath. Her silence was suspended as leaves rustled nearby and the murmur of the Willoughby guests floated atop the flowerbeds.

"But...?" he whispered, leaning closer to her. He was going to kiss her.

Her palms rested flat against his chest. With such expressive eyes, she would be horrible at cards. When she tilted her head back, Michael knew exactly what she wanted.

"You are a dream," she whispered.

Or that was what he thought she'd said.

For just then, a group of revelers interrupted their privacy as they traipsed along on an adjacent path. At their approach, she stepped back abruptly.

Her eyes had grown large. She covered her mouth with one hand, apparently stricken with herself. "What am I doing? Aunt Eleanor and Mama are likely frantic!" She glanced rapidly from left to right as though expecting one of her chaperones to jump out from behind the hedges. "Oh, Lord! I may very well have broken every rule drummed into me!"

She enchanted him, such an innocent temptress.

"Not every rule, Miss Bridge," he teased, causing her eyes to widen further.

"Captain Redmond!" She spoke before he could finish.

But he merely laughed. "I'm fairly certain you used

all the right utensils at supper."

She rolled her eyes and shook her head at him. He laughed softly.

Not willing to push their luck, he escorted her back to Lady Eleanor's and her mother's side. As he went to take his leave, he apologized for monopolizing the most beautiful lady present. "I shall be calling tomorrow," he added, "for that carriage ride in the park, Miss Bridge."

Lilly smiled and looked him squarely in the eyes. "But of course, Captain."

Chapter Four
Dinner with a Duke

1824

After giving Glenda a brief narrative of her prior association with the Duke of Cortland, Lilly struggled to dismiss him from her mind. She'd known there was always a possibility of seeing him in London, but not in a million years had she imagined running into him along the road! Even seeing him covered in dirt, nearly a decade later, she'd known who he was the very moment she'd caught sight of him. And when he'd spoken, his voice had thrown open the portals of time and swept her into the past.

She'd nearly fainted.

But that would not do. She was the responsible one here, the matron, a guardian. She mustn't succumb to the momentary urge she'd had to throw herself into his arms tragically. No propriety existed in such wantonness. Nor could she lambaste him for his cruel and heartless desertion years ago.

She'd addressed him as though he'd merely been an old acquaintance—one who'd aged better than a fine scotch.

And now, while Mary assisted Glenda into her gown for dinner, her stepdaughter peppered her with endless questions. Lilly must put an end to this. It was as though Glenda poured salt into a festering wound.

No, it was worse.

Lilly had not been prepared for this. She ought not to have mentioned the failed courtship. She should have dissembled, told Glenda she'd had nothing but a passing acquaintance with the duke. It had been foolish to mention anything more than that.

"Cease with these questions." She spoke harshly. "It was not meant to be. I returned to Plymouth and married your father." Voicing the details of her and Michael's affair and remembering the agony of his rejection had resurrected her broken heart. She'd rather not contemplate such anguish again.

"You are lucky Father took pity on you! Otherwise you and Grandmother would not have had a home after Grandfather died." Lord Beauchamp had never been discreet about his lack of regard for Lilly. It had undermined her relationship with her stepdaughter from the very beginning. It had also eroded her position with the servants.

Lilly glanced into the small looking glass above the bureau and tucked in a few strands of hair that had escaped her chignon. She wondered what Michael had seen when he'd looked at her. Did he see her as the matron she now was? Did he remember what they had shared? Had that long-ago spring meant anything at all? Obviously not, or he would have contacted her. He would have sent her a message. Returning to Plymouth at the end of the season had been the most miserable and humiliating time of her life. Just the thought of it, even nine years later, made her breathing hitch, her chest tight.

Lilly changed into a periwinkle-blue evening gown

with a modest neckline and long sleeves. Although somewhat worn, it was the best she had for now. Aunt Eleanor had suggested she invest in a new wardrobe and put herself on the marriage mart as well, but Lilly adamantly refused. She would never again give the caring of her person over to any man. Common wisdom and the law suggested women were better off when they had a man to manage them. Lilly knew better. Although men were stronger, and more powerful, they were also rather idiotic as far as women were concerned. As much as she had loved her father, he had been wrong. Beauchamp had been cruel, and Michael had…well, he had been inconsistent. No, Lilly was free to manage her own life. She would not relinquish this opportunity.

That being considered, she still wished she had something prettier for tonight. Not that she needed to impress Michael, but she didn't want to appear unfashionable while dining with a duke.

Glenda chose to wear one of the new dresses that had been made for her debut this spring. The very pale pink chiffon had barely-there puffed sleeves and tiny butterflies embroidered along the bodice. She wore new satin slippers, and Mary had styled her hair in an elegant upsweep with several chocolate-colored curls falling decoratively down her back.

When the ladies exited their room, a maid escorted them downstairs to the duke's private dining area. Rising from his chair, Michael then bowed formally as they entered. He now looked very much, a duke.

The mud from earlier had been washed away, and he was now dressed in evening finery. At the sight of his soft, clean hair and summer-blue eyes, Lilly's mouth went dry.

He had a manner of smiling without actually moving his mouth. His lips might barely twitch, but laughter lurked in his eyes. It was part of his natural appeal.

He did this as she sat down.

Awareness buzzed through him the moment Lilly entered the room. This surprised him. But it oughtn't.

She seemed small, beside her stepdaughter. Petite, quiet, and mysterious.

The younger girl, bold and unself-conscious, had no such inhibitions. She took one look at him, flushed crimson, and made a deep curtsy. "Your Grace. I am so very honored to have been invited to join you this evening. Such a distinction to dine in your exalted company. Our limited conversations have become tedious, as you might have guessed, what with it always being just the two of us."

Lilly rolled her eyes heavenwards and made a half curtsy. When she finally allowed her gaze to settle upon him, he nearly laughed at her expression. She'd not meant for him to see her roll her eyes.

Lilly, apparently, was still unsuccessful at hiding her emotions.

She hadn't changed all that much, then.

The servants rushed forward and pulled out the dining chairs for each of the ladies.

"The pleasure is all mine, Miss Beauchamp." The younger girl stifled a giggle and blushed profusely at his comment. It had been this way with marriageable misses everywhere since he'd become the duke.

He couldn't help but watch Lilly.

Her gaze darted around the room, as though she'd

rather look anywhere but at him. He was grateful she had been here, at the inn, to clear up the issues surrounding his identity, but he also resented her presence.

For years, anger had burned inside of him. She'd married another man. She'd not waited for him to return. During the darkest time of his life, she'd failed to honor their pledge to each other.

And yet, most unfortunately, Michael was still drawn to her. Lilly's striking silver-blond hair and warm golden eyes captivated him all over again.

She now belonged to another man. She had a stepdaughter. The girl must be her niece.

When they had courted, Lilly had told him about her dead sister's widower and the motherless girl.

"It's been a long time." Michael spoke softly, unable to look anywhere but at her. He willed her to meet his gaze as he spoke. Lilly stared down at her bowl as a servant ladled some stew into it. Had she forgotten so easily?

She answered, still not looking up. "I trust you are well, Your Grace? Today's adventure notwithstanding?"

Michael thought he could read the emotions in her eyes. Ah, but he had been wrong earlier. She was, in fact, better at hiding her emotions now. Meeting his gaze at last, she donned a mask of some sort. This was a different Lilly. This was the Baroness Beauchamp.

Michael searched her face before answering. He too, could be nonchalant. "I am doing well, yes. And despite today's calamities, I find myself most fortunate, indeed. For here I am, dining with two very lovely ladies."

Glenda blushed and then found her voice once again. "Was it terribly frightening when the highwaymen attacked you? Were there dozens of them?"

"It happened rather quickly, actually." Anger flared as he mentally revisited the heist. "Too quickly in fact. The robbers jumped from the trees overhead, onto the coach, and before we could do much of anything they had driven off with it." Shaking his head, he muttered, "Failed to carry my pistols today, idiot that I am."

Two little lines appeared on Lilly's forehead as she frowned. "Do you think the attack was random?" she asked astutely.

Michael contemplated his answer carefully. "It would appear so, but one can never be certain."

The mask slipped, and a flicker of concern crossed Lilly's once-again-expressive face. "Did they attempt to harm your person?"

"Not directly. But stranding a person in such a remote part of the highway doesn't take much concern for their safety in mind." He chuckled. He didn't wish to discuss his concerns right then. Some close friends in London would help him shed light on this outrageous attack. Hugh Chesterton, the Viscount of Danbury, would assist him in ferreting out information. This was no discussion to have with ladies.

"But all is well." He reassured her. Her concern had seemed very real. "Where is that delightful little pup I met earlier? She does not sit at the table with you?" He would tease a smile from her.

Ah, there it was, his heart jumped at the sudden glow. "Miss Fussy stays in the room for supper." Her grin tugged at something inside of him. "The morning and noontime meals, however, are a different story."

"And will Miss Fussy be making her come out as well?"

Lilly responded in kind. "Not until she's been to the modiste. She lacks the proper wardrobe currently. But then, of course, she shall be presented to the queen—"

Glenda interrupted. "What rubbish!" The poor girl apparently lacked a sense of humor. "Lilly, don't be ridiculous." After sending a disgusted look in Lilly's direction, she turned her attention back to him. "Don't give her any ideas, Your Grace. My stepmother has a rather unusual attachment to her dog. I told her we should not bring Miss Fussy with us to London. She creates rather a nuisance at times. Even so, Lilly refused to leave the dog behind."

This was apparently not the first time the two women had had this discussion. Michael observed as Lilly stilled and dropped her lashes. "That's enough, Glenda." The words were spoken softly, and yet they allowed for no argument. It was clear to Michael that Lilly loved her dog.

"I've a few hounds myself—somewhat larger than Miss Fussy." Cedric and Norris likely outweighed Miss Fussy by more than ten times her own weight. "Wish I'd had them with me today. I expect they'd have taken care of those bas—those highwaymen." He held his dogs in great affection. Lacking open space for them while in London, Michael had left them in the care of his steward back at Summers Park.

Michael suspected the small dog brought Lilly a great deal of comfort. She had been tenderhearted toward animals before. She'd greeted the occasional dog they'd come across while walking in the park, and at Edgewood Heights...He imagined her dog received a considerable amount of devotion.

Which reminded him. Lilly was married. There would be a husband at home or awaiting them in London.

"You are traveling alone, I take it? Is the baron in London already or does he plan to follow you later?" When the ladies glanced at each other, Michael felt compelled to add, "I was acquainted with your aunt several years ago, Miss Beauchamp, in London—before she married your father."

The responses to both his question and his statement were very different than he had expected. Miss Beauchamp gasped and then turned accusingly toward Lilly. "You promised not to tell anybody! Are you trying to ruin my season already?" And then the girl let out a wail, hastily excused herself, and ran sobbing from the room.

Lilly, dry-eyed, set her fork down and calmly stated, "That would be quite a feat, Your Grace, for the baron has been dead for over a year now."

What the devil? What had he said to send Lilly's niece running from the room? And the baron was dead?

Lilly was a widow?

Lilly stared at the closed door and sighed. "It must remain a secret that I married my brother-in-law. Although no matter at home, Aunt Eleanor has advised it may not be quite the thing in London. It was illegal after all." She raised one delicate shoulder and grimaced. "Glenda will realize I told you about it before. I ought to go after her but...she tends to find more comfort from her maid these days..."

Once Glenda's wailing had receded completely, those two little lines appeared upon Lilly's forehead again. Of course, she must have realized they would now be dining together alone.

It was perfectly acceptable. She was a widow, after all. In the past, this opportunity for them to be alone together would have been terribly romantic. Without another word, she delved back into the tasteless stew.

He forced his mind to return to her other revelation. "I am sorry for your loss." There had been no sorrow or regret in her voice when she'd announced the baron's death. Regret at the news of Beauchamp's passing eluded him as well. Lilly again avoided looking him in the eyes.

It was strange, sitting here with her. What had her marriage been like? Had Beauchamp loved her? Had Lilly given herself to her husband with the same passionate abandon she'd shown with him? Did she have other children? Did she have a lover? Who had Lilly Bridge become? Nearly a decade had passed. He didn't know Lilly *Beauchamp* at all.

And yet, she was Lilly. As in that moment in the Willoughby foyer, the pull between them still existed— for him, anyway. He forced himself to remember the aftermath. She was also the woman who hadn't waited for him. The woman who had bolted from town when he'd promised to return. She'd abandoned him when he'd needed her dreadfully.

Lilly placed her fork on her dish and folded her hands in her lap. "Thank you," she said, oh so politely. "We expected his passing. He had been ill for many years."

And then, finally, she met his gaze. "It has been so

43

very long, but I am sorry for the loss of your father and brother, as well." Upon this topic, she would be sincere.

Michael took a drink of ale and swallowed hard. He had rather hoped to hear these words from her long ago.

Upon returning to her aunt's town house in London to claim her, Michael had been handed a short missive. The butler had appeared disapproving. The missive had informed him of Lilly's betrothal. Letters he'd later sent to her home in Plymouth had gone unanswered. He'd stopped writing when her father finally sent him a response. He'd demanded Michael refrain from any further attempts to correspond with the baroness. "She is a married woman." The bold statement had been underlined twice.

At that point, Michael had travelled to Summers Park and seized hold of the duties required of him as the new Duke of Cortland. Keeping busy helped him to erase her from his mind. Erasing her from his heart hadn't been so easy.

With the ducal seat near Exeter, Michael had struggled knowing she was not so very far away. But she had married.

And that, even more so than the miles that separated their homes, had removed her from his life forever.

"Thank you." He brought himself back to the present. "It was a difficult time for many. Over half the servants at Summers Park succumbed. Scarlet fever is a ruthless enemy."

Michael's statement shocked her. Her father had only told her Captain Redmond had become a duke. He'd convinced her she'd been jilted. She'd known nothing of a scarlet fever outbreak! And now, she listened in dawning despair as Michael casually described the conditions he'd come upon when he'd arrived at Summers Park that fated summer.

Would she have resisted her father if she had known this? Surely she would have! Not knowing what had become of Michael, she had begged her father to allow her to stay in London—to no avail. Aunt Eleanor was to depart for a summer house party in the country, and her mother had been eager to return to Plymouth. Her father had insisted that as a duke, Michael would no doubt look higher for a wife. *The season is over, and the time for this nonsense is past.* He had insisted on the betrothal and her quick wedding to Lord Beauchamp. He'd been anxious to have her settled.

Her father's concern had had merit. For he had shortly after become very ill with a cancer. He'd died that year on Boxing Day, one day after Christmas. By insisting upon her marriage to the baron, her father had secured a home for both Lilly and her mother with Lord Beauchamp.

"You haven't yet married?" Lilly asked, even though she was sure she would have heard something if he had.

Nearly a full minute passed before Michael responded. "I am to marry in June."

It made no sense, but it seemed as though a part of her heart died all over again upon hearing his words.

She recovered quickly. "Ah, then, felicitations are in order." She sipped at her watered-down wine and then set the glass back down. Her hand shook slightly.

"Tell me about her." She would not spare herself these details. *Let me put this part of my heart to death once and for all.*

"She is Lady Natalie Spencer, daughter of the Earl of Ravensdale," he stated baldly.

Lilly waited for him to embellish upon his announcement, but he did not. "I remember the Countess of Ravensdale as a charming woman. She was a good friend of my aunt's." Lilly searched her memory. "I know they have several sons, but I don't believe I ever met any daughters."

"There is just the one. She came out last spring."

"She must be very special." Lilly felt as though the words would choke her. Oh, God, the girl must be close to Glenda's age.

Michael grimaced and then covered it with a wry smile. "Oh, she is." His voice sounded tinged with…irony? Perhaps he'd rather not discuss Lady Natalie with Lilly.

But Lilly could not let it go. "How did you meet?" she persisted.

Michael's eyes narrowed. "The usual. Last season at a ball…" He lifted his chin. "The Willoughby Ball, in fact."

"Oh." Lilly wasn't sure how she ought to respond to such information. That broken part of her heart now felt as though the heel of a boot was grinding it into the ground. Lilly pinched her lips together and stared at the top button of his jacket. It was a burnished gold. The backs of her eyes burned. Had he intended to strike out at her?

He smiled a bit vindictively at Lilly's apparent loss for words. "Both ironic, and yet fitting, don't you think?" he said.

Ironic and yet fitting? Gathering her composure,

she responded, "Whyever would you say that?" And then she met his eyes with a hard stare of her own. She had been harboring the notion that they would not address the past this evening.

Was he really going to do this?

If so, he'd have to do better than that. Her eyes challenged him. If his eyes could be ice, then hers could be fire.

Michael crossed his arms and leaned back in his chair, his cold gaze fixed upon her. "I believe," he said chillingly, "that was where I'd thought I'd found my future wife once before."

Blinding fury exploded within her. How dare he! How dare he! Standing up, Lilly pushed her chair back abruptly, not caring when it fell over. "I certainly hope you act with more honor this time then, *Your Grace*, as you failed to follow through with your promise on that first occasion!" She did her best to keep the tears in her eyes from overflowing. His words had been brutal. She should hate him!

Instead, confusion and shame threatened to engulf her. Knowing now, something of the ordeal he'd experienced with his brother and father, she second-guessed herself.

Had their separation been a betrayal on her part? Had *her immaturity,* and not his lack of honor, brought about the end of their courtship? Had *he* suffered as well?

Her conscience berated her for impugning his honor, but his cruelly delivered comment had hurt. She would not relinquish her anger yet. Before losing her composure completely by bursting into tears, Lilly walked to the door, spun around quickly, made a hasty curtsy, and said, "Good night," in a wobbly voice. There must have been a strong draft in the corridor, however, for the door slammed closed violently behind her.

Chapter Five
The Courtship

1815

True to his word, Captain Redmond arrived at the stately townhouse on Curzon Street the next afternoon. He carried with him three separate bouquets of flowers.

Lilly knew the moment he entered the room, for her heart seemed to skip a beat.

The very atmosphere changed with his presence.

He appeared confident and unconcerned by the other suitors surrounding Lilly. No military uniform today. Instead he wore tan breeches, a brown waistcoat, and a black jacket. His neck cloth was tied in a simple knot, and his jacket hung loosely upon him.

His boots, were, however, buffed to a high shine.

As unobtrusively as possible, she watched beyond the gentleman currently speaking to her, so she might observe Captain Redmond greeting her aunt.

Bending over Lady Eleanor's hand, the captain presented *her aunt* with one of the bouquets he carried. He then handed an identical one to *her mother*. The bouquets were original, mostly greenery, ferns with a smattering of geraniums. Lilly was curious as to the last collection of flowers he held.

Other suitors had shown no originality at all. They had all, of course, come bearing bouquets of lilies. The unique arrangements brought by Captain Redmond struck her in that it seemed, she thought, he was using his bouquets in a completely different way. He must know the language of flowers.

The geraniums, Lilly knew, meant esteem, and she was also quite certain ferns meant sincerity. The third bouquet he brought was made up of a profusion of colorful blooms, some names of which escaped her. There was one lily, several different-colored roses, forget-me-nots, and baby's breath. She knew a lily meant beauty and elegance, the roses represented different aspects of love, and the baby's breath was innocence. The other flower might be a peach blossom, but she wasn't sure. She would have to look it up.

Probably, she read too much into them.

Meanwhile, Lord Harris continued to describe, at length, the distinctive poets he was interested in, reciting lines from a few of their poems. Lilly nodded but continued observing Captain Redmond. He'd known she was watching him; she was certain of this by the look in his eyes when he finally approached her.

She interrupted Lord Harris's recitation. "Excuse me but a moment. I must greet a new arrival." Captain Redmond's eyes stayed locked upon her until they met halfway across the room.

Lilly curtsied, and he bowed over her hand. This time he *did* place a soft kiss upon her wrist. Shivers ran through her at his touch.

And this time, neither wore gloves.

She couldn't help noticing how elegant and strong his hands were. They appeared to have been darkened by the sun, but his nails were neatly trimmed. Despite wearing civilian attire, he looked just as imposing as he had last night. As he bent over her hand, she breathed in his scent—musky sandalwood and leather. She inhaled deeply. He intoxicated her!

He continued holding her hand even though he had completed his bow. "Miss Bridge, I trust you are well rested, having survived your first London ball?" The low, gravelly tones of his voice sent shivers down her spine.

Lilly had hardly slept a wink. She had been far too excited to sleep. Each time she had closed her eyes the image of Captain Redmond had enticed her into romantic, hopeful fantasies.

"I am, sir." She looked up at him flirtatiously. "And you have survived it as well."

The captain released her hand and presented the bouquet to her. "Just barely," he teased. His eyes were laughing.

"They are beautiful." She buried her face in the fragrant flowers. Then, touching a few of the petals, she indicated one she wasn't sure of. "What is the name of this one?" she asked.

He leaned in to get a better look at it and then held her eyes steadily. "It is a peach blossom," he said. He was telling her more, she knew.

"Flowers have meanings. Do you know what the peach blossom means?" she asked.

He answered her cryptically. "I do."

"But you will not tell me?"

"I will not."

"Oh…"

Just then Lilly's mother came forward, gushing about the so very original bouquets the captain had brought. He was the only suitor who had thought to gift her aunt and mother as well as the popular debutante. "So unique, and how thoughtful of Captain Redmond, don't you think, Lilly?" Mrs. Bridge went to take the large bouquet from Lilly. "Let's have Jarvis take care of these. He can put them in the morning room. They will be so lovely in there, with all of the sunshine."

But Lilly didn't want them stashed away with all of the other flowers. "No, Mother, have him put them in my be—in my chamber."

Lilly's mother paused for a moment, looked like she might object, raised her eyebrows, and then said, "Very well," before taking the flowers and disappearing into the foyer.

"Come and sit down, Captain Redmond." Lilly remembered her manners. "Are you acquainted with our other guests?"

Captain Redmond glanced around at the faces in the drawing room and nodded. Approaching a seating area which held a small group of young men and women, Lilly delighted in his amicability. "Danbury, Harris…Miss Crone." He bowed. "Miss Harris."

Lilly found an open settee nearby and, as her hand was tucked into the captain's arm, pulled him down to sit beside her. They sat very close. They were, in fact, touching.

Lilly was to learn that Miss Harris was Miles Harris's younger sister. The captain had apparently attended Eton with both Viscount Danbury and Mr. Harris. In addition to that, Penelope Crone was friendly with Caroline Harris. They all had a prior acquaintance and were a pleasant group. Conversation flowed easily.

Lilly turned to Captain Redmond. "Miss Harris and Miss Crone have offered to take me to some of their favorite shops tomorrow afternoon. I am so happy to make friends here. I love keeping company with my aunt and my mother, but it's not the same as spending time with friends of like age, wouldn't you agree?" Oh, Lord, she was babbling already.

"If I remember correctly, they will likely drag you into *every* shop in London." The captain teased the young ladies. "Harris has complained long and hard after accompanying these misses on a few of their more extravagant shopping expeditions."

He kept his hands firmly in his lap. Lilly's hand remained tucked into his arm.

The group discussed various upcoming balls and parties, a possible excursion to Vauxhall, and of course the weather, before Captain Redmond turned toward Lilly.

"I must retrieve the curricle for our drive this afternoon. Will you be ready in one hour?" He had taken hold of her hand when he'd turned. Both of their hands were lost in the folds of her skirts. He squeezed gently and massaged her palm slowly with his thumb.

Lilly was so conscious of his touch, she forgot what he'd asked her. What had he said? Something about leaving?

"Pardon?"

"I need to collect the curricle for our drive. Is an hour enough time for you to get ready, Miss Bridge?"

He knew.

He knew how his touch had affected her. She trapped his thumb in her hand and smiled daringly back. "An hour will be fine. I'm looking forward to it."

Lilly spent a quarter of an hour longer with the remaining guests before they finally stood to leave. She was excited for the plans they'd made to meet the next day but even more excited for her scheduled outing with Captain Redmond. She waved them a very cheerful goodbye and then dashed up to her room to freshen up for his return. When she entered her chamber, she was instantly caught up again by the beauty of his bouquet. Burying her face in the blossoms, she inhaled deeply before remembering that she did not know the meaning of the peach blossom.

As a flower enthusiast from childhood, she had a book conveniently tucked away in her escritoire. Not bothering to sit, she skimmed through it until she came across the section on the language of flowers. "Oleander...orchid...palm leaves...aha!" Lilly read aloud. "The peach blossom...I am your captive..." Pressing the book into her chest, she closed her eyes. He was too good to be true. Could this be happening to her? *He is my captive? Oh, no*, she thought. *I am his.*

She twirled around slowly and then tossed herself onto the yellow counterpane that covered her bed. Then, unable to contain herself, she kicked her feet in excitement and covered her hand with her mouth, lest her squeal of delight alert the entire household of her joy. Rolling over to her stomach she reopened the book to verify the meaning of the peach blossom once again, as though she couldn't quite believe it.

I am your captive...I am your captive...

A knock on the door had Lilly slamming the book closed and leaping to her feet. Her mother opened the door slowly.

"Be sure to take a pelisse with you this afternoon. The sun is shining, but the wind is brisk today." Her mother smiled as she entered the room.

Her gaze, as Lilly's had been, was immediately drawn to the colorful, passionate flower arrangement. She then looked at her daughter suspiciously. Mrs. Bridge knew her daughter well. She also knew the meaning of such sparkling eyes and flushed cheeks.

"You seem to have found a beau rather quickly, Lilly." Her mother had told her that she believed in love. She'd also advised Lilly to be wary of it.

Lilly would be no such thing. "He is the one, Mother. I know it. He is so utterly handsome, and kind, and sweet…and handsome! What should I wear for our drive? Should I change my dress? Should I allow him to see me in the same outfit I have on now? Oh, Mama, I am so nervous! I am also so very happy!" Lilly flitted around pulling out various dresses for perusal.

Her mother gently seized her by the shoulders, quieting her. Tenderly, she tucked a stray curl behind Lilly's ear.

"The dress you are wearing is fine." She paused and then caressed her daughter's cheek. "Take deep breaths and slow your heart, my dear." She held her until she seemed satisfied Lilly was no longer swept up in excitement. Then, she squeezed Lilly's shoulders affectionately and turned to pace the room. Her mother would not send Lilly off without some well-timed maternal advice. "A curricle only seats two people, so you won't be able to take your maid along as chaperone. Therefore, you must be *very* proper. Not too much smiling and absolutely no giggling. Everyone will see everything you do once you enter the park." She stared at her daughter sternly. "I don't want anything to taint your reputation. Do you understand?" Her mother's lips pinched in concern.

Nodding, Lilly would lessen her mother's nerves. "Of course, Mother, I shall be the soul of discretion. No giggling. Sit up straight. Nod at the people I know. Look beyond the people I do not." Lilly slipped on the pelisse that matched her dress and turned to study herself in the mirror. "It's only a drive, Mother. You mustn't worry so."

Her mother met her stare in the mirror and then surprisingly grinned. "He is very charming, isn't he, Lilly?"

Lilly grinned back. "And handsome!"

****

Captain Redmond heard a step and turned as Miss Lilly Bishop descended to the foyer. He wondered if there would ever be a time when he didn't feel this pull toward her. He couldn't help but be mesmerized as she pulled on her gloves and then tied her bonnet under his watchful gaze. She wore the same dress from earlier but had donned a pelisse to cover her arms and shoulders. Once ready, she glanced up and smiled.

Good God, she lit up the room.

"I hope I haven't kept you waiting for long." She spoke, oh, so very properly.

He'd been waiting nearly twenty minutes.

"Not at all." He smiled down at her as they stepped outside.

The curricle he drove belonged to his brother, Edward. It rode high off the ground, was painted shiny black, and had plush maroon-leather seats. Edward was not one to go about in bright colors, as were some of the bachelors that season.

Lilly took one look at the vehicle and then glanced at him with an impish smile. "Oh, this looks fun! I have seen these high flyers about town before but never thought I would actually *ride* in one." And then, as she further examined it, her expression turned into a curious frown. "How does one get in?"

Michael laughed and then showed her where to step. Placing his hands on her waist, he lifted her easily so she could step around the wheel and sit down. He then easily climbed up himself and sat beside her. His groom handed him the reins and jumped on the back, and they were off.

Since so many members of the *ton* were in town, and it was nearing the fashionable hour for driving, traffic was heavy.

As Michael paid heed to drivers and riders around him, Lilly sat beside him in companionable silence. He was amused to note she took advantage of the ride by gazing all about at the mansions lining the popular route. Most of the residences they passed were owned by London's wealthiest noble families. Flowers bloomed and trees burst forth with their spring blossoms all along the route. After a while, Lilly settled back and seemed to relax.

"I looked it up, you know," she said quietly beside him.

"And..." Michael prompted. He knew exactly what she referred to.

"I rather like the notion."

Michael glanced over at her. A smug little smile danced on her lips. She was a minx. An innocent one, but a minx nonetheless.

"Very unnerving, you must realize, for a military man, such as myself."

He felt her stare upon him as he focused on the

road ahead. At the same moment, the curricle jostled and one of the wheels hit a rut. She reached and grabbed onto his leg, just above his knee. Before she could remove it, Michael covered her hand with his.

"The question is…" He leaned to the side so his lips barely brushed the top of her ear. "Now that you have me, what do you plan on doing with me?" He waited for her to blush.

She did not disappoint.

Lilly stared down at their hands and then back into his eyes. Another slow smile spread across her lush pink lips. This one, almost seductive. How many different smiles did she have? He anticipated the opportunity to find out. "I have no idea, Captain. What do you suggest?"

Michael raised one eyebrow at her. "As you are a lady and I am a gentleman, I'm afraid I cannot say."

The blush deepened.

"In that case"—she recovered—"I shall devise some special form of torture for you. Hmm…What does a lady do when she wishes to torture a special gentleman?"

Michael chuckled and then glanced over at her. "Make him go—"

Then they both spoke at the same time. "Shopping."

Her giggle delighted him. Unable to help himself, Michael turned her wrist and raised it to his lips. He inhaled her scent greedily, wishing she did not wear gloves, before settling her hand back onto his thigh. They had arrived at the entrance to the park, and he needed to grasp the reins once again with both hands.

Directing the horses onto the well-worn path,

Michael forced his attentions back to driving. All around them were other curricles and phaetons, some fellows on horseback, and a number of very fashionable ladies and gentlemen strolling on foot. He would have liked to ride out of the city but would not risk Lilly's reputation. He wanted time alone with her though.

Lilly was impressed as several people seemed to know Captain Redmond. Some waved, and the captain would stop the curricle to greet them. He introduced Lilly as a dear friend, the niece of Lady Eleanor Sheffield. He seemed to be well liked, a respected member of the *ton*. But he was also well known for his military prowess.

Gentlemen congratulated him on his exceptional service in the war. He had apparently come home with honors and a promotion. Ladies eyed her jealously.

Not until they reached a clearing and had turned down a less populated path could Lilly have any sort of meaningful conversation with him.

"How old are you, Captain Redmond?" He seemed to have acquired a great deal of respect to be as young as she thought he was.

"I am one-and-twenty," he answered. "Does that sound so very old? You, I am guessing are barely seventeen."

"I will be eighteen in September," she corrected him. Hopefully, he would not consider her too young! The thought of going back to Plymouth, to the baron, hardly bore consideration. "This will be my only season." She would be certain he knew this.

The captain nodded and pulled the curricle to a halt. Turning to face her, he grasped her hands before speaking.

"Then we must make certain it's a successful one." Even wearing gloves, she felt warmth emanating from him. For a scandalous second, she thought he was going to lean forward and kiss her right there! And she would have let him! But he pulled back instead and cleared his throat. "Shall we walk along the water?"

Lilly hadn't realized where they were until that moment. She had been intensely aware of his arms rubbing her shoulder whenever he turned the carriage or pulled back on the reins. Through her petticoat and skirt, his thigh pressed into hers each time they'd turned. The seat was not overly wide causing such necessary intimacy.

"I'd like that."

She hadn't intended to tell him this was to be her only season. The words had escaped of their own accord. *But he needed to know.*

Captain Redmond jumped off and then came around to assist her. She placed her hands upon his shoulders, and he grasped her waist. Leaning down, she trusted him with her weight. He didn't lower her to the ground right away, however.

Quite unhurriedly, he slid her close to his body until her feet landed softly upon the grass. She moved her hands along his collar and then briefly touched the nape of his neck. She wished she weren't wearing gloves so she could feel his hair. She wanted to stay in this position, close to him, touching him, but knew it was quite improper. Captain Redmond's groom seemed busy enough with the horses but could see them clearly from where he worked. Much of society's worst gossip began belowstairs.

As she pulled her hands down, her fingers dragged

a trail along his cravat. Reluctantly, she pressed upon his chest and took a step back.

Holding one another's gaze with open longing, he seemed as breathless as she was from the encounter. His hair had fallen forward again, giving him that sleepy, sensual look. Liquid warmth pooled in her center, and Lilly thought that perhaps her heart might jump out of her chest.

After what seemed like several minutes—but was, in fact, only a few seconds—Captain Redmond gestured toward the water, and they began their stroll.

At last! They could talk without other eyes and ears about.

"Tell me about your family," she said. She wanted to know everything about him.

He tugged at his cravat, uncomfortable at first. Apparently, he wasn't used to discussing personal matters. But he would not disappoint her. "I have not seen my father and brother since before I joined my regiment, two years ago."

And yet he lingered here, in London.

He was silent as they neared the water's edge.

"What is the age difference between you and your brother?" Lilly persisted. She was going to have to help him along. His discomfort in talking about himself merely endeared him to her more.

"My brother, Edward, is four years older. He has always been my hero. I trailed after him for the better part of childhood. Before he went off to school, he showed me how to be a hellion, just like him." He chuckled softly to himself, almost as though forgetting she was there. "My father's property is huge. It encompasses two lakes, several streams, a very large forest, and more meadows than I could count. For a couple of young boys with active imaginations, these places transform into an entirely different world. We were pirates, Robin Hood, and battling knights. Many evenings we would forget to return home until after dark." He grinned sheepishly. "That earned us a thrashing every time."

She imagined him as a youth, trailing after an older boy. "So you and Edward are close then?"

They had stopped walking and were looking out over the slow winding river. He raised one fist to his mouth and looked away from her. "We have grown apart."

Ah, so there was some sadness in his life. No family, it seemed, could escape it.

"It is difficult when one sibling becomes an adult and the other is still a child." She could not help thinking about her own sister, who had married while she was yet in the schoolroom.

He cleared his throat and turned back to her with a smile on his lips. It did not reach his eyes. It was not his real smile. "The heir to a dukedom requires training. He is separated from everyone else and taught to live his life independent of other children. There is little room for mistakes. My brother was distanced from me by my father."

"Your father separated his sons from each other?"

"It was necessary...and my brother—well—he changed. He has grown to be much like my father—disciplined, rigid, aloof—but we all must grow up eventually." With her hand tucked into his arm, they strolled alongside the river's edge. "What of your family? I can already tell you have a good relationship with your mother—and your aunt seems to think highly of you as well."

He was changing the subject. Was he estranged from his father and brother? As the second son, perhaps he'd been neglected. She must allow him his privacy in this—for now.

"I had an older sister, Rose, born ten years before me. She was beautiful." Lilly glanced over at him, feeling sheepish. "She was tall and elegant with gorgeous chestnut hair." She touched her own hair self-consciously. "I always felt like the ugly duckling around her." She grimaced at how self-pitying that sounded. "She was as much a mother to me as Mama is." Why had she told him that? Why had she drawn his attention to the unusual color of her hair? She hoped he did not decide she was unattractive now. "We lost her three years ago. It sometimes feels like summer will never come again. My parents adored Rose. They were so proud of her. She was beautiful, perfect." Lilly shook her head sadly. "She was a wonderful mother."

He was looking at her curiously. "Ah, but you have become a swan."

She felt her cheeks turn warm. She *had not* been fishing.

"But Rose married and left me all alone." She feigned a sigh, to show him that she was mocking herself, and then looked up at him to grin. "But she had a beautiful baby. Glenda is an adorable child. I visit with her whenever I can."

"How old is your niece?" He sounded genuinely interested.

"She is all of eight years old and has already surpassed me in sophistication. She is not as playful as she once was. Ever since Rose fell ill…"

"The child remains with her father?" Captain Redmond asked.

"Oh yes, but his estate is not far from ours, just over an hour's drive. Her father is…" Lilly searched for the best way to describe Lord Beauchamp. "Somewhat reclusive, although he dotes on Glenda. He rarely ventures away from his property. We retrieve Glenda every other week and bring her home for a few days at a time." Lilly laughed and shook her head. "Even I will admit she is becoming spoiled! She needs a mother in her life, but…" She trailed off, realizing what she was about to tell him.

"But?" he prompted. He was a good listener. It was as though the things she had to say actually mattered! He was a captain! He'd fought in a war and returned safely. He'd won metals. And yet he wanted to know her thoughts—her opinions.

"My father wishes for me to take on the position!" There, now. She'd said it.

She was going to have to explain such an announcement. "I love Glenda, truly, I do, but I could never marry Lord Beauchamp." Never. Never, ever, ever. "First and foremost, he is Rose's husband. So horribly wrong! And secondly, he is so very old! Thirdly and most importantly, I am not comfortable with him. He has this mustache that is absolutely ridiculous…" Lilly trailed off.

She really had said more than she ought.

"It is not legal," he said.

Lilly shrugged. "My father and the vicar have discussed this at length. Apparently, the vicar believes the law contradicts the Bible, and so he is willing to abide by my father's wishes."

Oh, dear. She'd told him far too much. For a moment, she thought his jaw clenched. At the same time, his arm went tense beneath her hand. She would change the subject. She ought not to talk about such things with him...even if it did feel as though she'd known him forever.

"What about you?" Lilly asked. "Does your father press you to marry?"

"No," Captain Redmond answered, "I am not the heir. That particular expectation has been placed solely upon my brother." He sounded irritated. Lilly wondered if he was offended by what she'd said about Lord Beauchamp, her father, and the vicar. She really must learn more restraint! Nonetheless, the whole of the situation was a sore spot with her. She had no wish to marry her sister's widower.

"But—" He stopped and turned to look at her. His expression was serious, stern even. "—perhaps when I've found the right match..." He stepped closer and put one hand up to her cheek. Pausing momentarily, he glanced toward the hill behind them.

Not a soul in sight.

Lilly realized they'd stopped in a somewhat secluded location.

Lifting his other hand, he then tipped her bonnet back. Lilly inhaled the warmth of his scent. Nothing could stop this. Nothing could stop them.

Needing to be closer, she pushed herself up onto her toes and tilted her head back. Oh, yes, she thought, before parting her lips.

His face moved closer and blocked out the sunlight.

And then his lips were on hers.

It was exactly what she'd been craving.

"Oh," she whispered at his touch. His lips nibbled at the corner of her mouth, and she tasted the essence that was him. Not sure what to do with her hands, she fluttered them at her side before placing them on his hips. His arms wrapped completely around her as he deepened their kiss.

Lilly was lost to all reason. Her heartbeat pounded in her ears as she gasped for air. She clung to him, lest her knees give out. *Breathe*, she reminded herself. *Breathe*. She was *not* going to faint during her first kiss. She melted into him further.

Michael growled and explored her mouth. With their bodies pressed together, he felt hard all over, his arms like steel around her. And then his lips abandoned hers. Hot breath trailed from her chin, to her jaw, and then her neck.

Lilly had never felt anything like this. Surely, she was turning to liquid. Heat poured through her limbs and settled between her thighs. What was this? In that moment, she no longer felt she belonged to herself. She was a shared person, open to this man she'd only just met.

A cool breeze alerted her to the fact that she no longer wore her bonnet. A few strands of hair had tumbled out of her coiffure. The thought of her hair being down in public frightened her. Suddenly realizing their vulnerability, her vulnerability at being discovered in such a compromising position, Lilly stiffened.

"Captain," she said, "Michael, we must stop."

Michael stilled as they both sought to regain some composure. His head remained buried in her neck, but he had ceased whatever it was he had been doing to render her so unhinged.

"Lilly." His voice was somewhat muffled.

"Yes, Michael."

"You are definitely not going to marry your brother-in-law."

"Of course not," she said.

Chapter Six
Help for an Old Friend

1824

Why had Michael been so cruel?

Restlessness coursed through Lilly as she strode back to the chamber she was sharing with Glenda.

He had hurt her.

And worse, she now doubted everything she'd believed about him for nearly a decade!

Upon entering, Lilly found Glenda sprawled out on the bed and Mary, their lady's maid, folding and smoothing the clothing she had pulled from their trunks. The chamber they'd paid for had only one window, a large bed for two, and a trundle pulled out for a servant. There was one wooden chair and a desk.

Lilly paced agitatedly near the window. She was more than a little upset by her conversation with Michael. He hadn't returned to London because people had been dying! He'd been caught in a scarlet fever epidemic. He'd not willingly abandoned her after all, had he?

He would not lie, would he? What had she done?

Looking around to locate the leading string for Miss Fussy, Lilly beckoned Glenda to come with her. "Let's take Miss Fussy outside for a little exercise. It has been a long day of sitting, and I for one could use some air."

But Glenda was still upset with her. "When did you tell him? He knew you are my aunt! You promised me no one would be told! Already you have ruined everything!"

Lilly sighed. "He remembered from before. And you have no need to worry. The duke is not a man to spread gossip." He would not. In spite of his disgust of Lilly, he would not do anything to ruin an innocent girl's season. "He will not tell anyone. Come with me, Glenda. I cannot bear to sit inside all evening."

Glenda stared down at the pretty new slippers she had insisted upon wearing that evening. "It would not be good if your illegal marriage were to be made public. I would be ruined." Glenda's lips were pinched. She was not in a very forgiving mood this evening. "And I do not wish to go out of doors. There is too much mud. I will stay inside with Mary."

"Mary will enjoy the fresh air as well," Lilly said. "We'll never be able to fall asleep tonight if we idle in here all evening. Now come along, we won't go far. We'll be cautious not to step in any puddles."

But Glenda would not be convinced. "I am staying here, and Mary can help me prepare for bed, thank you." She sniffed haughtily. "It is important that I get my rest."

Well then.

Lilly paused for only a moment. She was just going to have to go out alone. It most likely was not a very good idea, but she could not remain indoors for even a minute longer. After all, she would not be *totally alone.*

"Do you need to go potty, Miss Fussy?" Her bosom companion of over seven years now perked her ears in excitement. An unlikely-looking dog, Miss Fussy was a small dachshund, low to the ground, long in body and short of leg. A few months after Lilly's mother's death, her aunt Eleanor had come for a short visit and brought Miss Fussy along as a gift.

The pup had been about three months old and weighed less than a cup of tea. As she held the tiny animal and allowed it to lick and nip at her fingers, Lilly's heart had jumped. How could one not fall instantly in love with such soulful eyes and expressive ears? Lilly had embraced the warmth she'd been missing since her marriage.

Miss Fussy had needed her.

After donning her favorite, well-worn cashmere shawl, Lilly grabbed the leading string and scooped Miss Fussy into her arms. Having such short legs, the dog was not very agile. It would be easiest to simply carry her down the stairs and through the tap room. Once outside, Lilly tied the leading string to Miss Fussy's collar, set her on the wet ground, and followed the little dog as she explored. The night air cooled Lilly's flushed skin.

Michael's unexpected appearance had brought a flood of forgotten emotions raining down inside of her.

And he was a duke now! Except her heart simply knew him as Michael. Her heart *knew* him, and it *wanted* him. It had come back to life, rejoicing the moment she recognized him in the taproom that afternoon. Foolish, foolish heart.

Michael was betrothed.

Betrothed to a young heiress, it seemed. She was probably beautiful too. Probably tall and slim and elegant. All of the things that Lilly was not. No doubt, she had perfect alabaster skin, whereas Lilly's was tanned and a little freckled from working outside in her gardens. Lilly sighed.

The sun had set, but the moon shone brightly. She wasn't ready to go back into that stuffy lodging room again. A slight breeze had Lilly pulling her shawl more tightly around herself.

As much as she loved to read, she struggled to read by candlelight. It tired her eyes. At that thought, she realized her eyes were watering. She impatiently wiped away a stray tear.

She wasn't crying. She'd stopped crying years ago. Tears were for a woman who was sad and disappointed. A woman didn't get sad and disappointed if she didn't expect too much. A woman didn't expect too much when she'd accepted her lot in life.

As the wife of the Baron Beauchamp, Lilly had learned exactly what that was to be. She was a replacement for her sister, a sorry replacement. But she hadn't even managed that. She'd become an object of disdain, to her husband, to Glenda, even to the servants. The less Lilly dwelled on all she had dreamed of as a girl, the less disappointed she would be now.

She would not shed her pessimistic outlook, even knowing the baron was gone forever.

Scooping Miss Fussy into her arms, she allowed the dog to lick her chin. She then tucked the dog's head down and kissed the soft furry spot between her ears. Miss Fussy snuggled into her, and they absorbed one another's warmth.

"You shouldn't be out here alone." An approaching voice interrupted her solitude.

Of course, it would be Michael.

"I'm not alone," she said, indicating Miss Fussy. "I have my most excellent bodyguard here." She smiled a little. It wasn't a smart idea to wander outside, in a strange place, in the dark no less, alone. But she was a widow now. Did her reputation even matter anymore? She supposed it wouldn't help Glenda if her stepmother were considered to be s*candalous*.

Michael eyed the dog a bit warily. Miss Fussy eyed him right back with a low growl and fur standing on end.

"You won't want to come much closer to her. You see, she is my protector."

What was she thinking? Walking about outside all alone? Likely more than one unsavory lecher patronized this inn's tap room. Michael was glad he'd caught sight of her out the window. Anyone could have followed her. Miss Fussy and her mistress did not look very fierce, regardless of the small dog's defensiveness. In fact, Michael thought, Lilly looked vulnerable.

He had behaved badly at dinner, goading her. He hadn't meant to be cruel, but all the hurt of her desertion, the years of heartache, had risen up inside of him upon seeing her again.

Which was ridiculous after all this time.

"I am sorry," he said softly, "for provoking you earlier. It was…unkind of me."

Lilly eyed him suspiciously. "It was," she granted. And then, "I'll admit you've had what seems to have been a rather awful day."

Appreciating her consideration, he smiled ruefully. "Oh hell, that's putting it mildly!" They stood together quietly for a moment, neither of them speaking. Then, "I couldn't believe it when I heard your voice. It was quite a shock…seeing you…" His voice trailed off softly, almost to a whisper.

Lilly seemed to force an uncomfortable laugh. "I nearly didn't recognize you! Nearly every inch of you was covered in mud!" But then she grinned. "It was even in your hair. And you stood there, issuing orders! You should have seen yourself." Miss Fussy squirmed in Lilly's arms. Crouching down, Lilly placed the dog on the ground.

"You finally got your pet." Whenever they had been in the park and come across a dog, she had always expressed her desire for one. And he had remembered. He remembered everything.

"She has been such a comfort to me."

"After your—after Beauchamp's passing?"

"Oh, no, I've had Miss Fussy for seven years now." She paused. "Lord Beauchamp could not refuse. She was a gift from my Aunt Eleanor after Mother died." Lilly took a few steps when the dog tugged at the leading string. "Father was right to ensure we were provided for. I believe he knew himself ill before Mother and I travelled to London that spring. He grew very weak, couldn't keep his food down, and then stopped eating all together. He died the day after Christmas."

"Both of your parents are passed?"

"Yes." She glanced at him with a rueful smile. "Mother was not the same afterwards. Lord Beauchamp allowed her to live at Beauchamp Manor for those last months, and I was glad to have her with me. But…" She swallowed hard. "She loved Papa more than life, I think."

Lilly followed the dog to the edge of the clearing.

It was in her nature to care for helpless creatures. No wonder the pup defended her so bravely. There was a time when Michael had imagined her the mother of his own…He shoved his hands into his pockets and strolled alongside her.

"Did you—Do you—Have you any other children from your marriage?" This was a difficult question, but he wanted to know. Had she loved her husband? Had she been happy?

She shuttered her eyes and looked away. "I have been happy to be a mother to Glenda." She paused and pinched her lips together, then picked the dog up again. Miss Fussy burrowed into Lilly's shawl. "It was not meant to be." She tilted her head back to look up at the sky. After a weighted pause, she continued, "Such a clear night. I think it will not rain tomorrow. Do you plan on hiring horses to catch up with your other carriages?"

Ah, it seemed perhaps all had not been right in her marriage. And Lilly would not share this with a former lover. She would not wish for his pity.

Michael offered her his arm. "Let's walk," he said. The wind had increased and added to the chill. Still holding the pup, Lilly hesitated and then tucked her free hand in his arm. Touching her brought a new wave of memories. Her hand felt more fragile than before. She seemed to lean into him for warmth as they walked along the edge of the cut-away forest. Perhaps she too, was remembering…

Michael cleared his throat. "To answer your question, Jackson doesn't have any horses available. We'll have to wait for the mail coach. Unfortunately, this puts me in London later than I was hoping. That is, unless Duncan, my valet, decided to return for us. But he doesn't even know...This entire situation is unprecedented, I'm afraid."

"I've never heard of a duke travelling on a mail coach before." Lilly glanced down at the toes of her slippers, peeking out from under her dress. The ground was soft here, still damp from the rain. And then she surprised him. "Parliament opens in a week. You lords have some dicey questions to address this session. Have there been any uprisings on your properties? I had heard they were mostly in the north."

"Not on my properties, but nearby. I don't agree with the Corn Laws, but most of my colleagues see them as necessary." His previous worries arose at her words. "Must keep the aristocracy strong, you know," he added sarcastically.

"But they have accomplished just the opposite!" Lilly nearly gasped. "When I have visited with our tenants and nearby farmers, the wives do not keep their opinions from me. The tax is the source of much resentment. There is more unrest to come."

"I wish it weren't the case, but it's likely you're correct." Anger stirred him. "There are other ways to bolster one's estate. The old ways are failing. We must look to innovation to keep people working. Build factories that make industrial parts and textile works. I can hardly keep up with all of them, but it's necessary for me to do so." He was surprised she followed politics. Most women did not. He knew that Lady Natalie did not, despite her father's involvement.

Lilly nodded in approval. "Some of the tenants talk of emigrating to America. It baffles me that so many peers support the Corn Laws. It's as though they have placed sacks over their heads."

Michael clenched his fists. "Precisely why I need to be in London now." In agitation, he stepped away from her, picked up a stick, and hurled it across the field. "The highwaymen got away with some rather important documents. I don't know if it was inadvertent or not. I had counted on using them as evidence to garner votes. All that work…gone. I have a few allies but not nearly enough. It's going to take a miracle to bring in the votes needed to pass the amendment." And then he paused and turned back toward her. "Do you remember Viscount Danbury, Hugh?" At her nod, he continued. "He's planned some strategic gatherings— formal dinners, that is—this week. The Earl of Ravensdale has as well. We're hoping to use the social occasions to convince a few of the less adamant peers to our way of thinking."

"Ah…" Lilly nodded. Had she realized that the Earl of Ravensdale was his fiancée's father? "And these dinners commence…?"

"In two days," Michael finished for her.

"Well, then, you simply must be in London in two days then." She spoke firmly, with a stubbornness he remembered. "You will travel into town with us. There is enough room for you and one of your grooms. The others, and your man of business, can ride in with the mail." She grimaced. "Glenda won't mind if we eliminate a few stops. In fact, she will likely appreciate the opportunity to arrive in London sooner. She is impatient for the season."

Michael would have liked to have been able to decline her generous offer. Two days in her company could not be a good idea. He was an engaged man. Was it possible to spend time with her and not want her even more? Already, he'd sensed that pull, that magnetism they'd shared in the past. When she had taken his arm, he'd again experienced that notion of completeness.

But she was no longer the woman for him. No, that ship had sailed, so to speak. The pain of Lilly Bridge was far behind him now—where it would stay.

What *was* important were the votes. He needed to be in London as soon as possible so that he, Danbury, and the earl could work toward changing some influential minds.

"I would be grateful, my lady, if you are certain it's not too much trouble. To arrive in London on time, however, we'll have to keep stops to a minimum."

"Of course, *Your Grace,* we can make such a small sacrifice for a worthy cause." Lilly nodded agreeably. He had addressed her formally, and she had returned in kind. "I suppose if we are to leave early in the morning, we ought to be getting ourselves off to bed—I mean, I should get back to our chamber, to my chamber…" He'd flustered her.

"Your driver was in the taproom earlier. I'll apprise him of the change in plans, if that is amenable to you?"

"Yes, please," Lilly said. "And Michael…"

"Yes?" His heart skipped a beat at her use of his name. No one called him "Michael" anymore.

"Can you procure some pistols?" Her brows furrowed as she seemed to consider he had already been the target of one attack.

He'd be damned if he'd be an easy target for another one. "I already have."

****

Early the next morning, after a quick breakfast in

77

the duke's private dining room, Michael assisted Lilly, Glenda, and their maid, outside and into an ancient, but well-made, passenger coach before climbing in behind them. Looking the worse for wear, Arty climbed onto the carriage driver's box with Lilly's driver, Mr. Fletch. Fletch seemed happy for the company. Michael had procured a pistol for each of them, as well as himself.

Glenda and Lilly sat facing forward with Miss Fussy on Lilly's lap, and Michael took a seat across from her, beside the maid. Mary was not a small woman, so he didn't have a great deal of space. Glenda had brought along some embroidery while Lilly carried a few books in a satchel. All of them were a little sleepy so the first half an hour passed quietly.

Michael would have appreciated the tranquility a great deal more had he realized what was to come. For Glenda, once alert and awake, chattered enough to make up for all of them.

She began her assault by peppering him with a barrage of questions about London and the *ton*. After attempting to answer one, and then another, and being interrupted with the next, he quickly realized he was not necessary to the conversation and happily lapsed into a contemplative silence.

The girl chattered exhaustively about all things to do with fashion—high-waisted dresses, morning dresses, walking dresses, evening dresses, pelisses, bonnets, gloves, and lace fichus. Half of which he had no idea what they were. She informed him that, as a debutante, she must wear only very light colors, but did he think she would look better in pastel pink, or periwinkle blue, or perhaps in lilac? Which shade of lilac, a rose shade or more of a purple? She went on and on…

Lilly appeared to be asleep, but occasionally he caught her tightening her mouth in an attempt to conceal her mirth. The little wench knew Glenda was boring him endlessly. And since he was awake, and a gentleman, he was forced to nod occasionally and smile. Of course, Lilly, the minx, would find pleasure in this. The worrisome thought was that perhaps Glenda was not so very different from Lady Natalie!

Once such a notion entered his head, Michael forced himself to examine it.

In truth, he hadn't spent much time alone with his betrothed. They had danced together several times at the endless balls he'd attended last season, and he had admired her and told her so eloquently. He had cheerfully fetched numerous glasses of lemonade for her, many of which had gone untouched, and she'd politely once pointed out to him that she preferred chicken to beef. Of course, she was always present when he dined with the earl at his town house. After dinner, the ladies always disappeared, and the men drank port or brandy and discussed politics, usually.

What else? What did he and Lady Natalie talk about?

Ah yes…

"I think I shall allow my gloves to go just past my elbows as my arms are smooth and very white. Lilly will have to wear very long gloves to cover her skin. I tell her all the time she shouldn't spend so many hours out of doors—it isn't good for one's complexion—but she just disappears into the sunshine anyway. Once outside, she sometimes removes her bonnet as she works. Oh, yes, she must wear very long gloves indeed.

The long gloves must be tied with a string at the top so they do not slip…"

Fashion. Lady Natalie often mentioned shopping trips. Oh, God, he sincerely hoped she wasn't the slave to fashion that Miss Beauchamp was.

Lilly frowned at the comment about her wearing long gloves. He could tell she wanted to correct the girl but could not while feigning sleep.

This gave Michael the perfect opportunity to observe her. She was thinner. He liked how her hair contrasted with the tanned color of her skin. She looked exotic. Lilly had been passionate about all things to do with flowers when they'd first met. She'd had quite a passionate nature.

They had explored that nature whenever possible.

Chapter Seven
Exploring Lilly's Nature

1815

Following that first drive to the park, after that first kiss, Lilly's life revolved around the occasions when she would see him again. Her mother cautioned her against wearing her heart upon her sleeve. Every morning, in fact, over breakfast, she chastised Lilly for making herself too available to the captain.

"Men," she told Lilly, "even gentlemen, appreciate the thrill of the chase."

But not Michael.

He was different.

Her mother then changed tactics and began taking extra pains to ensure for meticulous chaperonage. She either performed the duty herself or instructed the maids with strict rules regarding the diligence required.

The freedom Lilly had experienced at the Willoughby ball was not to be experienced at any subsequent events. Her mother never allowed her to dance with Captain Redmond more than two times, and, when they attempted to walk out onto a terrace or patio, either her mama or her aunt watched them—never far away.

The moments in which they *were* able to steal some privacy, without a watchful chaperone, were limited to open carriage rides and an occasional moment in the drawing room with the door open. Her aunt or mother always nearby.

And Lilly had made some friends.

Somewhat isolated since her sister's death, Lilly hadn't had many such opportunities back in Plymouth. She'd nearly forgotten the pleasure to be had with ladies her own age. Furthermore, they'd so enjoyed their first shopping trip, it had become the first of many such outings.

Rarely a day passed that she, Caroline Harris, and Penelope Crone hadn't made plans of some sort. And they complemented one another's personalities.

Caroline, bubbly and outgoing, had a tendency to point out absurdities as they toured about town. Penelope frowned upon the absurd and was very opinionated. She liked to discuss and ridicule the rules women were forced to follow—rules, she never failed to point out—that had been established by men. Between the two of them, the girls added a sense of whimsy and inventiveness to Lilly's days.

These outings also made a much-needed distraction from her feelings for Michael, which at times, overwhelmed her. Being able to enjoy herself, apart from him, grounded Lilly and reassured her mother. There was a certain vulnerability a lady felt when one other person became so essential to her happiness.

One particularly sunny morning, while wandering through various shops with their maids discreetly behind them, the girls coincidentally met up with Mr. Harris, Viscount Danbury, and Captain Redmond. This chance meeting was fortunate, for they realized quickly that, when gadding about in a group of both ladies and gentlemen, chaperones weren't nearly as intrusive.

Amongst a cluster of such friends, a courting couple could find themselves afforded some unexpected leniency. Michael, clever as he was, took full advantage of these opportunities. It was as though the springtime was made for them—made for their love.

Toward the end of the season, Michael told Lilly he wished to show her his estate in the south. He told her he would speak with her father but wished for her to see his home, first. It wasn't dreadfully far from London, near Southampton, but the journey would take two days by carriage. They would need to make the trip in a manner that would not harm Lilly's reputation.

During tea one afternoon, Aunt Eleanor solved the conundrum.

She suggested the captain make a house party of it. If she and Mrs. Bridge chaperoned the group of young people, the break from town would be considered utterly respectable.

Michael didn't want to delay.

He would leave the next day with Danbury, and they could address any repairs necessary before the party arrived. Lilly and the other guests would not leave town until Sunday. Three days later!

Melancholy at the thought of not seeing Michael for all of five days, she attempted to suggest they all travel together.

But her mother restrained her exuberance. If Lilly did not show some patience in all of this, her mother promised her, they could forego the journey altogether.

Her mother didn't understand. What with all of this *longing* for him and *aching* for him!

There was some consolation, however, in that

Viscount Danbury had planned a party at Vauxhall for that very night. The evening promised to be romantic, indeed!

Every season Danbury and his mother hosted their friends in a private booth. Upon hearing that the viscountess would be present, Lady Eleanor and Mrs. Bridge relinquished their rather demanding duties as chaperones with relief. It had been a busy season, and they were run down from attempting to keep up with the young people so far. They welcomed a quiet evening at home.

The weather was perfect that evening, and as the sun dipped behind the horizon, a warm breeze barely stirred the leaves on the perfectly placed trees. There was no threat of rain, not a single cloud. Nearly bursting with excitement, Lilly stood at the railing of the barge with Michael by her side.

She wore another new dress, purchased by her aunt, this one more risqué than her others. Aunt Eleanor wasn't nearly as prudish as her mother could be.

The bodice, although not quite scandalous, displayed a tantalizing hint of cleavage and the back was cut daringly low as well. Made of a vibrant blue silk chiffon, the simple cut of the nearly backless dress was more sophisticated than anything she had ever worn. When they had departed from her aunt's town house, Lilly wore a shawl, covering the exposed skin on her back. Had her mother seen it, she would not have allowed Lilly to set foot out the door.

Whether it was due to the dress or the fact that Michael was departing the next day, Lilly's mood was unusually daring that night. Up until that point, they'd managed to steal but a few kisses since the initial ride in the park. And those kisses had been short and sweet, as there had always been a chaperone nearby.

Like every other lady attending the gardens that night, Lilly was warned not to separate from her group when exploring the meandering paths in the forest. Even Aunt Eleanor told her to remain only on the paths that were illuminated with lanterns. The other trails, she'd said, could be quite hazardous to a woman's virtue.

Of course, these warnings merely served to pique Lilly's curiosity. And by the time she'd climbed into the carriage, she was already hoping she and Michael might find themselves lost together on one of these very same dangerous trails.

A roguish look from Michael suggested he had similar designs.

Danbury had reserved one of the more extravagant boxes for their party which allowed for a protected vantage point in which to dine and watch the revelry. The viscountess insisted that anything else would have been common and vulgar. Gently bred young ladies did *not* eat in public.

For the first hour or so, everybody stayed in the supper box, drinking champagne and sampling the sliced ham and strawberries provided. There was an orchestra and dancing and a great deal more to see, however, and the younger people soon announced their intent to explore the famous gardens.

Michael and Lilly, Harris and Penelope, and Danbury and Caroline stepped out into the merriment with warnings that under no circumstances were they to allow themselves to be separated from each other. Nodding reassurances toward the viscountess, they were quickly swallowed by the river of revelers strolling among the amusements. Colorful paper lanterns illuminated their way, casting the night in a mystical light, with shadows laden with opportunity.

As they drew close to the music, Michael swung Lilly around playfully, in a very un-*ton*-like dance. Her curls, so carefully pinned up earlier, quickly came undone and tumbled down her back. The sensation of locks of hair caressing her exposed skin lured Lilly into shedding inhibitions which had been drilled into her for years.

With the music, the people, the champagne, the lanterns and shadows everywhere, the festival atmosphere enchanted Lilly. She laughed and danced freely. Her body humming all the while.

Michael's fingers brushed along her back often and with a possessiveness he'd not shown so openly before. And as he watched her, a tension built inside him.

He'd known she was beautiful all along, but tonight…well, there was something different about her. She'd somehow woven a spell around him, his very own Aphrodite. He kept hold of her, jealously, as they were pulled along the throng of merrymakers. Even before she'd had any champagne, her eyes watched him boldly. There'd been a hunger in her gaze, very similar to what he himself felt. He knew she dreaded the short separation awaiting them both tomorrow.

As did he.

With youthful exuberance, she threw her head back to watch the fireworks. But she was not so caught up in them as one might believe. For after just a few explosions, she glanced out of the side of her eyes toward him. Her slow smile was a secret invitation that only he could read. In that moment, he knew, *with every fiber of his being,* that there would never be another woman he would want as badly.

He would be the man to awaken her deepest passions. He would one day feel her tremble with need for him, skin on skin, and bury himself inside of her. He craved to touch every part of her, knowing she burned for him too.

Since that first glance, he'd known their connection was special. Tonight, however, brought with it an awareness that the emotions he experienced were much more than a passing attraction.

He wanted to be the person with whom she shared her soul.

He loved her. He wanted her love as well. No, he needed her love—desperately.

With a suddenness that surprised her, he grasped her hand and pulled her away from the crowd onto a nearby path in the woods. She followed him, lifting her skirts so she could keep up with his pace. As the fireworks popped and exploded in the sky, Lilly ran with him brazenly.

Spying an opening, exactly what he had been looking for, he drew her off the main path and into the darkness. Like a hidden portal, it beckoned them into a conveniently secluded retreat. There was a thick branch, growing sideways, keeping them from disappearing any deeper. Michael maneuvered Lilly so she leaned against the branch. And even though they both breathed heavily from their mad dash, he did not pause to rest.

Instead, he hungrily sought her kiss.

He'd waited for this all night—good God—all

spring. That's what this tension had been. Being so near her and not being able to make love to her had tormented him for weeks now.

Like a flower in full bloom, her lips opened, soft and welcoming. She pressed herself into him, demanding more. Like a vixen, she nipped at his tongue lightly with her teeth.

Michael had never imagined she could abandon herself to him so utterly, so completely. She clutched at him as though he was a lifeline. Closer, she wanted him closer.

He'd not resist her demand.

He didn't just kiss her. He tasted, he probed, he explored. His tongue discovered the tender skin on the inside of her cheek, the roof of her mouth. His hands were equally inquisitive.

One of them caressed its way down her naked back and then slipped inside her dress. His other hand reached up to cup her breast and squeeze it gently, testing its weight. So perfect. So soft.

His mouth drifted down her neck, tasting all her sweetness as he went. Lilly's head was thrown back. She panted in faint little gasps.

"More," Lilly whispered, her hands in his hair. Her words fueled the inferno already blazing inside of him. "More."

Michael complied, pulling her short, puffed sleeves down her arms, exposing both of her breasts to the sultry night air. In awe of her, he held himself still, simply gazing at her in the shadowed moonlight.

And then she licked her lips.

Putting his hands on her waist, he abruptly lifted her up to sit on the branch. Unable to stop himself, his mouth sought out the puckered tip of one breast. As he suckled, his hands clutched at her dress and petticoats. Understanding, in perfect harmony with his needs, she lifted her legs and wrapped them around him. He wanted to free himself and press into her warmth and dampness. She would be wet. She would be ready for him.

But she was also shivering.

She was so sweet. She was a virgin. She would one day be his completely.

But not tonight.

"Lilly." He gasped for breath. "I need to stop."

She tightened her legs around his waist. "No!"

"Lilly," he said again, burying his forehead under her chin. "Not here. Not now." He was but a hair's breadth from coming completely undone.

As a hint of sanity began to niggle its way back into Lilly's passion clouded thoughts, she dropped her legs from around his waist.

They sat quietly, holding each other as their breathing slowed. Michael turned his head and pressed his ear against her chest. The beat of her heart squeezed at his own.

"I will speak to your father." He finally found his voice. "When will he arrive in London? If not soon, then I will journey to Plymouth myself."

"He should be here when we return from your house party." There was a smile in her voice. She was everything he ever wanted.

Remembering he was leaving tomorrow, he pulled her closer once again.

"I wish I could go with you." It was as though she read his mind.

Michael laughed and moaned a little, both at the same time. "I'd have to take you to Gretna Green first, my love." He then lifted his face to gaze into her golden eyes. "Be patient, Lilly. We have the rest of our lives."

She nodded, touching his face. She seemed to marvel at his whiskers. His jaw was roughened slightly as his recent shave had been early that morning. Her eyes were warm and loving.

"I can't wait to see your home. I will love it, you know, simply because it is yours."

"It's been a while since I've been there." Michael was uncertain as to how much work awaited him, but he would make the repairs himself, if necessary. He wanted it to be perfect for her.

Before his resolve left him, Michael pulled Lilly's dress up to return her to modesty. With his assistance, she hopped off the branch and then attempted to straighten her skirts. He watched her, smiling, as she did her best to tidy up. She had leaves in her hair, and her skirts were twisted tightly around her.

"Hold still, love," he said. He plucked the leaves and twigs out of her hair and then tugged at her dress in a few strategic places. "Now, turn around."

As she did so, she looked over her shoulder watching him. "You're rather good at this, you know." She sounded surprised as he brushed some dirt off the back of her skirt. "Now come here. Let me fix your hair. It's all mussed up."

"Who's to blame for that?" he teased but did as she asked and then delighted in her touch as she massaged his scalp lovingly.

He would have her touch every day. Soon.

Over the past several weeks, they had cultivated

this connection, this…relationship. He had never imagined being blessed with a wife whom he could love so thoroughly. He was a lucky man indeed.

****

"When I've visited before, I paid more attention to the farming side. I barely looked in the house…God, I hope it's not in ruins."

Danbury chuckled and shook his head. The two men had been friends since they attended Eton. They reminisced for a while as they made their way out of town, and then Hugh sighed loudly.

"You are going to offer for her, then?" he asked as they rode leisurely heading south.

Michael looked over at his friend and nodded. "As soon as her father arrives in London."

"That's what I was afraid of. How can you be ready for this? You've just returned from war, and already you are taking on a wife. Hell, man, you'll be setting up your nursery come Christmas." It was well known that Hugh considered marriage a necessary evil. Even then, only for gentlemen well into their forties, or fifties…if one could get away with it. "For Christ's sake, you're too young for this! *I'm* too young for this! If you marry, my mother will never let me hear the end of it. Don't do this to me! Sow some wild oats first, for heaven's sake."

Michael pondered his friend's words. Danbury's mother, sister, and aunts had been pressuring Hugh to marry since he'd inherited the title three years ago. He was the last of his line, and the burden to secure it was heavy, indeed. Michael knew Hugh though, and the more they pestered him to marry, the more he would avoid it.

"It's not like that for me, Hugh." He understood his friend's concerns. "There is no pressure from anybody. In fact, my father and brother couldn't care less what I do." At the same time he said this, a part of him anticipated introducing them to Lilly. They would love her. They would realize he was ready to settle down and perhaps, even, worthy of some respect. He hated that he craved their respect.

"They care," Danbury contradicted him. "In their own way. You just never see it. Your brother and father are two of a kind. Stoic. Undemonstrative sort of fellows. They think they're doing right by you, allowing you to live your own life. You'd appreciate them if you had my lot.

"But that's not what we're talking about." Danbury pressed his point. "We're talking about Miss Bridge. Marriage. Children. Forever after and all that."

"I know."

"And?"

"I know I am young. Good God, *she's* only seventeen. But I also know she is *the one*. I can't let her go—I won't let her go." Michael looked over at Danbury again. "When you've met the right lady, you'll understand." Then unwilling to continue this line of conversation, he said, "Let's pick up the pace, man. We'll never get there at this rate."

****

"Oh, Miss Bridge." The lady's maid gasped as she assisted Lilly out of her nightgown that morning. "You've got love bites!"

"What?" Had Betty said *love bites*? The memory of Michael's mouth upon her skin came quickly to mind, and Lilly glanced down in horror.

"Use the looking glass, Miss Bridge, you'll see—on your shoulder and...well...lower."

Oh, dear Lord. The maid had the right of it. Purplish, reddish marks marred her skin, exactly where Michael's lips had been. Other areas were reddened from his whiskers. Good heavens, there was even a mark on her breast. "Oh, dear Lord!" This time she spoke the words aloud.

Half of her was livid with Michael for doing such a thing to her. Had he known? Had he realized what he was doing?

And then the other half, the wanton half of her, was thrilled. It was as though he had marked her for his own.

But she then had to face that third half of herself. That half her mother had instilled so thoroughly. These very marks that thrilled her somewhat were also a recipe for ruin! If her mother saw them she would be livid! And her father! Good heavens, if he were to know about any of this, he would likely try to kill Michael. What if he called him out? What if her father and Captain Redmond dueled?

Nobody must find out! She turned to the maid.

"Betty, are they permanent? Can we make them go away?"

"Nay, not permanent, but they do last about a week." The maid surveyed Lilly's skin closely. "We'll conceal them with a high neckline and long sleeves today. As they fade, perhaps we can cover them with face paint." Looking out the window, she sighed. "'Twould be more comfortable if the weather weren't so warm, Miss Bridge."

"It doesn't matter, Betty. No one—and I mean not

93

a single living soul—must ever see these…these…oh my God, I don't even know what to call them. You are certain they are not permanent?" She implored the maid for reassurance.

Betty laughed. "Yes. They will disappear. More of a nuisance for now, miss."

Lilly slipped into her chemise and then dropped onto the bench in front of the mirror. She then sat anxiously while Betty lifted Lilly's hair to examine the extent of Michael's handiwork. "Let me find a dress to cover this up. Not to worry, dearie. Nobody will be the wiser as to what your scoundrel has been up to."

Lilly assessed herself in the mirror and then reached for a cloth that had been soaking in cool lavender water. Dabbing at the tender skin, she was amazed at Michael's audacity. As she touched each mark with the cool rag, she recalled the sensations he'd aroused with his lips and hands and whiskers. A flush swept through her body, reddening her face and neck even further, as she relived a few of those moments.

Lilly held the cloth up to her face and inhaled deeply.

Before coming to London, she had dreamed of finding some fantasy man who would save her from marrying Lord Beauchamp. Such a man had been hazy, heroic, handsome, and unreal. Nothing could have prepared her for the emotions that had flared up between Michael and herself.

He was so much more than a fantasy.

He had lived an entire life without her. He was dashing, rakish, and wanted by many other women. She had seen the jealous looks sent her way. Debutantes and even some older women glared at her with envy.

And he was hers.

Better than a dream come true, for she couldn't have dreamt up a man as honorable and complex as Captain Redmond.

Mrs. Redmond...Mrs. Captain Michael Redmond. And then she wondered. Was the wife of the second son of a duke a lady? She should know such things.

Lord and Lady Michael...ah yes, she loved the sound of that. If Michael was a lord, surely she would be a lady. Was he a lord?

Caught up in her daydreams, Lilly donned the high-necked dress Betty had chosen but was drawn back into the present when she saw her reflection once again.

She looked ridiculous! Why, it was nearly June!

Nobody would be so buttoned up in June...except perhaps her matronly aunt...and her mother. Good Lord, her friends would think she'd gone batty!

Betty twisted Lilly's hair into a tight chignon and laughed. "Don't mind my saying so, but Miss Bridge, you hardly have any pins left for me to do your hair with." Lilly just smiled at Betty in the mirror.

"I guess I'll have to go shopping then." With that, she smirked and bounded out of the room to find some breakfast.

She was ravenous.

Chapter Eight
Close Quarters

1824

Even with eyes closed, Lilly felt Michael's gaze upon her. Of course, he would have guessed she wasn't sleeping. She focused upon remaining still, likely too still, when his boots grazed her ankles as he stretched his long legs.

His touch, even accidental, would always affect her. She nearly moaned at the thought.

Instead, she tucked her feet farther beneath the seat.

Michael's followed.

Unable to help herself, she opened her eyes and caught him watching her.

His eyes smiled; they laughed even.

Glenda had finally fallen quiet, focusing all of her attention onto her embroidery circle. And Mary, snoring softly, truly was asleep. As she'd slouched deeper into the elegantly upholstered bench, she not only took up her own half, but some of Michael's—*His Grace's*—half as well. Meanwhile, his boots, hidden under Lilly's skirt, held her feet captive beneath the seat. How many times had they played games like this during their courtship?

And what in blue blazes did he think he was doing

anyway?

He was betrothed!

What kind of a woman did he think she was? Lilly glared at him.

He tapped the side of her ankle with one of his boots. Oh, this was too annoying!

Lilly wanted to throw something at him, but Miss Fussy slept soundly upon her lap. Since she couldn't reach down and grab a book to launch in his direction, she would have to use her wits.

"Glenda, what type of stitch are you working on today? You ought to show the duke some of your designs." Lilly spoke innocently. "You have your basket of samplers with you, don't you?" Of course, Glenda had her samplers...she never went anywhere without them.

"Oh my, yes, Your Grace. How rude of me to work on this while you have no such distraction for yourself! I will make it my personal obligation to keep you entertained all morning."

Glenda lifted out a basket bursting with various colors of fabric, each embroidered with flowers, butterflies, kittens, ducks, etc. "Now this one I did when I first turned twelve." She leaned forward and handed the sampler to the duke.

Michael was forced to sit up and take the piece of fabric. This required him to remove his boots from Lilly's feet. The chuckle she couldn't keep from escaping drew a frown from him.

Glenda continued, "When I first learned embroidery, I worked on perfecting my cross stitches. See how the thread crosses over itself. It is quite a beginner stitch really. Although it can become rather complex when one does a cross, over an X. Do you see the corners, Your Grace?"

Michael, not one to abandon his manners, graciously studied the wispy, yet colorful material, with something of a grimace on his face. "These?" he asked politely, pointing at the border.

"Oh, yes. Those are the more complex version of the cross stitch. It is known as a Smyrna cross stitch, but Lilly just calls it the double cross stitch, don't you, Lilly?"

"Yes, Lilly," Cortland said sarcastically, "have you perfected the—what is it called? The Smyrna cross stitch?" Lilly had not favored embroidery as a debutante. Did he remember?

Lilly had no intention of participating in this conversation. "I have never in the past perfected, nor do I plan in the future to perfect the Smyrna stitch, or any other stitch for that matter. But do go on, Glenda. Show the duke your next sampler." At which point, Lilly closed her eyes and commenced feigning sleep once again.

Feeling victorious, she wiggled her toes and stretched her legs into the space separating the two benches. Michael's feet were planted firmly upon the floor.

The rest of the morning Lilly listened in amusement as Michael endured the drawn-out recitation of Glenda's embroidery progression. Ah, yes, she had won this round.

Mary continued snoring softly.

****

The party stopped around noon to change horses and enjoy a quick luncheon. Miss Fussy made good on

98

the opportunity to do a thorough search of the yard.

This particular inn had mounts available for use, but Michael was hesitant to leave the ladies to travel alone. Highwaymen lurked in the area, and the idea of the three women being overtaken was not something Michael wished to contemplate. They would continue in their travels together. Although the ladies had a driver to protect them, they would be safer with Arty and himself along.

No, Michael reasoned to himself, they were making good time. There was no reason, at this point, to hire a mount. Maintaining their current pace, they would arrive in London late tomorrow. That would provide him with barely enough time to attend his political dinners.

Just as he glanced at his watch, Lilly and Miss Fussy appeared from behind the building walking briskly. The little dog's tail wagged so vigorously, her entire body wiggled with it.

"We ought not to linger if you are to make London in time." Lilly glanced around and gestured for the other women to hurry along. "We've ordered a basket from the cook so we can eat in the carriage—that is, if you don't mind?"

She appeared rather adorable, her hand clenched around the strap restraining her dog, rushing the women out of the inn and back into the carriage. For some unknown reason, watching her put something of a lump in his throat. "No," he said, "A sound plan actually."

Lilly placed her dog into the coach and then lifted her foot to climb in herself. The yard was muddied, though, and slippery from the previous day's rains. Just as she lost her footing, Michael stepped forward and grabbed her from behind. His arms wrapped below her bosom, and he pulled her tightly against him. "I've got you." He spoke the words softly. He assisted her to stand again before dropping his hands to her waist.

Lilly was stunned at the shock she'd felt when he'd held her against his body. Even through his coat and shirt, not to mention her layers of clothing, she had felt his strength—his warmth. Michael's arms had once been the safest place on earth.

Drawing a shaky breath, she firmly placed her feet on the ground and reached up to hand herself into the coach once again. She wanted to slap his hands away as he assisted her up. He was a betrothed man. She would not allow herself to…to what? To remember? To feel? To trust?

"Thank you," she muttered. At least she hadn't landed in the mud. That would have been too humiliating. Once in the carriage, she found Glenda sitting beside Mary facing forward, leaving the backward-facing bench for Lilly to share with Michael.

"Since we're eating, I thought Mary should face forward," Glenda explained. "Remember that last time? She got ill, remember? When she ate those kippers while riding backward?"

Lilly remembered.

Nobody wanted Mary to get sick.

So Lilly slid to the opposite side as Michael climbed in behind her. This most certainly was not what she'd had in mind. She needed to find a topic of conversation to distract herself from his…maleness.

"The sky looks to be clear today. I think we will be lucky and not meet up with any rain." Oh, that was brilliant, Lilly. Sparkling conversation indeed.

Glenda agreed, and then Mary turned and opened her window to allow some air to flow into the carriage. Everybody else turned to do the same with theirs.

As the carriage pulled onto the road, Mary and Glenda proceeded to distribute the bread, cheese, and fruits from the basket. Eating while riding was a delicate enough task, normally, even more so for Lilly as she attempted to do so without bumping into Michael any more than necessary.

He seemed to have no such qualms.

He touched her as though all was right with the world. As though she were a stranger on the mail coach. He was such a man!

Resigned to his proximity, Lilly gave up and simply delved into the offerings.

It must have been the wine, for once fully sated, she found she'd enjoyed the meal thoroughly. Leaning back, she pondered. "Why does food taste so much better when eaten out of doors?" The breeze flowing through the carriage was cool and fresh.

"Must be the novelty of it." Michael's gaze teased. Was he too remembering other picnics they'd shared together? He leaned forward and searched the basket. "What, no lemon tarts?" They had been her favorite.

Lilly cocked her head at him slightly. He'd remembered.

"I haven't had a lemon tart in ages." Lord Beauchamp hadn't allowed the kitchen to keep sweets available. Even after his death, cook had followed his decree.

Lemon tarts.

Such a small detail for him to have recalled.

Feeling at ease, comfortable even, against her

better judgement, Lilly leaned back and glanced sideways at Michael. "Do you still visit Edgewater Heights? I imagine you travel often." She'd remembered him saying his father owned estates throughout most of England.

"It's currently leased out," he said flatly. "Business decision. It's getting dicey, keeping the dukedom profitable. Requires new investments and such. Important to keep up with the times."

"Oh…" Lilly remembered the home he'd taken such pains to show her.

It had been set in a lush valley, a few miles from the sea. She remembered he'd acquired a gentle mount for her to learn to ride with him. They'd explored his lands leisurely.

There had been old ruins to climb around on, hills they'd rolled down, and a lovely stream which dropped down creating the prettiest waterfall. They had gone swimming under it…and more. "That's so sad. I imagine the tenants are happy living there. It's such a lovely home."

It would have been their home. They would have raised their children and grown old together there.

But no, Michael had become the duke. They would have moved to his estate near Exeter and kept residence at the ducal seat. She would have been a duchess.

Except upon becoming a duke, Michael hadn't come for her.

It wasn't meant to be.

They weren't meant to be.

"Do you spend most of your time at Summers Park then?" she asked.

"As much as possible. If I'm not checking on the

other properties, though, I am often required to be in London," Michael answered matter-of-factly.

Imagining the ducal seat, Lilly could not help but contemplate what it had been like for him to return to his father's home in the midst of an epidemic.

"How did you do it? How did you cope with the aftermath of the fever?" Lilly had been angry with him for not finding her, but she wasn't such a fool that she didn't understand he'd likely been under a tremendous amount of stress. She only wished she could have been with him.

She could have helped him.

Had he thought her too immature? Had he, in truth, considered her too far below him once becoming a duke? Considering all they'd shared together, she had serious doubts about this now. It was just that her father had been so very convincing.

Had there been influential people in *his* life who had persuaded him to look higher for a wife? Or had his feelings been so fleeting that he simply hadn't thought her worth the trouble?

For a few moments, it seemed as though he were not going to respond to her question. Glenda and Mary had both given in to the effects of the wine and leaned against each other sleeping soundly. Mary snored in a soft, even tone.

A disagreeable emotion flickered across Michael's features before he answered her. Did he never speak of it?

"Edward was dead when I arrived. I found Father in the last stages. He was delirious, calling for my mother, calling for his mother. He kept calling me Edward." Michael stared out the window as he spoke.

"I think I must have been in shock, that first day. I did nothing but fight panic. Father passing, in fact, did something to move me to action." He told Lilly about some of his favorite old servants, some who had survived and some who had not. "When summoned home, I had no idea what I was walking into. We buried so many—my father and Edward were just two of them. There was no time for mourning...

"Having spent time with army physicians, I had learned disease might possibly be transmitted through the air as well as through items the patients had touched. Those of us unaffected covered our mouths and noses with fresh linen. Once the dead were buried, I ordered the clothing and bedding burned. It took over three weeks for the outbreak to subside." When he turned away from the window to glance at her, his eyes were haunted.

As he spoke, Lilly thought of what she had been doing during that time. Locking herself in her room, refusing to speak with her father about Michael or Lord Beauchamp. She'd been pathetic, feeling sorry for herself, all the while Michael had been fighting death. Michael had probably saved hundreds of people with his actions. When she hadn't heard from him after one month, she'd given in to her father.

"I am very ill," her father had told her. He was dying and needed to be assured that she and her mother would have a home. He'd convinced her a duke would not marry her. She needed to face reality. Her father had pressed her into marrying Lord Beauchamp, and she'd felt she had no choice but to succumb.

All the while Michael could have died!

"You did not become ill?" she asked, fearful even

though he was today sitting right here besides her.

"No."

They rode in silence for a while, each contemplating those days so long ago.

"I didn't know, Michael. I had no idea."

He stared beyond her, not meeting her eyes.

"I couldn't come to you. I placed the entire village under quarantine, how could I break my own rules? Many doubted me as it was. We didn't even allow the mail to come through. It seemed drastic, but I couldn't take any chances."

Lilly swallowed hard. Oh, God, she'd been such a fool. She'd thought he'd inherited and decided to look higher for a better wife, a woman raised to be a duchess. She'd had nothing to offer him, only herself.

She'd thought it had been because of her, because of him.

But she had been wrong.

What would have happened if she had resisted her father? She had believed her father when he'd told her that Captain Redmond, as a duke, would not feel obligated to keep the promises he'd made to her. He'd told her men did that sort of thing all the time, especially when a lady was as easy as she had been.

She'd been awash in shame and guilt.

She'd believed her father when he told her she no longer had a choice. He'd wanted her settled. He'd needed to know she and her mother would always have security and a home.

Lilly raised her fist to her mouth and turned away from Michael. She'd thought she hadn't any choice, but had she?

"I didn't know…" she said in a whisper.

"Once I returned to London, the caretakers at your aunt's home gave me a letter from your father, informing me of your marriage. I considered traveling to Plymouth, but you had already married."

Oh God, oh God, oh God...Lilly had never imagined such a scenario. Could she have waited? Her father had been dying. There had been absolutely no contact with Michael whatsoever. Surely she could have waited though? Had *she* been the reason their romance had ended? Had *she* been the fickle one?

Her heart fell.

If so, then she'd more than paid for it by marrying Lord Beauchamp.

Dearly.

Lilly turned her back to the window and studied Michael. He was leaning forward, his elbows resting on his knees, his hands clasped loosely. Even with the breeze flowing through the carriage, there wasn't enough air. This was a nightmare. "I'm so sorry, Michael." What else was there to say?

He glanced over at her and then looked back down at his hands. "There's been a lot of water under the bridge. We can't turn back time." He did not look back at her. "Glenda has a mother; I'm sure you were a devoted wife. I am to marry Lady Natalie, an excellent alliance for sure."

How cruel life can be sometimes. If only her father had arrived in London earlier. If only Michael's family had not come down with the fever. If only Rose had lived. If only she'd never met him. If only...

Too many if-onlys.

Chapter Nine
An Abundance of Yearning

Edgewater Heights, 1815

The journey to Edgewater Heights took forever. At least, that was what it had felt like to Lilly. She'd tried reading, crocheting, even embroidering (God help her) to help the time pass more quickly, but none of it could keep her attention for longer than a mile. It seemed molasses moved faster than the horses pulling their carriages. And must they stop at every inn? Really, hadn't Mother just relieved herself a few hours back?

Lilly squirmed and shifted the entire two days it took to traverse to Captain Redmond's home. It was dreadfully hard to act like a genteel lady when one hadn't seen one's true love for *nearly an entire week*!

As they passed the final village before Edgewater Heights, Lilly's excitement grew to a tangible thing. "Calm down, Lilly," her aunt had told her. "You're going to make yourself sick, for heaven's sake!"

That painted a pretty picture.

Lilly imagined herself, leaping from the carriage into Michael's loving arms and then promptly retching her luncheon all over the place.

Perhaps she ought to *try* to settle down.

Everything was so beautiful though!

Tall, lush trees, green grass, and lilac bushes

covered the valley where Edgewater Heights nestled. The carriages creaked more than usual as they crossed a delightful cobblestone bridge and then turned down through the wooded drive. And then they rounded a bend, and she saw the house.

It wasn't a mansion, but it wasn't a small country house either. Ropes of ivy profusely climbed the three-story manor nearly to the roof. Arched windows cradled flower boxes, recently planted, and the scent in the air was that of the sea mingled with fresh lilacs. Several steps led up to the large wooden door.

And standing in front of the house, Captain Redmond—*Michael*—awaiting their arrival. She must have attempted to stand, for her aunt's arm pressed her firmly down into her seat.

"Contain yourself, girl. Show him you have more than a thimbleful of dignity."

"Of course." It was as though the world had changed from grays to colors again.

The carriages came to a halt, and Michael stepped up to assist the ladies.

First, her mother. "Welcome to Edgewater Heights, Mrs. Bridge." Captain Redmond handed her down and then bowed politely.

Next was her aunt. "It is a pleasure to see you again, Lady Eleanor." He waited patiently as her aunt allowed him to assist her off the coach. He bowed to her politely.

Then finally, *finally,* Lilly leaned out the door. Michael's hands went to her waist, and he carefully lowered her to the ground. In his gaze, she saw mirrored the yearning she felt.

Michael wanted to gather her close more than

anything, but for propriety's sake, of course, he did not.

Instead, he bowed over her hand and pressed his lips to her wrist. "Welcome to Edgewater Heights…Lilly." Emotion nearly choked him.

Mr. Harris, Caroline, Penelope, and one of the lady's maids had all climbed out of the other carriage and were stretching and making pleasing remarks about the property. Placing Lilly's hand on his arm, Michael went about greeting the other guests and inviting them inside to freshen up while the servants took up the luggage. He introduced the women to his housekeeper, Mrs. Smith, and she asked them to follow her so she could take them to each of their quarters. Danbury volunteered to show Harris to the wing where his room was located.

In fact, it was a sizeable house. The staff had been madly cleaning windows and floors, airing rugs, washing linens, and sweeping out fireplaces for the last three days. Having worked alongside many of them, Michael was certain everything was in as good a condition as possible. Lilly went to follow the housekeeper, but Michael held her back.

"I'd show you to your room, if I may, my lady."

"Oh Michael, I'm not a lady." Lilly laughed at that, her eyes sparkling.

"You're *my* lady." He pulled her close, rather abruptly, and buried his face in her neck. "I am so happy to see you." He spoke the words in a rushed whisper before quickly pulling away. He didn't wish to harm her reputation. Covering her hand, he led her up the other side of the U-shaped staircase.

Lilly gazed around the foyer curiously. The carpet was worn, but all the wood had been shined and polished. There wasn't any dust to be seen, and lemon oil scented the air. "It's beautiful, Michael! It is grand, and yet, it feels like a home."

Satisfaction settled upon him at her words. Once they reached the landing, he guided her past several doors. They led to the master's suites. He would have loved to ensconce her in the suite adjoining his but knew that was out of the question—for now. So instead he took her to his next favorite room.

He opened the door and gestured for her to enter. The carpet, the drapes, the linen, and the counterpane had all been replaced especially for her visit. The room was clean and modern and comfortable. The window boasted the best view in the house, south over the gardens. Beyond the gardens, one could see the forest and far off in the distance, on a clear day, the sea.

A footman stepped in behind them and placed Lilly's trunk at the end of the bed. Michael addressed her. "I have designated one of the servants to act as lady's maid for you. I wasn't sure if you would bring Betty along or not."

"How kind of you, Captain Redmond. We did not, in fact, bring Betty along."

"I shall send her up shortly, then, if you wish to freshen up?" Michael sounded very formal. She waited for the footman to leave and then after he had partially closed the door behind him, Lilly threw herself into Michael's arms. In her enthusiasm, both of them tumbled onto the large bed.

"Oh, Michael, I have missed you so!"

This was one of the aspects he loved most about her. Her exuberance for life—her utter lack of forced ennui. She did not play games with him, and yet her innocent sensuality wreaked havoc on his libido.

Michael wrapped his arms around her and couldn't help smiling. Holding her close, inhaling her scent, and kissing her skin felt like the most natural thing in the world.

"You cannot imagine all the work that needed to be done here." This was so very inappropriate, he knew. Lying on her bed with the door halfway closed. If anybody were to discover them, she would be thoroughly compromised.

And then he would have to marry her.

Which he intended to do anyway.

"So you were too overwhelmed with the estate to miss me?" she teased.

His answer was to roll her onto her back and kiss her thoroughly.

Being away from her had been torture. He'd never imagined he would feel such need for another person. Lilly Bridge in his home, in his arms, provided him with a feeling of completeness. As though he had been starving and then served the perfect meal. She filled that hollowness he'd carried around since he couldn't remember when.

"It was either that or turn around and return to London, Lil," he admitted, reluctantly pulling away from her mouth. "I want everything to be perfect for you. I didn't want you to come here and be disappointed." He held her face tenderly and touched his lips softly to hers. Once, twice, again…

"Someone's coming," Lilly whispered. Growling in frustration, he pushed himself off the bed and pulled her up to stand.

Turning to the vanity mirror, Lilly smoothed out

her dress and then tucked a few wayward strands behind her ears. Michael ran his own hands down the front of his jacket but realized they'd likely not fool anyone.

A few of her hairpins remained on the center of the bed, which was now rumpled as well.

"Knock, knock." Her mother's voice sang through the open door as she pushed it open wide. Aunt Eleanor, Miss Crone, and Miss Harris were right behind her. "Lord Danbury gave us instructions to Lilly's room. We thought we would locate her before finding our way downstairs for tea."

Both Mrs. Bridge and Lady Eleanor glanced knowingly at the rumpled counterpane, and then Lady Eleanor raised her brows questioningly.

Lilly, who appeared somewhat rumpled as well, flushed under her mother's scrutiny.

Michael walked across the room and indicated the view outside the window. "This room has one of the best views on the estate." He'd had to turn away quickly in an attempt to subdue his own arousal. Stealing his thoughts, he imagined himself swimming in very cold water. "If you look beyond the forest, you might get a glimpse of the sea."

"Captain Redmond, your estate is absolutely divine!" Miss Crone sang.

"After being in the carriage for two days, I cannot wait to walk around and explore," Miss Harris chimed in as they reached around each other to take in the view.

Michael glanced over his shoulder and saw Mrs. Bridge was sending him a definitively icy stare. "Captain Redmond"—she spoke in a clipped voice— "would you step into the corridor so I might have a

112

word with you?"

It wasn't a question. It was more of a command.

Even though Michael intended to ask for Lilly's hand when her father arrived, he realized that now, more than ever, he must defer to her family's sensibilities. He did *not* wish to sully their relationship in any way. He also wanted to have a good rapport with his future in-laws.

"Of course, madam." He followed her out of the room.

Once they had exited into the sparsely decorated hallway, she closed the door and faced him.

"I realize, of course, my husband is not present to do whatever it is men do to defend their daughters. But I assure you that *Lilly—Miss Bridge to you, sir*—will not be taken advantage of without severe repercussions. She is a *gentlewoman*, Captain, and I insist you treat her as such. If there are any…*any*…further improprieties at this house party, than we shall pack up the carriages and depart as quickly as we arrived." Mrs. Bridge had worked herself into something of a temper. In the past, she had always been quiet and amenable.

Michael quite respected this side of Mrs. Bridge. There were not many women who would take on an army captain so handily.

"Is that understood, Captain Redmond?" she asked firmly.

Michael stared her straight in the eyes and answered in the affirmative. "Please accept my apology, madam. You have every right to expect proper behavior from me. I respect your daughter immensely and would never willingly do anything to tarnish her reputation." He paused a moment to choose his words.

"I would reassure you my intentions are honorable toward your daughter." Ruefully, he glanced toward Lilly's chamber. "Despite earlier…evidence…I will admit that it has been…somewhat—" Captain Redmond cleared his throat, which suddenly felt as though it were closing up. "—difficult to not see Li— Miss Bridge…as it were…"

Mrs. Bridge narrowed her eyes suspiciously.

"Honorable intentions?" she asked, expecting more of an explanation.

Michael took her hands in his and affirmed, "Very honorable."

After contemplating him for a long moment, she nodded, seeming to find his response acceptable. "Well then." She cleared her throat. "That's all well and good then." With that, she turned away and reentered the bedroom.

With Mrs. Bridge gone, Michael discovered his heart was beating rapidly. This surprised him, and yet, he *had* just declared himself to her mother.

He'd been stupidly reckless to lie upon that bed with Lilly. Admittedly, it had been *she* who had tackled *him* in an abandoned display of exuberance and passion. A wry smile twisted his face. Touching one another again had stoked them both into a blazing inferno.

That was no excuse, however. He would need to keep his—and her—impulses under better control.

Overhearing the ladies chatting and laughing within the room, he decided it was a good time to search out Harris and Danbury.

He strode down the hallway with a little extra bounce in his steps.

Lilly was here.

****

The next morning, Lilly appeared delightful and prim in the scarlet riding habit she had told him she'd purchased special for this occasion. Her hat tilted to the side, and a jaunty feather caressed one side of her face.

The younger guests were to venture out on horseback and explore the estate. Lilly, Michael knew, had no experience riding, so he'd acquired a gentle, well-mannered mare for her. He planned to teach her. It was a pleasure of his, and he wished her to share it with him.

Lilly's hand tucked into his arm as they strolled to the stables, and although she was smiling, she was quiet. Michael, himself, had been more reserved the night before in attempt to quell her mother's concerns.

"You're not nervous about riding, are you?" he asked.

"Oh, a little, I suppose. Although I am looking forward to it."

They continued walking toward the stable, an unusual silence between them.

"You are out of humor with me?" Michael asked, attempting to decipher the cause of this uncommon lack of chatter on her part. Not that Lilly talked more than she ought, but she usually bubbled with enthusiasm. He'd grown used to her gaiety, her normally effervescent personality. "You are unwell?"

Lilly dropped his arm and stepped away from him. She then glanced all around, not wanting to be overheard, took a deep breath and said, "I have been too forward, too loose with you. My mother says I ought to be ashamed. She says if I continue in the manner I have, then—I—you will, well, you will not respect me. You will decide I am—that I am—" Obviously distraught from her mother's words, she refused to meet his gaze. Instead, she stared off across the fields.

Her mother had chastised her.

She had embraced Michael *on a bed*.

She had *thrown* herself on him.

He had loved every moment of it!

Michael grasped her shoulders and turned her to look at him. He then spread his legs wide, lowering his height, so he could see directly into her eyes. He massaged her shoulders and then slid his hands down her arms.

Tension emanated from her. She was doing her best to hold back tears.

The last thing in the world he wanted was for her to be unhappy.

"Ah, love"—yes, *love*—"I *love* your passion. All of this is new and, in truth, perhaps even…frightening for you. It is for me." He swallowed hard as he searched for the right words to explain himself. This was uncharted territory. "When I see you, I ache to touch you. I ache to kiss you. I want to do much more than that. You are the first thought in my mind when I wake and the last before I sleep." He smiled ruefully at her. "Remember? I am your captive…" He tipped her chin up to be sure she listened with her heart. "I think you feel the same for me?" At her nearly imperceptible nod, he continued, "This is love that we share, Lilly. Please don't be ashamed. Never be ashamed with me."

Lilly placed one hand along his jaw. "It is love, isn't it?"

This time Michael nodded.

"But I think," he said, "we shall have to practice more discretion, especially when your mother is about."

"It is so very hard." Lilly sighed. "When I am not with you, all I think of is you. When I *am* with you, *I* ache to touch *you*. And the more I keep myself from touching you, the more I want to!" She paused and then said, "This 'loving' business isn't as easy as one might think!"

Michael laughed. She spoke without airs. What a gift it was to have found a woman who spoke plainly to him. Lilly was never coy. She was merely Lilly.

His Lilly.

He considered asking for her hand that very moment, but propriety demanded he speak to her father first. He would obtain the gentleman's permission and blessing. Lilly loved her family very much, and he did not wish to create any animosity. He'd already, obviously, given her mother cause for concern.

"Is it uncomfortable for you as well?" Lilly asked him.

Michael thought about the numerous times he'd found himself deuced uncomfortable. "It is, Lilly, for me as well."

Chapter Ten
Enchantment

After one day riding, Lilly was truly and completely hooked. Sitting high off the ground, flying along the pasture, she experienced a freedom unlike anything she'd imagined. But that was not what enchanted her.

Trusting the horse, talking to her horse—depending upon her so completely—created an experience that seemed to be of another world.

She had never been allowed a pet. Her father believed animals were meant to dwell out of doors. If they did not provide food or labor, they weren't worth the cost of their keep. Such being the case, Lilly had never experienced the unconditional love an animal has for its master.

Michael had found the perfect mare for her. She was named Willow.

Neither very young nor very old, she had lovely manners and a gentle spirit. As Lilly spent time with Willow, she realized the mare not only allowed herself to be ridden but seemed to enjoy the affectionate pats Lilly placed on her neck. The horse even nuzzled her when she brought carrots to the stables. At one point, Lilly found herself talking to the horse, petting the beautiful creature and placing a kiss on her head while out riding. This new sport was yet another aspect she anticipated while daydreaming about her future with Michael. Only it no longer felt like a daydream. It was beginning to feel more like a plan. Like her and Michael's plan—both of their dreams—coming together.

And to preserve that dream, they needed to behave.

The last night of the house party, after dinner and a lively game of charades, the older women announced that everybody ought to retire. As they planned to depart early the next morning, a good night's rest would not go amiss.

Lilly doubted she would sleep at all. Michael was not travelling with them. He needed to stay on for a few days before returning to London. At the thought of being separated, once again, her heart hurt. It physically pained her.

Long after the maid had brushed and braided her hair and then been dismissed for the night, restlessness kept Lilly awake. She tried closing her eyes and imagining the flowers she wished to plant at Edgewater Heights but found that only increased her angst. After grappling with herself for what felt like hours, she donned her dressing gown and tiptoed out of her room.

The moon was full and high that night, shining through the large windows to illuminate her way as she padded down the stairs.

It was a warm evening, and she needed fresh air. Even with windows kept open, the house was yet a little stuffy from the heat of the day.

Yes, this was exactly what she needed.

Hoping the large main door wouldn't creak, Lilly lifted the latch and slipped outside.

She inhaled the balmy air gratefully and wandered

around on the lawn. The gradual slope of the hill might just be steep enough…Oh, surely it was!

She traipsed over the rise of a hill and then lay down in the cool dry grass.

Feeling impulsive and childlike and free, she turned her body sideways. She was going to roll to the bottom. Propelling herself at first, the momentum of the slope gradually increased her speed. For a split second, her heart raced as she rapidly descended.

As one always does, however, upon reaching the bottom of a hill, Lilly lost momentum, and she rolled to a gradual stop.

Oh, that was delightful, she thought, sitting up.

Lilly bounced to her feet and returned to the top of the hill to do it again.

****

Michael had acquired the habit of staying up later than his guests. Sleep did not come easy knowing Lilly slept under the same roof. And it was imperative that they wait.

The first night, he had read up on new agricultural technologies. The next evening, he caught up on correspondence with distant friends with whom he had served in the war. He'd been quite productive, really, over the course of the entire week.

This last night would be no different. In fact, it was bittersweet. For the next time he returned to Edgewater Heights, he planned on bringing a wife—Lilly.

He did not know when that would be.

Would her father require a long engagement? God, Michael hoped not. They would likely travel to Portsmouth for the wedding. He also felt compelled to take Lilly to Summers Park to meet his father and brother.

Michael chuckled to himself.

He actually *anticipated* making such an introduction. Smiling ruefully at his own enthusiasm, he finished off his port intending to retire for the night.

But as he lifted the candle, it flickered. And the front door squeaked. The latch was old and tended to creak. What the devil?

He closed the study door behind him and went to investigate.

He'd not imagined it. The front door was now unlatched. Testing it, Michael peered outside and, just as he was closing it again, glimpsed a flash of a white nightgown and flaxen hair, illuminated by the moonlight.

He blew out his candle, shut the door behind him, and ambled in the direction she'd disappeared. What the hell was she doing running around in the middle of the night in her nightclothes? She was barefoot as well!

But when he realized what she was doing, he nearly burst out laughing.

Obviously, Lilly experienced sleeplessness as well.

He waited, watched her roll down the hill again, and then ran effortlessly down the hill to catch her.

This time, before she stopped rolling, Michael threw himself onto the ground in her path.

At their collision, she gasped in fright. "Oh, Michael, you scared me to death!" She was breathless, and blades of grass were caught in her hair.

Her eyes shone. Michael was very close to her, their bodies touching, shoulders to toes.

"I scared you?" Michael attempted to be stern. "I look out my front door and see a ghostly apparition, resembling my most honored guest, Lilly Bridge, levitating through the grass of my front lawn, and she says *I* gave her a fright?" He loved looking at her. His gaze touched all the places he'd like to taste.

Lilly stilled. She smiled at him and then grimaced. "I couldn't sleep. It was so very hot today, and all I could think was we are leaving tomorrow and I have enjoyed this visit more than anything in the entire world. Once outside, the grass felt so cool, and then I lay down. And then I realized I was on the hill and remembered how I wished I could roll down it earlier and so…" She made little swirly motions in the air with her fingers and looked at him smugly. Her eyes danced with merriment. "When guests come to stay, they can entertain themselves by rolling. It will be great fun, and everybody will want to visit us."

He liked the sound of that. *Their* guests…

So much so that…"Are you up for an adventure?" He had shown everyone the stream which meandered through the property, but they hadn't made it to the waterfall and pond.

"Oh, yes, Michael. I could stay up all night. If I did that, then perhaps I will sleep in the coach tomorrow."

"Come with me then." He assisted her to her feet.

Stopping at the small groundskeeper's house nearby, he gathered a few blankets he had stored there and then locked the door behind him. Lilly was curious but did not ask any questions. He tucked the blankets beneath one arm, took her hand with the other, and led her onto a hidden path.

Except the path was laid with crushed rocks.

And Lilly was barefoot. Taking stock of the situation, he handed her the blankets and scooped her into his arms. "Hold tight, love."

Lilly put one arm around him, and with the blankets tucked on her lap, she reached her other hand over and placed it on his chest.

Before long, the sound of the waterfall grew louder, crescendoing when they reached the edge of the pond.

Keeping hold of her still, Michael lowered her feet to the ground.

"Up for a swim?" He grinned, anxious for her reaction.

Lily's eyes went wide when she glanced at the pond. Even though the moon was full, the water looked dark and cold.

"In the dark?" She indicated her gown. "I don't have even a chemise…Michael, I'm in my nightgown."

He merely shook his head mockingly. "Tsk, tsk, tsk, I thought this was an adventure!" He let go of her and sat to remove his boots. Then his stockings. He'd removed his waistcoat and cravat much earlier that evening, and so when he stood back up, he wore only his breeches and shirt. He proceeded to untuck the shirt, and in one easy move, pulled it over his head.

Lilly's breathing became shallow. The naked skin on Michael's chest was nearly as tanned as the skin on his arms and hands. Watching him fold his shirt and carefully place it on a handy log, Lilly had no qualms watching his muscles ripple and stretch. There was a tantalizing V of black curling hair forming a trail into his breeches.

"The water isn't as cold as you think," he reassured her. "A hot spring empties into it beneath the falls." He then took a couple of steps, hopped onto a boulder, and dove cleanly into the darkness.

Sensing magic in the night, she searched the moonlit reflections on the water until Michael's head appeared. Like a seal, his black hair slicked back and glistened. He treaded water, looking up at her.

"It's dark enough, Lilly. No need to be modest." And then floating backward he added, "I promise I won't look, love. Swim with me."

In his eyes, Lilly saw the tiniest hint of uncertainty. He hadn't been certain she would swim with him, but he had hoped…

She would not disappoint! Lilly looked about and agreed that it really was too dark for anyone to see much of anything.

"You won't peek?" she asked.

"I won't peek. Go ahead. Just give me a holler when I'm allowed over there again."

Lilly considered where she was. At an enchanted waterfall, on Michael's property, in the middle of the night, alone.

With Michael.

She unbuttoned her dressing gown and laid it upon the blankets. She could not swim in her nightgown. It wouldn't dry by morning, and how would she explain that to her mother? She looked back at the water to make sure Michael was not watching, and then pulled her nightgown over her head. Wearing nothing, she held it in front of herself and crept back toward the water.

It had been ages since she had swum. When Rose had been at home, before marrying, she would take Lilly to a small lake near their father's property. There was a private cove where, if so inclined, one could cool off in the summers. Her sister had taught her how to push air out her nostrils while under the water in order to keep the water from going in. She had taught her if she kicked and waved her arms, she could stay afloat, and she had eventually excelled at crossing back and forth across the pond from one end to the other.

It had been a very long time ago, and it had always been only the two girls. Even then, they'd swum wearing some underclothes, a chemise and a pair of drawers. This was utter madness!

"The water is deep enough to dive?" she called out to Michael, clutching her gown modestly in front of her nakedness.

"It drops off quickly. You can jump or dive," he called back.

As though quite literally walking off a cliff, Lilly tossed her gown aside, climbed onto the boulder, took a deep breath, and dove in.

He was right. The water wasn't icy cold as she'd expected. In fact, it was lovely.

She twisted her body underwater and then kicked herself to the surface. "Oh, Michael, this is heavenly!" she shouted. She didn't hear him but felt his presence when he surfaced only a few feet away.

She playfully splashed him and then ducked away when he retaliated. After several minutes more horseplay, they each floated on their backs, gazing at the stars.

"My brave angel." Michael spoke softly into the night air.

Lilly trailed her fingers along his arm just below the surface of the water. "I don't have to be brave when I'm with you." She smiled over at him.

Pure love shone from the eyes looking back at her. "Follow me?" he asked.

"Of course." In that moment, she would have followed him to the ends of the earth.

Michael dropped his feet and used his arms to tread water. "We are going to swim under the falls. The water from the falls will seem as though it is pushing you down, but don't let that scare you. Simply duck under the surface, and swim to the other side. Can you do that?" There was a twinkle in his eyes. This was a special place to him.

"Under the falls?" Lilly asked skeptically.

Michael laughed. "Follow me."

He kicked off and moved his arms in strong even strokes away from her. Unwilling to be left behind, Lilly let her body remember the motions and followed him, her feet kicking out behind her.

She was glad he had warned her of the pounding water. It was so powerful that it did, in fact, push her downwards. Responding to an instant of panic, she kicked her legs harder and eventually surfaced on the other side, coughing and sputtering. She hadn't been able to take a full breath before going under.

"Good girl." Michael's hands encircled her waist, and he pulled her up next to him.

She could only see darkness, but the water was warmer here.

"The hot spring?" Her feet found a ledge of stone to grip, but it was Michael who kept her from slipping away.

He moved the hair out of her eyes and massaged her shoulders under the water. "Right below us." His voice sounded gravelly in the warm, humid air. Her naked body was pressed against his by the force of the water.

Nothing in life had prepared her for the sensation of her skin rubbing against all the male hardness that was Michael. Her feet stood firmly on the rock surface of the ledge, but in truth, she felt like she was floating.

Michael slid one hand down her spine and cupped her bottom. Her face tilted up toward his, and intuitively, his lips found hers. "Lilly," he whispered into her mouth, kneading her flesh gently.

Her hands wound around his neck, and her feet floated up to cinch around his waist.

She felt *him*.

There.

And it seemed like the most natural thing in the world.

Her mother had been right about her. She *was* a wanton! Good heavens! She liked this. No, she *loved* this!

And she was not sorry. She would soon be his wife. She knew in her heart their love was pure. She would surrender to him and not be ashamed.

When Lilly wrapped her legs around Michael's waist, a shudder ran through him. As he held her, touched her, and kissed her, he trembled. Together, they were the only two people who existed in the world...in the universe even.

Like a blind man, he moved his hands to her face, touching her with his fingertips and then his lips. As he trailed a path to the sensitive skin of her earlobe, Lilly's bones turned to liquid. Her head fell backward, and she barely realized she was floating on the water, clutching Michaels arms to support herself. He continued trailing kisses down her shoulders, her chest, and eventually to one of her breasts.

Carnal sensations unfurled within her.

The pulling of his mouth invoked a throbbing between her legs. It was an ache that promised intense pleasure. All that separated her from his desire was the wet fabric of his breeches. "Tell me to stop, Lilly," he gasped.

His ragged voice could barely be heard above the roar of the waterfall. She was aware of her hair, like strands of silk, flowing in the water over her body and his hands.

Lilly released his arms and pulled his face down. "No, Michael." She panted between her words. "Don't stop. It's too right...too perfect." She implored him with her kisses. She savored him with unfettered abandon.

"I want to love you forever." He spoke into her seeking mouth.

She nibbled at him, exploring the skin inside his lips and along his teeth. "Then love me now," she demanded.

A low growl escaped his throat, and his hands became bolder still. He reached down between them, tentatively brushing the soft skin of her thighs until he found the folds between her legs. He fondled her softly, lightly, and then applied a more subtle pressure.

The ache inside of Lilly intensified. "Michael?" This pleasure nearly brought her to tears. She was so very close to *something;* what it was she did not know. She reached for it, pressing herself into his hand. The world no longer existed. There was only the two of them, only this place.

She clung to him as though he were her lifeline.

Supporting her back with his other arm, Michael reassured her. "I've got you, love. Let go."

And then she felt one of his fingers slip inside of her, nudging her in a sensual rhythm. Lilly shifted along with him, chasing something, so close. She found herself chanting his name with each breath. He did something else with his hand, widening her further, and then…

The world shattered.

Instead of the black nothingness of the cave, flashes of white burst behind her eyelids. She jerked her head and shuddered, again, again, again. Gradually, her muscles relaxed, and she slumped against him.

Michael spoke as though in awe. "I wish I could see your face right now." He held her head tenderly against his chest. He'd not removed his hand.

Lilly's answer was to search for his mouth in the dark. She knew he'd not found his own pleasure. "I want you. I want all of you." Her words echoed in the cave.

Sensing his hesitation, Lilly dropped her legs and reached forward to unfasten Michael's breeches.

Her gesture eliminated any further reluctance on his part.

Impatiently, he pushed her hands away to undo them himself. He was considerably more efficient at the task than she would have been. But when they were loosened, she reached forward again. This time she wrapped her hand around *him.*

He groaned, and together they placed the tip of his staff where his hand had just been.

"You are sure? You are quite, quite sure?"

Michael's voice sounded hoarse and gravelly.

In answer, Lilly wriggled forward. "I am," she said. "I am yours, Michael. I will always be yours."

Her words freed him.

Michael began slowly, almost leisurely sliding along her entrance, as he had earlier with his fingers. But this was different. His member was larger, fuller, and yet it was made to fill her completely.

He paused a moment and then, taking a ragged breath, thrust hard.

Lilly gasped out loud, almost a sob.

"I'm so sorry. Lilly, I'm so sorry." He froze, as though any further movement would cause her more discomfort.

Lilly inhaled slowly to regain her bearings. She enjoyed this closeness, but *that last part* had most definitely not been pleasant. With Michael still inside, she waited as the pain receded. Finally, she spoke. "Was that it?" she asked. "Are we done?"

She felt Michael begin to shake, and then could have slapped him when she realized he was trying not to laugh.

"We're just beginning, sweetheart." She heard the smile in his voice.

And then he was moving again.

He started slowly, testing her. "So sweet," he whispered. He seemed to be in tune with her needs, listening carefully for any sounds of pain or resistance she might be experiencing.

Right here. Right now. This was meant to be.

Relaxing into the water and into Michael's hands, Lilly began moving with him as that promising ache began to build again. Small waves sloshing around them grew to larger surges, as Michael held her against the smooth rock of the cave and pressed into her deeper, deeper.

The fullness increased.

Sensing only her core, where she and Michael joined, Lilly moved with him to find completeness.

The world became smaller still.

And then Michael reached down, past her belly, and touched her lightly. It was all she required for those crashing sensations to wash over her again.

Like a wave hitting the sand, Lilly broke into a million pieces.

But Michael's pace increased. He thrust twice more and then one last time, into her very center, and cried out as though in pain. His seed, he was releasing his seed inside of her.

How can such closeness be possible?

Shaking, her lover wrapped his arms around her.

If this was her last night on earth, she could never ask for more; surely it was enough. For she would always know that for one enchanted night, she had, in truth *lived*.

Chapter Eleven
Regret

1824

They rode the next mile or two in complete silence, neither really knowing what to say now.

What's done was done.

Lilly watched outside as trees and pastures flew by the window, disappearing frame by frame. She had no idea how far they had travelled since Michael's revelation. It was almost as though she were in shock.

"When I was twelve"—Lilly finally broke the silence—"my father took our family for a holiday. We were to stay with his sister who lived in a village near the sea.

"I remember as we rolled into the village thinking it looked like a painting. The homes were surrounded by perfect whitewashed fences, and flowers were lined up neatly beside them. A garden bloomed in front of every cottage.

"In the center of the village, the stores were built very closely together, and there were wooden sidewalks so one could visit the shops without having to step in the mud. It was the prettiest village. I decided it was where I wanted to live when I grew up."

Michael had turned on the bench. He watched her closely as she spoke.

"It was the most beautiful place in the world, I had decided." She grimaced. "Our first night there, we were awakened in the night. Father threw on his clothing and boots and ran out the door, my mother imploring him to be careful. Outside of the window, not very far away at all, the village was engulfed in flames."

She fell silent for a moment, remembering.

"Father didn't return until very early the next morning. He was covered in soot. The air smelled of smoke even though the fire had burnt itself out.

"We stayed at my aunt's home for a few days after that, my mother and father helping his sister's friends, comforting some who had lost their businesses or homes. Finally, my father allowed me to walk with him, back out into the streets of what had once been the village.

"There was nothing there. What had once been white and pure had become filthy charcoal and black mud. All that was left was the view by the sea.

"I remember asking my father where the people would live. They had no homes, no clothing, no businesses left to earn their living. Their very existence had burnt to the ground."

Michael tilted his head, encouraging her to continue.

Lilly took a deep breath and said, "I feel rather the same today as I did then…Something that was once beautiful has been destroyed, and there is nothing anyone can do about it."

She felt Michael's eyes upon her as she looked back toward the passing scenery and wondered if he felt the same. They'd lived nearly a decade apart from one another. She had had a husband. Another man had taken the privileges Michael had thought were to be exclusively his.

And now she was a widow.

"Did the village rebuild?" he asked, "or did they begin new lives somewhere else?"

Lilly remembered watching the remains of the village grow smaller and finally disappearing when they drove away. "I don't know. Some of both I imagine."

"What was the name of the village?" Michael asked.

Searching her mind, she pondered aloud, "I think it was Pelican Point, or Pelican Perch, something like that. We never returned. My aunt moved to live with a dear friend farther north shortly after."

They rode in silence again. And then he surprised her.

"I thought about torching Summers Park," Michael volunteered. "After the fever," he clarified. "I wanted to burn everything the disease had touched."

"Why didn't you?"

"It's a magnificent structure, actually. It's endured for hundreds of years. Who was I to destroy it?" He paused. "Too much history there. It is a beautiful place—structurally sound, very well built. No reason to demolish it because of a few bad memories."

Bad memories.

He'd experienced tragedy and horror in that time.

Glenda startled them both by speaking up just then. Apparently, she had been listening. "I had this dress once—most beautiful dress in the world. Pearls along the bodice, lace trim around the hemline, and I had embroidered tiny white stars throughout the entire skirt.

Then that Nathan Plumery spilt wine down the front of it at the harvest celebration. Do you remember that, Lilly? Mary never could get that stain out. Had to give the thing to Mary's sister. Now that," she finished grandly with a sigh, "was a tragedy."

Ironically, Michael and Lilly both looked at each and smiled faintly. Lilly resisted the urge to lean into him and take comfort in his arms.

They traveled until it was nearly dark, and everyone was relieved when they pulled into a coaching inn for the night. Lilly wished she could find somewhere to be alone but would not, of course.

They had made very good time, however, and if tomorrow went accordingly, they should arrive in London on schedule, just before dusk. And then she could say goodbye to Michael once and for all.

****

A less than enthusiastic quartet climbed wearily into the travelling coach early the following morning. The previous night they'd taken their meals upstairs and then gone right to bed.

Which had been fine with Lilly.

She'd spent too much time in his company already. His fine eyes, his strong presence, and his charismatic laughter served only to mock her now. Mock her cowardice. Mock her stupidity.

Mock her life.

As they pulled onto the road, Lilly drew out a book and donned her spectacles. She couldn't afford to dwell on the revelations of yesterday. If she did that, she'd be swallowed up by bouts of self-pity in no time. She had already done enough of that in her life.

After reading several pages, however, and not

comprehending any of it, Lilly surrendered to her traitorous mind.

What was Michael thinking today? Did he have any leftover feelings for her?

She had believed when she'd given him her body, it had been something sacred. Did he remember it that way as well?

He hadn't married in all this time. Surely not for lack of opportunity. At one-and-twenty Michael had been heart-stoppingly handsome. Now, at thirty, he was devastatingly attractive and a duke to boot. His features were still just as striking, but his face now somewhat chiseled, the line of his jaw more defined, his beard coarse. He was sinewy, hardened by work or exercise. And his eyes, those beautiful eyes of his, held wisdom and more than a little cynicism. Her dear Michael was now every inch the aristocrat.

Surely, he'd had mistresses? Likely, many of them since he'd remained unmarried. Or maybe one special lady…? This thought hurt more than contemplating the former.

Stop it, Lilly! She chastised herself for even contemplating such unproductive thoughts. She would never know. By now, he'd experienced a lifetime of living in which she'd never been a part. She had no place in his future either.

"Do you think, Your Grace"—yes, that's what she must call him; he was no longer her Michael—"the highwaymen who attacked you were politically motivated?" Her question came out of the blue. She must think about something else. The mystery of the hijacking suited perfectly. "They very nearly succeeded in delaying your arrival in London and got away with all of those documents. That could have been their purpose, all along."

"A little drastic, don't you think?" He raised one skeptical eyebrow.

"More drastic measures have been taken for less, I'm sure. One never knows. Were the documents really so very important?"

Michael *had* considered this possibility. "I'd arranged to present them to other members. I've gathered compelling evidence that could possibly sway a few to change their votes. Those few votes could make all the difference in the world. If I cannot show them our evidence, though, our arguments are considerably less convincing. And without those votes, the amendment will fail."

"Can you think of any political enemies who oppose you strongly enough to take such action?"

Michael could almost laugh at that. "It could be anyone on either side of the issue. As a duke, I am required to live by the laws. And as we've discussed, the Corn Laws bring hardship to the poor. But as a member of Parliament, one who opposes the laws, I've already angered many who believe they are the answer to all of England's economic woes."

"But has anyone *in particular* threatened you? Has any person given you misgivings as of late?"

Michael had a few such gentlemen in mind. Normally, he would never speak of such things with a lady, but this was *Lilly*, and she obviously had some awareness of political issues. His mind taunted him with the notion that she'd discussed intellectual matters with her husband.

She was no longer the naïve and innocent girl he'd

once known.

And now she wanted to *help* him. Good Lord! She was attempting to deduce who had held up his carriage.

"The Earl of Hawthorn has sent me several letters imploring me to reconsider my position. At first, they were cordial, but his later missives have carried some venom." He'd suspected Hawthorn the moment he'd stepped out of the carriage at gunpoint.

"Have they included any threats?" she asked.

"Not that I remember."

"Where does the earl reside when he is not in London?"

"His home, Maple Hall, is just south of Reading."

Lilly raised both her brows upon hearing this. They were to pass through Reading within a matter of hours. "Wouldn't you like to peek into his coach house to see if, by chance, your carriage is housed there? Perhaps you could recover your papers!"

"Would Hawthorn be idiotic enough to keep evidence of the crime on his own property? Would he implicate himself so blatantly?" Michael was skeptical. It was too easy.

"You tell me. I do not know the man. Would he?"

The idea of investigating, possibly recovering his property, tempted him. Unfortunately, he no longer travelled alone. There were three women, two men, one small dog, and their boatload of luggage to consider. Still, though, he ought to take advantage of their proximity to the earl's estate.

"I could hire a mount at the next inn." How could he not at least take a look? "Your idea has merit."

"You'll need assistance. I can come along and be your lookout." Lilly offered her services brazenly. Both

Mary and Glenda looked at her as though she'd suddenly sprouted wings.

Before the words were even out of her mouth, Michael was shaking his head. "Absolutely not." His tone forbade contradictions.

Best to cut ties with Lilly now, before she crawled any further under his skin. As it was, he already felt a renewed connection with her, and notions leading in that direction were impossible. He didn't blame her any longer. At least he didn't think he did. Blaming himself wasn't useful either.

He would part company with them in Reading.

He'd spent months berating himself for not getting word to her despite the quarantine. For all intents and purposes, circumstances made it look as though he'd abandoned her. He'd taken her innocence and then not contacted her for nearly a month. Had there been repercussions from the night under the waterfall?

There had not been.

Michael had, in fact, made certain to discover this for himself. When informed that the Baroness Beauchamp was most definitely not with child, he had been greatly relieved.

He'd also been irrationally disappointed.

Lilly was his past. Lady Natalie was his future.

****

With his luck changing, Michael acquired a respectable mount when they arrived at the Reading posting inn. He gave strict instructions for Arty to see the women to their lodgings in London and to be certain of their welfare before taking leave of them. The women had gone into the inn for lunch and to freshen up.

He would say goodbye to Lilly with Glenda and the maid looking on. It would be for the best.

Handing the mare off to Arty, Michael turned to go in search of the private dining parlor where they would be eating.

Except, that would not be necessary.

A flash of Miss Fussy out of the corner of his eyes, alerted him that Lillie had remained outside. She would care more about exercising her pup than dining in leisure. She played with the dog, unaware he was looking on.

This time, he would tell her goodbye. There must have been smoke in the air nearby, for his eyes burned as he memorized her features.

When he arrived at her side, he didn't speak right away. A breeze carried a hint of her perfume in his direction. It was the same: hyacinth and citrus. Warm and delicate—like Lilly. A lump formed in his throat.

"My outrider will continue with your party." He spoke rather stiffly. He didn't look directly at her.

Lilly nodded, understanding his discomfort. She'd given him her body, once, but that was ancient history. He owed her nothing now. The promises they'd made to one another were null and void. They had been for years. It was best that they part.

The fool! He planned on travelling to the Earl of Hawthorn's estate alone!

"That's fine. Thank you, Your Grace." She thought he should take somebody along with him but didn't want to feel the sting of his rejection again. So, she simply responded evenly.

But she had other ideas…

"I do appreciate all you have done for me. You did

not have to offer me conveyance along with your party. Your assistance has been invaluable." His voice was distant, that of a stranger almost.

"My pleasure," she said, "*Your Grace*." She didn't mean to sound petulant. She wanted to be able to think they could remain friends, but that was impossible. There was too much sentiment left between them, for her anyway—to many memories for her to be friendly and cordial.

As strong as she thought she had become over the past years, she would rather not watch him marry another woman. She was not a glutton for punishment.

She turned toward him and attempted a smile. "I do wish you luck in everything. I hope you recover your documents so you can pass your amendment, and I—well, I wish you happiness in your marriage." She could say no more lest she make a fool of herself and allow her tears to come. She bent down and clapped her hands. "Come now, Miss Fussy. Come to Mummy!"

The dog ignored her for a moment and then ran and jumped into her arms. Her legs shook as she rose to stand. She could not go back into the inn and make conversation with Glenda and Mary. Hopefully, they were nearly ready to depart.

Michael bowed toward her. "Goodbye, Lilly." No regret in his voice, only a steely determination to be on his way. This was worse than she could have imagined.

Lilly nodded in his direction and then turned with her dog to climb into the carriage. She wished the carriage could whisk her away from him, leaving clouds of dust in their wake.

But wishes were just that. Wishes.

And her dignified exit was eclipsed by the fact that

she had to sit in an unmoving carriage awaiting the arrival of the other occupants.

In the end, it was she who watched Michael mount his horse and ride away from her.

Chapter Twelve
Recovering the Goods

Michael had acquired directions to the earl's estate while at the inn and was cheered to discover it was only a few miles south of Reading. And so, after less than an hour of riding at a comfortable pace, he found himself at the end of the long drive. What were the chances the earl was in residence? With the opening of Parliament a week away, it was possible he himself had not yet departed for London. Unless, that is, he had plans to court votes the same as Michael.

Best to assume the earl was in residence.

Michael dismounted and walked the horse into the trees so they would not be visible from the road. *Damn, Lilly had a point.* It would have been convenient to have a second along.

He didn't like leaving the horse alone.

After securing his mount, Michael remained under cover of the trees as he edged around the perimeter of various sheds and outbuildings. The large brick structure was easily identifiable as the coach house. It was built adjacent to the stables.

A back door was left open, and no servants were in sight. Again, Michael wished he had thought this endeavor through more ahead of time. He'd been too bloody distracted by Lilly to think critically. What if his carriage was, in fact, hidden inside the coach house?

One couldn't simply hop onto a carriage and drive it away. Horses required harnessing, and that took time. Time Michael wouldn't necessarily be allowed. In those moments, he could likely be accosted by one or more of the henchman who'd attacked them yesterday.

And yet the thought of locating his team and coach and then abandoning them once again did not sit well with him either. Michael had brought his pistols with him, but he was only one man. Albeit a damned irritated one!

It took a moment for Michael's eyes to adjust as he peered into the open doorway, but even in the shadowy building, there was no mistaking what he saw.

Parked as though it had recently been out for a Sunday drive sat his very own personal carriage, the ducal insignia displayed prominently. Michael was tempted to march up to the main house and confront the earl. But…again…he was but one man, and already the earl had shown no qualms at resorting to violence.

Creeping into the cool silence of the large structure, Michael quietly peeked into the windows of his coach. It appeared the contents had been untouched. His boots and greatcoat, along with the other men's hijacked attire, were carelessly tossed on one of the leather benches inside.

His valise and the papers lay on the other.

Unwilling to risk losing the documents a second time, he hastily stuffed the loose papers into his valise and then turned to exit the building.

He could not retrieve the carriage by himself. He was going to have to go back to Reading and return with a magistrate. Hawthorn must be insane! Horse theft was a hanging offence, by God.

"I didn't think we'd be so lucky as to actually find anything here."

Michael nearly jumped out of his skin upon hearing Arty's voice.

"What the devil are you doing here?" Michael's voice rasped. He'd given the man explicit instructions.

Arty shrugged, sheepishly. "The baroness told me to follow you. She insisted you needed me more than they did and then ordered me off her carriage. Didn't want to argue with the lady, Your Grace, though I'm sorry not to have been able to carry out your orders."

Michael tilted his head back and took a slow deep breath. Impertinent wench! Then he glanced over at the carriage again.

"The team isn't in here. Have you by chance checked the stables?"

"I have, Your Grace, and our team is in there—your team—Your Grace," he said. Up until the other day, he'd never had much reason to speak with his employer directly.

"Did you see anybody?"

"A couple of boys—grooms."

Most of the earl's staff might have travelled with him to London. It was anybody's guess as to the location of the stable master.

Michael was a duke, however, and he planned to exploit this fact. He explained his idea to Arty, and the two of them marched to the stable.

"You there, boys," Michael called out. "Why isn't my conveyance ready for travel? The earl said it would be in good repair and ready for departure today at noon. It's now half past!"

The boys looked at him in utter confusion and

alarm. They then looked at each other.

"Don't you realize I am the Duke of Cortland, and that is my travelling coach in there?" He pointed at the coach house. "I want it ready for departure in fifteen minutes!"

"The blacks inside are your team, Yer Grace?"

"All four of them! Now move!" Unwilling to draw their employer's ire, the boys scampered to the coach house. Cortland turned to Arty. "Better make sure they do it right," he said.

Arty smiled, sauntered into the coach house, and began issuing instruction to the boys.

The conveyance was ready within one quarter of an hour.

Before heading back toward town, Michael and Arty retrieved the hired mounts so they could return them to the posting inn. That was the only stop they would make. With a deadline awaiting them, Michael had no time to waste with magistrates.

All in all, it had been quite a coup.

For later that night, Michael and his footman rode into Mayfair, both of them sitting on the driver's box, just after sunset. It was not so late, though, that he would miss the first of Danbury's political dinners.

****

Marveling at the events of the past forty-eight hours, Michael pondered the guests at Viscount Danbury's table. Danbury, of course, sat at the head of the table while his mother, the viscountess, held up the other end. She was an eccentric woman, known by the colorful plumes she wore in her startling white hair. At times, the feathers added up to twenty-four inches of height and a similar number of inches to the girth of her head. Every time she stood near candles burning in wall sconces, he was fearful she would go up in flames. In that moment, she discoursed avidly with one of Lady Natalie's older brothers. Michael was uncertain which one, however, as they were all similar in looks. He imagined once married to their sister, he would remember each of them by their given names.

The Earl of Ravensdale had done well securing his line.

Seated beside Danbury was Hector Crone, Baron Riverton. His baroness, Lady Riverton, and daughter, Penelope, sat at the other end, near Danbury's mother. Riverton was an amiable fellow who hadn't committed to either side of the issue. Michael and his allies hoped to win him over that evening.

Lady Natalie sat to Michael's right and her father on his left. He'd spent considerable time engaging his bride-to-be in pleasant conversation, only to find himself repeatedly comparing her to Lilly. It seemed every word Lady Natalie spoke had been rehearsed. Her ability to discuss the weather, fashion, and various events of the season would, nonetheless, keep her above any criticism as a duchess.

He'd be bored to tears if, once married, their conversations remained so limited. Hopefully, after some time as his wife, she would speak what was on her mind and in her heart—to him at least. He intended to grow to love her eventually. He intended to have warmth in his marriage.

His discussions with her father were a great deal more interesting. Lord Ravensdale, through hard work and thoughtful investments, had rejected the concept that aristocrats avoid trade and had successfully increased profits on all of his estates. He'd come into his title unexpectedly while employed as a barrister. Ravensdale's own father had been a disowned younger son who, after marrying below his station, hadn't maintained contact with his aristocratic roots.

Michael had met Lord Ravensdale during the first year he'd become Cortland. Upon discovering the older man's wisdom and strength of character, he'd come to value the earl's mentorship.

Although the men discussed some politics at the table, they did so only in a general sense. They would wait until the ladies removed themselves before going into any detail regarding their strategies and proposed alliances.

Michael had been pondering what Hawthorn had wanted to accomplish with the highway robbery. It was no secret the man was something of a fanatic when it came to the separation of the classes. Many of his servants had left his employ for that very reason. He'd been labelled an eccentric, a strange character. Michael suspected the man belonged in Bedlam.

Except he was an earl.

Likely, the robbery was not going to be his only attempt to block them. Although neither Michael nor his servants had been injured, Hawthorn had proven he was not above using foul means to accomplish his ends. They would need to keep a watchful eye on the bastard.

Had it not been for Lilly, Michael would have been considerably delayed and his agenda completely upended. He also would not have gone after Hawthorn and, without Arty's help, would have been unable to recover his coach and team in such a timely fashion. It was difficult to keep his mind off her. He ought to call on her aunt tomorrow to assure himself of their safe arrival. She deserved no less than his gratitude.

And then he would make no further efforts to see her.

****

Arriving at the achingly familiar townhouse, Lilly and Glenda were greeted with enthusiastic affection by Lilly's aunt, Lady Eleanor Sheffield. Lilly hadn't seen her since her mother's funeral and was saddened to see how much the lady had aged. Her eyes still sparkled with mischief, however, as she exclaimed over Glenda that she would be the talk of the *ton* this season. Aunt Eleanor pulled them into her cozy drawing room and sent Mary and her own servants to assist in bringing in the luggage and unpacking it in the girls' rooms.

The weather had cooled that evening, and the fire roaring in the overlarge hearth was welcome indeed. Tea and sandwiches were brought in as the three settled in to catch up with one another.

Lilly hadn't prepared herself for the memories that assaulted her the moment she entered her aunt's home. Nine years ago, Michael had called upon her often. He'd come during receiving hours and taken tea with Lilly, her mother, and her aunt. He had also dined with them on several occasions with everyone expecting his presence among the family to one day become permanent. There had been a few moments when they had been left alone in this very room and managed to engage in various…other…activities.

A lump lodged itself in Lilly's throat. She was glad for Glenda to fill her aunt in on the events of their journey. Glenda told her Aunt Eleanor about the duke who had been robbed by highwaymen on his way to town. She told her all about how he had been handsome and very charming and had known Lilly before becoming a duke. She told her he had ridden in their coach with them for a day and a morning and had been very pleasant indeed.

Aunt Eleanor was not so old she did not remember who this duke was. She watched Lilly in concern and then tentatively said, "Captain Redmond, now the Duke of Cortland, is to marry the daughter of a dear friend of mine in May. As I am the bride's godmother, all of us, of course, shall be invited to the festivities."

Lilly schooled her features to hide her inner turmoil. She did not want her aunt to suffer guilt for celebrating with her friend. But, oh, God, life could be cruel indeed. Lilly had not bargained for such a complication as this!

"It is Lady Ravensdale, then, who is your friend?" Lilly maintained a peaceful demeanor.

"It is, dear. I've known Josephine for years. Along with their daughter, the youngest, there are four sinfully handsome sons." Pausing in her enthusiasm, she peered closely at Lilly. "This connection, does it cause you distress, my dear? If so, then we must avoid the family. I was hoping enough time had passed, but if not, be truthful. I'll not cause you torment over it." The older woman's eyes regarded her in concern.

Lilly refused to deprive her aunt of her dear friend Josephine Spencer—who just happened to be Lady Ravensdale—who just happened to be Michael's betrothed's mother. "I shall be fine, Aunt. I am, however, weary from the long drive today. Would you be disappointed if I excused myself early? I can hardly keep my eyes open."

"Oh, but of course, you must go right up to bed! You remember the room you took before? I have put you in the same. And I still have Betty with me, and she is so pleased to act as your maid again!" Aunt Eleanor rose to her feet and placed her hands on both sides of Lilly's face before Lilly could exit the room. "I am so very, very happy you have come to stay with me. We are going to have the most delightful of seasons!" She looked Lilly straight in the eyes, searching for any misgivings or second thoughts. "Everything is going to turn out fine. It always does. Get a good night's sleep, and then we will discuss our plans tomorrow!" She kissed Lilly on the cheek and then shooed her off to bed.

Lady Sheffield, never considered a beauty, even in her prime, was nonetheless attractive in that she was confident in both manner and bearing. Despite having lived alone since her husband's death, decades ago, she was never seen in any manner of dishabille. With her gray-steaked reddish hair upswept in a regal style, Aunt Eleanor hadn't really changed at all. A little grayer, perhaps; a few more wrinkles…But she was the same woman who'd brought her Miss Fussy. A heartening warmth welled up in Lilly's chest upon this realization.

Betty awaited Lilly in the familiar chamber, having already turned down the bed and unpacked her nightgown. Lilly *was* grateful to see her, but in truth, she wanted to be alone. One of her blasted headaches was threatening.

She needed to recover from seeing Michael again.

Even so, she gave Betty a hug and accepted her assistance in preparing for bed.

The maid confided to her that her ladyship had

been thrilled to learn of their upcoming visit. The winter had been drab and dreary. After brushing out Lilly's long silver-blond hair and plaiting it in one long braid, Betty went about the room, organizing items on the dressing table and collecting the clothing Lilly had worn that day. When she finally departed, closing the door behind her, Lilly sighed in relief.

It had been too much. Too many memories. Too many reminders of what could have been. The headaches had set in shortly after marrying the baron and still came upon her when she was overwrought. Life was cruel and unfair, and the baron had been a monster, but she had survived.

Learning the truth, learning Michael had come back for her after all, shook her to the core. Because she'd learned it was she who was to blame for their separation. She could not blame her father, nor her mother, nor Michael himself.

It had been her own fault.

In this room, she'd experienced both euphoria and devastation. Euphoria early in their romance and devastation when Michael had failed to return—failed to come and speak with her father. They had waited two weeks in London before her father insisted upon returning to Plymouth. Once she was home, there had been another week before her wedding. And when he'd still not contacted her in that time, she gave up hope completely and married a man she did not love.

Chapter Thirteen
A Reluctant Bride

1815

Mr. Bishop arrived at Aunt Eleanor's town house the day after Lilly, her mother, and her aunt returned from Michael's estate. Her father had been anxious to get home to Plymouth but, upon speaking with his wife, reluctantly consented to await Captain Redmond's return. He would not consent unless he wholeheartedly approved, he informed them both sternly.

Lilly was nervous and excited for her father to meet Michael. Once she'd told her mother Michael intended to speak with Father upon his return, it seemed, all talk turned to an impending wedding. Lilly and her mother even discussed where the ceremony ought to be held. They concluded since the family chapel in Plymouth was not so far from the Duke of Cortland's home in Exeter, it would be the logical and sentimental choice.

Her mother's excitement nearly eclipsed Lilly's. She would have dragged Lilly over to the modiste to order a wedding gown, but Lilly drew the line. A niggling part of her thought it might be bad luck to anticipate matters so completely.

She would await Michael at Aunt Eleanor's. How long could it be? And so she waited one day…

Two days.

Three days.

Four days.

Where was he? Had there been problems at Edgewater Heights? Did he encounter difficulties while travelling? Alternately, Lilly would be mad with worry and then outraged that he dallied. Did he not realize how anxious her father would be to return home?

In defiance of society's sometimes unreasonable expectations, Lilly sent a missive to his London bachelor's quarters at the end of the fourth day.

Captain Redmond,

My father is in London and anxious to meet with you. He wishes to return to Plymouth immediately, so please make your visit soon! I do not know how much longer we will be staying at my aunt's townhome, so expediency is of great importance.

And I miss you very much.

Yours,

Lilly Bridge

Not one word. Lilly hadn't heard a single word from Michael. It had been nearly two weeks, and he had failed to appear or even send a letter explaining his absence.

Doubt set in.

Had he actually told her he loved her? She couldn't be certain now, and the more she thought about it, the more she questioned her memories. Had he? Surely, she would remember the exact time and location. She would remember what she was wearing and the exact time on the clock. Wouldn't she? Surely she would!

Dear God, what had she done? Could it have been only she who was in love? Had she been so blinded by his charm and good looks?

And then she remembered special moments with him, magical moments, filled with secret smiles and tender looks. He'd trembled when he'd held her.

Surely that had been true emotion.

Or, as a niggling doubt entered her mind, did all men tremble when they were sexually aroused? Could he have possibly been only physically stimulated while being indifferent to her emotionally?

During that awful two weeks, Lilly spent so much time crying into her bed linens, it was a wonder she hadn't soaked the mattress completely. After a few days of this, Betty had wondered aloud that she had any tears left at all.

Her eyes were puffy, and her stomach tied in knots. She would hear a carriage in front of the town house and feel a giddy sense of relief, but when inevitably it wasn't him, she fell into an even deeper despair than before.

Two full weeks passed, and her father announced he would wait no longer. It was time to return to Plymouth.

And although she was devastated, Lilly also felt a sense of relief. He would contact her eventually. Unless he was dead. Which he had better be!

No, no, no, Lord, she didn't mean that! Everything was wrong now. Even her own thoughts.

Having been too upset to eat much over the past few weeks, Lilly listlessly climbed into her father's coach the morning of departure. A part of her kept watching, hoping. But there was nothing. No last-minute arrival with a perfectly reasonable explanation for being tardy. In a dress that hung loosely, now, on her diminished frame, Lilly departed London with little hope to cling to.

Several times, as they drove, her mother pulled out her handkerchief and dabbed at her eyes. "What did you do, Lilly? Why did he not come? Is it as I feared? Were you too forward? Were you too fast? Did you not listen to me when I told you a man would lose interest if you gave yourself to him too quickly?" And then she would moan and turn her head to look out at the window.

With two days of this, Lilly's mood plummeted further.

Lilly's father, who normally rode his own mount outside, traveled most of the distance inside of the carriage with Lilly and her mother. On the second day, he made an announcement.

"I have received word from Lord Beauchamp. He is willing to take you on as his wife."

Lilly had been slumped pathetically against the side of the carriage with her face leaned against the window when her father began speaking. Upon absorbing his words, however, she sat up straight and alert.

"But Papa—"

He did not allow her to interrupt him. "I am not well, Lilly." He looked to his wife who nodded in agreement. "I do not know how much longer I have on this earth. Something is growing inside of me, disrupting the functioning of my organs. Nothing can be done."

"That cannot be! You do not act as though you are sick!" And then looking at him, she saw that her father was much thinner than he had been when she and her mother had left Plymouth earlier that spring. How had she not noticed? Had she been so wrapped up in her own concerns she did not notice her father was failing? "Surely the doctor can do something!"

But her father was already shaking his head side to side. "I have seen three different physicians, and all of them have given me the same prognosis. I will be lucky to survive till the year's end."

Her mother was dabbing at her eyes again. Lilly sat silently, trying to absorb the truth of her father's words.

Lilly was torn by the shock of sadness upon hearing her father speak of his own demise and the fear of being forced to marry Rose's widower.

"You must see my predicament, Daughter. I cannot have peace until my affairs are in order. I must secure a home, a living, for you and your mother."

Again, Lilly went to speak, but he held out his hand. "I realize you believed this young captain of yours was planning on offering for you, but it is rumored both his father and brother have passed. If that's the case, then he is now the Duke of Cortland. Which explains, of course, why he did not come as promised." He sent her a hard stare and then spoke in a stern voice. "He is a duke now, Lilly, far above our social status. Even if he was still inclined to do so, he's most certainly been advised against marrying so far below his station. You must accept the fact that he has not come. He is not going to. He may have planned on offering for you before but…His absence speaks louder than words ever could."

Lilly held her hand over her mouth. A duke? He was a duke now? And both his father and brother, dead! *Oh, Michael, why have you not come to me? Why have you not come to tell me in person? Did you not think I would understand*? Would she have? Could she have released him with her blessing?

And then a sob escaped. He was not coming. He was never coming!

Her mother crossed the space between the two seats and wrapped Lilly in her arms. "Oh, my darling, it will be all right. Remember the Lord doesn't give us hardships we are unable to bear." Lilly felt her mother's lips upon her forehead and then soothing hands upon her back, but all she could think was that there had been no mistake. Michael had intentionally abandoned her.

He would not marry her now—he *could* not marry her now.

"I've notified the vicar, and he's willing to perform the ceremony as soon as we arrive home. It will be a relief to know you and your mother will be cared for after I am gone."

These words only pierced her heart further. What would they do without Papa? She searched her father's face. He believed this news about Lord Beauchamp was something she might welcome.

Now that the scales had fallen from her eyes, she realized her papa did indeed look tired and somewhat haggard. Not only was his frame shrunken, but his hair looked thinner too. There was a yellowing around his golden eyes, so very much like hers. His gaze pleaded with her.

"You will do as I ask?" Now he spoke to her in a voice that was vulnerable.

"Marry Lord Beauchamp?" she confirmed.

"Yes, it would ease my mind immensely."

Perhaps if he had less to worry about his sickening would slow. Perhaps all the worry he had felt for her these past two weeks had worsened his condition.

"I will, Father," she said. And with those words a light went out inside of her. That love she had felt for two short months was put to rest. She would marry Lord Beauchamp after all.

Unless, a part of her whispered, *Michael came to me after all.*

Please God! Please?

****

Exactly one week later, following a brief and somber ceremony, Lilly rode in another coach. This time with her husband.

A husband who was not Michael.

She made a mental attempt at summoning some pleasure, anticipating a closer relationship with her niece, but she hadn't the energy.

She sighed.

Lord Beauchamp glanced up from his reading with narrowed eyes. "You're slimmer than you were last Christmas." He spoke grudgingly. "Almost like Rose, only she was taller."

"I wish Rose was here." If Rose were here, then Lord Beauchamp would not have needed a wife. Perhaps her father would not have sickened.

Lord Beauchamp's eyes seemed even glassier than normal for a few moments, then realizing he had not responded to her, he nodded and went back to his letters.

Even while Rose had been alive, the baron had never been a particularly amiable man. And in the years since her death, he'd grown even more morose. His reddish hair, even his horrible mustache, were now streaked with gray. His eyes were dull, his skin white and pasty, and his lips pinched thin, always disapproving. Lilly turned her head away from him.

God help her, she was terrified to contemplate her wedding night.

Surely her brother-in-law had no desire to consummate their marriage. Surely not! There had been no discussion on the topic, but of course, it was to be a white marriage, wasn't it?

When they arrived at Beauchamp Manor, Lilly climbed out of the carriage, stiff and tired. Since returning from Edgewater Heights, she had gradually come to feel her heart was exhausted from lost love.

It pumped only what was required to keep her alive.

Having rained for most of the day, the weather precluded the servants from lining up outdoors to greet their employer's new wife. They stood in a formal line along the entrance hall instead. Lilly hadn't paid a great deal of attention to the manor when visiting before. Her attention had been diverted by spending time with her sister, and then later, with her niece. Now, as she entered, she looked around and thought it gloomy and the air stifling. A life-size painting of her sister hung on the wall near the staircase—the perfect English rose.

The painting had been commissioned around the time of her wedding, and her smile spoke of happiness untold. It ought to make Lilly happy, seeing an image of Rose like this, but on this occasion, it did just the opposite. In fact, Lilly turned her gaze away from it quickly.

Except that Rose was memorialized throughout the house.

On every pedestal was a vase. In every vase, roses.

Fresh roses in some, dried in others. No wonder the air was thick with perfume. It was pungent with the scent of roses.

Lord Beauchamp cleared his throat so he might have her attention. Lilly obeyed his nod and faced the servants.

"Mr. Richards, Mrs. Bertie, this is the new baroness, Lady Beauchamp. Lilly, Richards and Bertie have the house well in hand. If you are in need of anything, direct your requests to either of them. Mr. Richards and Mrs. Bertie manage the household to my standards. You need not interfere."

Lilly blinked in surprise. Surely it was the lady of the house who managed the home? But she would not argue today. Exhausted from the turmoil of the past month, she lacked the energy to address such a trivial matter right now.

The baron then introduced a dozen or more servants to her. She nodded and greeted them but knew she would not remember most of their names. Today had been a nightmare with no end in sight. And yet, tomorrow held only bleakness.

"I'll show you to your chamber." The baron winged his arm in her direction.

Lilly had been introduced to too many servants to remember, but her young niece was nowhere to be seen. "Is Glenda napping? I was looking forward to seeing her." The prospect of spending time with her sister's daughter was like a candle in the darkness.

"She and her current governess, Miss Hokes, are with an aunt of mine in Wales this summer." His voice sounded matter-of-fact. "Glenda will return here for a few weeks and then depart again for school. Miss

Hokes will leave us for a new post at that time. Your father suggested you perform the duties of a governess to Glenda while she is at home."

A governess? Not a mother? Was that not part of why the baron needed a wife? So that Glenda would have a mother? Lilly looked over at the man she'd married. He continued holding out his arm for her to take. His pale face showed impatience.

She was not comfortable taking his arm. There'd never been a need until today. It felt…awkward.

He was different from Michael in many ways. His googley eyes and boney face were fine for somebody else's husband. Just not hers. If only he weren't so…baronish—so stuffy and meticulous. If only he were softer looking and exuded even a hint of warmth.

If only he were Michael.

For the thousandth time that day, she tried not to think about the night ahead.

After reaching the third story, they walked past several doors until he finally opened the second to last.

"Wasn't Rose's room on the second floor, adjoining yours?" This room, although pleasant, was far from the master suite. Ought she to be grateful for this?

Lord Beauchamp dropped her arm and solemnly walked to the window. "I could never put another woman in Rose's room. It will always be hers. You will refrain from entering it. Ever. You must understand my feelings on this matter?"

"I…yes…I suppose." *But it has been three years!*

"I do not want the room disturbed, do you understand?" She could see him swallow hard, as though holding back emotion.

Feeling distressed and uncertain, not to mention a

little homesick already, Lilly nodded.

"Your trunks will be delivered and unpacked shortly, I presume. You may rest and then meet me for dinner downstairs in two hours. Ask one of the upstairs maids if you find yourself in need of anything." He hesitated a moment. "It is to be hoped we can go on well together. Your father explained the bad luck you had in London."

"He did?" Her eyes went wide at this information. For some reason, she hadn't thought her father would have informed Lord Beauchamp of her relationship with Michael.

"He told me everything. And as much as I abhor such behavior, out of the regard I still have for your sister, I am willing to give you my protection. It is something she would have wanted."

A deeper foreboding began to take root. "What, exactly, did my father tell you?" She felt like she were being lowered into a grave—cold and alone and ashamed.

And she felt betrayed. Had her mother suspected she'd given herself to Michael completely? And if so, how could her parents have shared this with Lord Beauchamp, of all people? He was a virtual stranger to her, and now he was to know of her most personal secrets?

"He told me you've likely been ruined." The words came out clipped and monotone. "He told me I may very well have married a whore—one who could possibly be carrying another man's child." His tone dripped with judgement. "But, as I've said, Rose would have wanted me to extend to you the protection of my name."

This was why Lord Beauchamp had deigned to marry her? As a favor, no—as a tribute—to his love for Rose? He was martyring himself—for her?

"Nevertheless, I shall endeavor to make your existence here…tenable." This was the nicest thing he'd said to her all day.

Turning on his heel, he strode toward the corridor. "Do not be late for dinner. I abhor tardiness." With that, he exited and closed the door.

Lilly dropped to the bed, stunned. Was this why her parents insisted upon such a hasty marriage? Surely it must have been, for her father was not on his deathbed yet. Lilly wanted to cry again but had no energy to do so. Neither was she to be given a chance, apparently.

There was a short knock on the door, "Yes," Lilly said.

A servant who looked to be the age of her mother entered and made a short bow. "My name is Hilda, ma'am. I am to be your maid. The master told me to see if you needed assistance before dinner. Do you require a bath?"

Lilly thought about the two long flights of stairs the servants would be forced to carry water up and shook her head. Although a bath sounded lovely, she would limit them if possible. It would do her no good to draw the ire of the servants in her new home by creating additional work for them.

Chapter Fourteen
Lilly Returns to London

1824

Lifting the knocker, Michael felt an odd familiarity. He'd resolved to make this one morning call to Lady Sheffield's town house in order to assure himself of the ladies' safe arrival. He'd also apprise Lilly of his success in recovering the documents and carriage from Hawthorn's estate. She would want to know.

He hoped coming here was not a mistake.

How many times had he eagerly waited on this very step the season they had met? More times than he could remember.

The intensity of anticipation, of longing he'd felt upon each of those occasions, was not something one forgot. Even when it had only been a matter of hours since they had last been together, his heart had raced and his breathing had quickened while he stood waiting to see her again. Every time it had been the same. Her mere presence made him feel alive.

Had—that was—*had made* him feel alive.

This time was different. In fact, he ought to forego talking with Lilly altogether and instead, confirm their safe arrival with the butler or perhaps with Lady Eleanor.

165

The door opened and with it, long forgotten emotions from his last meeting with Jarvis. A lifetime servant of Lady Eleanor, Jarvis protected the home with the demeanor of a mean but very refined bulldog. His singular eyebrow, along with deep forehead creases, accentuated the butler's frown. Two chins rested above the man's cravat, and Michael suspected another lurked beneath. Although the butler was short in stature, he more than made up for it with the bulk that strained his formal servant's attire.

On that last occasion, Jarvis had informed Michael the family, including Miss Lilly, had returned to Plymouth. It was obvious Jarvis presumed, as had the rest of her family, that Michael had been avoiding a parson's trap. Michael had wanted to strike out in frustration upon hearing the butler's words.

And today, nearly a decade later, Jarvis's demeanor revealed his opinion of Michael had not changed in the least.

"Hello, Jarvis. I'm here to see Lady Eleanor or Lady Beauchamp if she is in." Michael handed him his calling card. The card wasn't necessary. Of course, Jarvis recognized him immediately.

The butler grudgingly allowed Michael to enter the foyer. "A moment please, Your Grace." He spat the words before making a half bow and then disappearing quietly.

Michael glanced around at the familiar paintings, which likely hadn't been moved in decades, before realizing he was experiencing the same anticipation he had felt nine years ago.

What the devil?

If he could leave without making a fool of himself,

in that moment, he'd be out the door already. Instead, he cooled his heels for all of ten minutes before Jarvis returned to announce Lady Eleanor and Miss Beauchamp had gone out for the afternoon. Lady Beauchamp, however, had consented to meet with him in the morning room. "If His Grace would please follow me." Jarvis's impeccable manners conveyed distinct mistrust.

Michael followed Jarvis to a room he had entered dozens of times before. Even the scent was the same. As Michael stepped in, Jarvis backed out, conspicuously leaving the door ajar.

His eyes took a moment to adjust to the darkened room. Although several windows opened to the back gardens, all the drapes were pulled shut. Lilly was curled up on one end of the settee.

Dressed in a simple blue muslin gown, she did not stand when he entered but greeted him with a pinched smile. Miss Fussy snored softly upon her lap.

"Please sit down, Your Grace. I am pleased to have learned your arrival in London was not delayed." Lilly's hand tenderly stroked the hair on her little dog's back. She seemed to wince slightly as she spoke. Sitting forward, she reached for the bellpull but then hesitated before ringing it. "You will join me for tea?"

Michael sat beside her on the sofa but turned his body so he could face her. "I would be delighted."

Jarvis entered mere seconds after she rang. "Dear Jarvis, I realize it is early yet, but would you be so kind as to have tea brought in for His Grace and myself?"

Michael remembered this about her. She didn't order people to do things. She asked. She'd always become irritated in the presence of a person who did not subscribe to this philosophy.

Upon Jarvis's exit, Michael studied her quietly. He had come to express his gratitude again, but instead, he said, "You did not allow my man to travel with you."

"However...?" she urged him.

"However?"

"Yes, you paused distinctly as though there was more information needed to follow your thought." She sounded quite innocent.

Shaking his head, Michael reclined and then crossed one ankle over his knee. "Well...as it turned out, I needed Arty after all. And for that, I suppose, I must express my appreciation."

A smug smile danced tentatively on her lips. He was glad of that, glad to see her tension ease.

He felt it imperative to add, nonetheless, "But I was concerned for your travels and needed to reassure myself of your safe arrival."

"We reached London last night, tired but otherwise fine." Lilly, again, spoke softly. "My aunt has taken Glenda to her modiste. She is commissioning a gown for her—for the Willoughby ball—just as she did for me." She looked down and continued massaging the dog's fur.

Michael remembered her gown. He remembered how she had sparkled.

She did not sparkle today, however. In fact, she nearly faded into the material of the sofa.

"What did you discover at Hawthorn's?"

"Hawthorn's?...Oh yes." Lilly would want details. "By God, Lilly, he had it stored right there in his coach house. And the entire team too." She seemed to take pleasure in hearing this, so Michael told her all the particulars of the caper. She managed a slight laugh when he described how Hawthorn's grooms had assisted them. "Couldn't have done it without you though, Lil." He uncrossed his legs and leaned forward. "And though I could shake you senseless for sending Arty, I'll admit he was essential to my success." He felt sheepish, as he bowed his head and steepled his fingertips. "I am grateful for what you did—vouching for me to Jackson, providing me with transportation, everything—even ordering Arty to follow me."

When she did not respond, he glanced back up and realized she was not even looking at him. Her eyes were closed.

"Lilly, are you unwell?" Her manner disquieted him. Taking her free hand, his concern grew at how cold she felt.

Lilly paused in stroking the dog and raised a fist to her closed eyes. "It is nothing. I get these awful headaches sometimes." Miss Fussy hopped down and ran over to a large pillow in the corner of the room. Lilly pinched the bridge of her nose.

She was so pale. Michael held her hand in his and kneaded her palm, her fingers, her wrist. At his touch, she eventually relaxed into the sofa. Once her hand had warmed up, he took the other and massaged it.

"Lilly," he whispered.

She'd apparently fallen asleep. Her head had tilted to the side, and her lips parted. Soft breaths came slow and even. Studying her hand in his, a deluge of emotion rushed over him. He lifted it to his lips and held it there.

A breeze caused the drapes to flutter and sway. It was still early spring, and a chill, if not a downright frostiness, hung in the air. Michael tucked her hand onto her lap and located a crocheted blanket. Arranging it over her, it struck him she might be more vulnerable than she would admit to.

At seventeen, she had been brave and daring. Now she carried with her a frailty that was new. When they courted, long ago, the world had been her oyster. She now seemed as though she carried it on her shoulders.

Michael kneeled on the floor and removed her well-worn half boots. He then lifted her feet onto the loveseat and tucked her skirts around her cozily. Standing up, he decided he had best make his leave. He would have Jarvis send for a maid, so that she would not be alone.

He turned to leave but then paused.

Unable to help himself, he leaned down and placed his lips upon her forehead. At the same time, Miss Fussy jumped back up to burrow in with her mistress.

At least he was leaving her in good hands.

****

Lilly's wedding night, 1815

She was dreaming.

With her back pressed against the stone wall, she stood in the cave, behind the waterfall, and Michael was kissing her. But the kisses were wrong.

The lips scratched her, harshly demanding something she did not wish to give. Her teeth ground into her own gums, and she tasted blood. Blood?

Her eyes flew open in panic.

Enough moonlight flooded the room that she could see that it was Lord Beauchamp!

Her new husband had apparently decided, after all, to claim his marital rights. Surprised, angered, and a little frightened by his treatment, she pushed him away.

"That hurts. Please, stop. You are hurting me." His breath reeked of spirits as he thrust his tongue into her mouth. She tried turning her head away, but he would not allow it.

It was just light enough that she could see his eyes. They were clouded with, not desire, but some form of hysterical lasciviousness.

"Rose."

His hands went to pull her nightgown up. His own weight hampered his effort so he had to tug at the offending garment a second time, ripping the material as he did so.

This was not right.

This felt horrible. Horrible and degrading. His frenzied hands moved over her body with what felt like, a bruising intent.

She began to feel very afraid.

Although not a large man, Lord Beauchamp was considerably stronger than Lilly. She tried pushing him off, but he thwarted her efforts. He seemed disoriented, even to himself.

"Rose." He said it again.

Did he think Lilly was some apparition of her sister? And yet she knew he'd never treated Rose this way. Rose would never have allowed it.

There was no tenderness. There were no sweet kisses or whispered endearments.

Only this...attack!

And then all hope left her.

The very small amount of optimism Lilly had grasped at for this marriage shattered when he entered her. He took her rudely, showing no care or feeling for her has a woman, or a person even.

What was she supposed to do? He was her husband, and yet, his rough treatment caused her to whimper in pain. At the sound of her crying, he paused. An acute awareness filled his eyes, followed by disgust.

"Your father's suspicions were true, then." Upon penetrating her, of course, he'd not met any resistance. There was no indication of her virginity. There would not have been any. Rage contorted his features. "You *did* give yourself to that bastard in London, didn't you?" he snarled. "Don't pretend I have taken your innocence when there was none to give!"

He jammed himself into her again, even more viciously. Tears flowed down Lilly's face and onto the pillows. Before achieving his release, he jerked out of her, spilling his seed on her thigh. "If you think to pass his bastard off as mine, you're sorely mistaken." Standing by the bed, he fumbled with the falls on his pants. His face had turned a splotchy red color she could see, even in the dark. She stared at him in shock. He spoke again, through labored breaths. "I had hoped your father was mistaken. I had hoped you would be..."

"You had hoped I was more like Rose. But I am not! You may have this marriage annulled now. I did not come to you a virgin." She closed her legs and let them fall to the side. Her knees shook, and her thighs ached. She tried not to think of the burning sensations he left inside. "The church will annul our marriage. We've simply made a mistake, a dreadful mistake!" Her voice wobbled, but she had stopped crying.

"Of course I will not. I made a promise to your father, knowing you were possibly already ruined." He rubbed his hands together. "I won't allow you to bring such a scandal upon your parents, upon Rose's parents and Glenda's grandparents...I will allow you the protection of my name, but nothing more. You...*you* are a whore!

"Do not expect to be treated as anything better. You've made your bed, and you shall lie in it. God help us if you are indeed with child, for it will never be my heir. I shan't have it raised in my home. It will never bear my name. If you are with child, you will go into seclusion, and afterwards, it will be sent away."

Lilly closed her eyes tightly, as though she could imagine herself away from here.

"I find myself in a distressing situation, madam." His voice was judgmental and condescending. "Your father is a man of whom I respect greatly. And your mother, she gave birth to the woman I will love till my dying day, to my Rose.

"We are married, and yet, I cannot respect or esteem you in any way. But what am I to do with you?

"I will not treat you as a wife, as a baroness," he continued. She glanced up at him upon these words. "Your father has confirmed to me, in no uncertain terms, he is in fact, dying. I assured him both you and your mother would be cared for, that you would have a place to call home, here at Beauchamp Manor."

Tears filled Lilly's eyes again at the mention of her father. He desperately had wanted her to establish security for herself and her mother. But at what cost?

"And you are family to my daughter." He looked at her thoughtfully. "How am I to treat you as a wife? How can I begin to give you regard as my baroness when you have so thoroughly disgraced yourself? I find myself unable to comprehend doing so."

Lilly did not speak, torn between anger and guilt.

Yes, she had acted impetuously with Michael, but did she really deserve this treatment? Did she deserve this...*punishment?* What did he expect her to say? *I'm sorry I was not a virgin for you? I'm sorry I am not Rose?*

"This does not mean, however, that I will not exercise my rights." He looked down at his fingernails as though examining them. Apparently uncomfortable meeting her eyes while making such a statement, he continued. "I find I do have...needs, and I will not avail myself of a harlot when there is one within my own home." Finally looking back up at her, he magnanimously declared, "We'll simply have to make the best of it."

Lilly flinched when he reached toward her. She hated him. She could never welcome his touch. His lips pinched together in a tight smile, and he chuckled before turning away.

Footsteps echoed as he finally left her, blessedly alone.

Lilly sat up and with shaking hands, lit the candle beside her bed. There was nothing she wanted more at that moment than to submerge herself in a very long, hot bath. She wanted to scrub herself of his touch again and again. She went to the basin and, with the washrag and towel left from earlier, attempted to wash away his touch. He had taken her so roughly that, ironically, the rag came away with streaks of blood. Although the blood was not from the loss of her innocence, it may as well have been. She would never feel pure again. Lord Beauchamp, her husband, had succeeded in making her feel, indeed, like a whore.

****

Although somewhat dire, her circumstances were not as bad as they could have been. She was *not* with child. She'd had her courses the week she awaited Michael's return.

But she was trapped.

She could not run away from her marriage. She must consider her father. She must consider her mother. She must consider Glenda.

Caught in the paralysis of her responsibilities and guilt, she took no action to alter her situation. Her father would be distraught if he knew what had happened, and what with his illness, how could she add to his worries?

Over the next several months, her parents visited a few times, and she saw that her father's health was, indeed, failing.

Lord Beauchamp had, as warned, intruded into her room on some occasions during the first year. When he touched her, Lilly had learned to close her eyes and imagine she was somewhere else—anywhere else. She did her best to remove herself from reality.

The less she said, the less she did, the shorter the visit was. They weren't always violent, but they were always demoralizing. And he a*lways* made certain he would not give her a child.

She knew it unworthy of her, but she'd felt it was nothing but a blessing when he'd been diagnosed with consumption. And as the illness took greater hold of him, the nightly visits terminated. She only felt guilty when she was with Glenda.

She would do what she could for her niece. There must be some purpose in her life.

Chapter Fifteen
Old Friends and New

1824

The Willoughbys, as was tradition, hosted the first ball of the season. With the betrothal, arrangements had been made weeks ago for Michael to attend with his fiancée's family. After dining at the earl's home, they traveled by carriage and arrived at the ball together. Lady Natalie seemed more relaxed in his company and even managed to carry on a polite conversation for most of the ride. She asked after his friends, for she had met Harris and Danbury on more than one occasion and knew they had attended school together. She seemed pleased to hear both Harris and Danbury would be attending tonight. She expressed how nice it was to have close friends at these events so one wasn't always forced to make conversations with virtual strangers. Michael nodded and agreed.

Did she consider *him* a stranger?

Although he watched her lips move and stared into her eyes as she spoke, Michael's thoughts were elsewhere.

If he could have ducked out of this damn ball, he would have.

It was understood, however, as Lady Natalie's fiancé, he was to partner her for the first dance and later, the supper dance. He was expected then to escort her into the supper area and attend her during the meal. To suddenly back out of his commitments at this late hour would be a slight to both the lady and her family. He hadn't any choice and was thus compelled to attend.

Thoughts of Lilly, however, plagued him.

He could not help but compare the seventeen-year-old girl from his past, brash and open, loving him unreservedly, to the woman he'd visited the other morning.

With maturity, her beauty had taken on a gossamer quality. Sitting in her aunt's home, she had seemed ethereal, fragile, brittle even, before falling off to sleep. Pursuing her was futile, and yet, he hungered to know the woman she had become.

Although clouds threatened, rain held off as the sleek carriages lined up outside of the Willoughby mansion. Men and women of all sizes and ages, dressed in their finest evening wear, materialized like butterflies emerging from their cocoons as coach after coach moved slowly past the grand entrance. The gentlemen ushered ladies inside regally as befitted the exalted members of the *ton*. The Ravensdales, along with their guest the Duke of Cortland, were no exception.

Drawing the eyes of many, the betrothed couple made a striking pair. Natalie, only about six inches shorter than Michael, stood tall and elegant with her golden hair drawn up in a jeweled tiara. While she wore a pale-yellow chiffon gown, Michael wore mostly black. Duncan had used a touch of pomade to slick his black hair back, and it had held so far. Their wedding, scheduled for May, promised to be the pinnacle of the season.

Two of the earl's sons were present as well. Michael had been pleasantly surprised to find them gentlemen modeled after their father. The other two sons, busy addressing concerns at a few of the earl's northernmost properties, had been unable to come to London for the season. His future brothers-in-law were not a pack of dilettantes who spent their time whoring and drinking away their father's fortune. So many sons of aristocrats failed to find worthy pursuits. It was a shame, really.

Lilly was nowhere to be seen in the reception line.

Had he expected to catch her watching him, once again, as he had all those years ago? The fleeting thought caused his heart to skip a beat.

It was good she was not here.

Without her as a distraction, he could concentrate on conversing with key political figures and cultivating new connections. Lady Natalie's hand was tucked loosely into his arm as they mingled strategically, greeting old friends and meeting valuable new acquaintances. When the dancing commenced, he felt more himself as he led his betrothed onto the floor.

Natalie was graceful, calm, and poised. She was beautiful, and yet he wasn't constantly tamping down amorous thoughts while holding her. Her father had raised her to be intelligent and perceptive. She would make an excellent duchess. He was happy to realize she wasn't as enraptured with fashion as Lilly's niece was, after all. He didn't know how he would have coped with that. Following the first dance, he returned Lady Natalie to her mother's side and relaxed with the youngest of Natalie's older brothers, Joseph.

As a family with four marriageable sons, the

Ravensdales' popularity went unrivaled. This particular bachelor son, Joseph, seemed somewhat distracted. Before Michael could escape to the cardroom, Joseph leaned in and spoke conspiratorially.

"Say, Cortland, do you by chance have an acquaintance with any of the ladies standing near that fern. I must have an introduction to the brunette. I've never seen her before, and if I must dance with some of the debs tonight, I don't find her objectionable...not objectionable at all."

Michael laughed and turned in the direction Joseph indicated.

Oh, hell.

The brunette in question was none other than Miss Glenda Beauchamp. Although Glenda was rather stunning in an icy-blue confection of a dress, Michael's eyes landed on the more diminutive woman beside her.

Wearing a plain navy dress with long sleeves and a high neck, Lilly appeared paler than usual. With her hair pulled back severely, she clutched the shawl wrapped around her shoulders as though it were a lifeline. She attempted, it seemed to Michael anyway, to appear staid and matronly. Had she but realized the truth—it was impossible to hide her beauty.

"I do," Michael said thoughtfully. "Old friends of mine. Shall I present you?" They weaved their way across the room, and Michael confidently stepped into their circle.

Glenda welcomed him enthusiastically with sparkling eyes. She was a rather pretty girl—a child, really. Just so she didn't wish to converse with him of fashion or embroidery.

"Your Grace, how wonderful to see you again!

Isn't this a beautiful ballroom? The candles and ribbons are so very festive!" She spoke to Michael, but her eyes stole several furtive glances at the younger gentleman beside him.

Michael bowed over her hand. "Miss Beauchamp, lovelier than ever. The ballroom needs no decorations when it is graced with ladies as ornamental as yourself. You are enjoying the festivities then?"

"Oh yes." She again glanced toward Joseph Spencer.

"May I present my future brother-in-law, the youngest son of the Earl of Ravensdale, Mr. Joseph Spencer? Spencer, this is Lady Eleanor Sheffield's great niece, Miss Glenda Beauchamp, newly arrived from Plymouth."

Michael watched them bow and curtsy to one another, both more than a little flustered. It didn't take long, however, before she'd promised young Spencer the supper dance. Joseph was writing his name on Glenda's dance card when Lilly caught Michael's eye. Apparently, she'd been eavesdropping on the conversation. She sent him an indulgent smile. Was she remembering a similar introduction?

Michael addressed her directly and proceeded to present her to Joseph as well. Lilly curtsied and gave Glenda and the young rogue her permission to take a turn about the ballroom. "Do not," she said, "go outside."

Michael stifled a chuckle. "You are looking more yourself this evening, Lilly. I take it you are in good health again?"

"Lady Beauchamp," she hissed.

"Pardon?" Michael asked.

"Please, especially in public, address me as Lady Beauchamp." She explained, "I do not wish to defend our past acquaintance or be the subject of gossip. Glenda must remain untouched by scandal. Her dowry is not very large, and it is imperative that...well, I am hoping she can make a good match this season."

"She is young yet, Lil—Lady Beauchamp. Surely it's not necessary for her to find a match her first year out?"

Lilly paused, reluctant to explain. "It would be best if she could. We are no longer...welcome at Beauchamp Manor. The new baron and his family have taken up residence and...we were lucky to have been allowed a year of mourning before they took possession. I have a small portion which has been settled upon us both, but a season does not come cheaply. After the spring, I am to be Aunt Eleanor's companion, and Glenda is used to a more...pampered lifestyle."

Michael was stunned. "Wasn't the security of your future the very reason your father wished you to marry the baron in the first place? Is there no dower house available for you? Damn it, Lilly, what kind of man fails to provide for his family in the event of his early demise?" What kind of man had Beauchamp been? Knowing his home was entailed to a distant cousin, the man ought to have made better arrangements for the women he left behind.

"Your Grace, *please*, let it rest. It is done. I can only guess Beauchamp never imagined his time would be cut so short." She glanced around, keenly aware of people chatting around them.

This was most definitely *not* a suitable place for

this conversation. He ought not to be having this conversation with her at all. Michael presented his right arm, indicating they walk. He pulled her across the ballroom, down a short corridor, and then outside through some terrace doors. Anger burned within him.

No, more than that, he was incensed. Knowing Lilly had married in order to be cared for properly for the rest of her life was understandable. He'd accepted the fact. But discovering she had been left financially strapped and must now act as companion to her elderly aunt, when she herself was not yet seven-and-twenty did not sit well with him at all. Her husband had been consumptive, for Christ's sake. The excuse that he had been unable to make proper arrangements for Lilly and his daughter didn't wash. It revealed a selfish character indeed!

And this ought not to be Michael's concern—but it was. Lilly was a woman who deserved to be protected. She deserved to be reminded of how beautiful she was every morning. She deserved to have *carte blanche* at dressmakers all over town.

She deserved to be loved.

Michael dragged her along, leading them to a small gazebo, away from the sound of the orchestra and the gaiety within the ballroom. Distant laughter carried over the garden. Once inside the gazebo, he indicated she sit on an ornamental bench and then paced across the small space a few times before turning to look at her.

"Tell me about your marriage," he finally said. Something didn't seem right. She'd been married to a baron, for God's sake, and if George Bridge had had confidence in the man's solvency, Lilly most definitely ought not to have been left in such straits. George Bridge had been stubborn and manipulative, but it had been for the sake of his daughter and wife's fiscal security. He'd be turning in his grave if he had heard what Lilly was saying tonight.

"Did Beauchamp care for you well, while he was alive?"

Lilly shifted and looked at her hands. "Please, Michael don't do this. There is nothing to gain by going into this…" She wouldn't look at him. He would see the truth in her eyes.

"I want to know, Lilly. I need to know." He went down on one knee before her so she would have no choice but to look into his eyes.

Lilly kept her gaze focused downwards, as though studying the polish of his boots. Her lashes fanned out on her delicate skin. As a younger man, he'd been determined to make her his—to protect her forever. And now he sensed she'd needed him more than he could have imagined. What had happened?

He touched her jaw lightly. "Please, tell me your husband treated you kindly." Was he pleading? God, it was what he wanted to hear—what he needed to hear.

She allowed him to tilt her chin upwards. "Of course," she said brightly.

Too brightly.

There it was—the brittleness. She was lying. Michael took hold of her hands. "Tell me the truth. Please, Lilly, tell me…It's all right. It's only me."

As he waited, a cloud drifted over the moon, making it impossible to see her expression. And then her voice, tight and reluctant, pierced the darkness. "It was…not an…amicable marriage. But it is behind me now."

Michael waited.

But Lilly remained mute, averting her face once again. With each second that passed, rage heated within him. Rage directed at a dead man.

And if he were truthful, directed at himself.

What kind of a person could ever be unkind to Lilly? Even though it had not been a love match, Lilly had been, still was, a tenderhearted, lovely, *lovable* girl. He was reminded, all at once, of everything he had loved about her.

She believed the best about others until they proved themselves unworthy. She welcomed new friends eagerly but had been extremely loyal to her family. She loved animals, for God's sake, and flowers! What excuse would her husband have for treating her poorly?

And then it struck him, like a fist to the gut *he knew.* "You were not a virgin."

Lilly emphatically shook her head from side to side. "Please, Michael, *please*, none of this matters anymore. Let it be." She tried to pull her hands from his. She attempted to stand, but when Michael had knelt, his knee settled on the hem of her dress, effectively trapping her. Nausea and self-disgust engulfed him.

She had suffered. She had suffered at the hands of her husband. She had suffered at the hands of her husband because her innocence had already been taken.

Taken by himself.

Raggedly, Michael pulled her into his arms. To comfort her? To comfort himself? He was not sure. He'd been so caught up in his own troubles and later angry with her for not awaiting his return, he had selfishly not considered such an obvious dilemma for Lilly.

She had been so young. Of course, her husband would have expected her to be untouched. Had her parents suspected? Had they known? Mrs. Bridge had watched him suspiciously on several occasions. She'd interrupted them more than once as they'd hastily jumped apart and attempted to set themselves to rights.

"My fault," Michael stated flatly. His face pressed against the tender skin just behind her ears. Tendrils of her hair caressed his face. So soft—his Lilly—so vulnerable.

Lilly shook her head. "No," she denied. "We did not know, neither of us could have known."

He held her tenderly. She stirred, as though to pull away, but he could not let her go. He wondered when she'd last been held. When she'd last been comforted by another human. He rubbed his hand along her back until she relaxed again.

"Lilly?" he prodded. And then, "Please? Tell me." She'd never denied him anything before. In that moment, she was simply...Lilly. Nothing else mattered.

A shaft of moonlight settled upon her. She squeezed her eyes tightly shut and then gave in to his request, voicing her memories.

"He hated that I was not...untouched," Lilly began. "He would never treat me as his w-w-wife...He said, instead, I was his...his..." She began to shiver, and Michael held her tighter. "He refused to annul the marriage. He said, because of the scandal it would create for my family and for Glenda."

As she spoke, Michael felt his eyes begin to sting.

"He came to my bed, after I was asleep, but not in a loving way, not in a way…and he did things so I could not have a child…He…said he'd rather die without an heir than for a whore—there was nothing I could do! My father was ill, and there was my mother…and Glenda…" The tremors running through her grew stronger. She ducked her head away from him, as though filled with shame.

Because of him…

Because he'd not come for her…

And he'd blamed *her*…

It could have been an hour. It could have been a minute. Guilt and shock stole even his sense of time upon realizing what she'd gone through.

After what felt like a lifetime of silence, Lilly squirmed and pushed him away.

His arms dropped listlessly.

"It is useless to visit this, Michael. I am unharmed. It happened. It is done." When she raised her eyes, they held resignation. There were no words to soothe her. Nothing he did now could change the past.

"I am alive, and he is dead," she persisted. "And I am free. Free to live a peaceful existence with my aunt. It will be so much better than…before…I will appreciate it greatly. We will do simple things: shop, go to garden parties, and perhaps even travel to the continent. She has given me *carte blanche* over her garden. I shall be content. You need not feel guilty, nor pity me, Michael. Please, leave me alone…Go to your fiancée. She is a lovely woman and probably wondering where you are this very moment."

Of course, she was right. Her words made sense, even though his mind had not ceased echoing her words.

He invaded my bed, after I was asleep, but not in a loving way.

He did things so that I would not have a child.

There was nothing I could do!

Hatred toward Baron Beauchamp was only eclipsed by the loathing he felt for himself.

What a selfish cad! What a goddamned bastard he had been! So utterly irresponsible and selfish. He'd only considered his own pain at the time. He'd only considered what he had perceived to be *her* betrayal.

No wonder her smile was brittle. Michael had taken her innocence, and then that damned husband of hers had taken everything else.

What else had he done? He had to ask her, in case he had been informed incorrectly.

"You were not with child? You never carried my child…?" Sitting back on his heels, he implored her. How self-absorbed he was! He should not have left the matter of ascertaining her childlessness to somebody else. He should have gone to her himself! He'd made love to her! He'd promised her they would be together forever. He'd given up too easily, far too easily.

"No, Michael." She shook her head. "There were times I had foolishly wished…but thank God, I was not." An even more poignant sadness settled into her eyes, and she looked at her hands. "I *was not*."

The unresolved issues from their affair were violent and messy. Seeing her, talking to her, touching her was akin to reopening a wound he hadn't realized was festering. It was painful but, perhaps, necessary.

And then Lilly straightened her spine. Her eyes implored him. "When we were together at the waterfall…so many times I have returned there in my mind. My mother warned me about men, you see, that they would say anything…What I'm trying to say, to ask, was it…was I…When I couldn't believe any longer that it had been about love and…" And then, "Michael, I have felt so ashamed of what I did. If it had not been love, then what was it?" Lilly covered her face with her hands. "Just tell me, even if you must lie, tell me it was more than that. I have spent years berating myself—"

Her torrent of words stopped when Michael tore her hands away from her face. In fevered desperation, his mouth sought hers almost violently.

She let out a cry and entwined her arms around his neck.

In less than a moment, the years fell away.

She was his dream, his soulmate, his past, his future.

She was his everything.

He trailed his mouth along her jaw to the tender skin behind her ear. As he did so, she tilted her head back and a choked sob escaped her.

It was only a moment, a moment of madness, but he couldn't help himself. She was a lifeline, an oasis, a portal to joy.

He was not a free man.

Gasping, hating himself, Michael tore himself away from her.

"Good God, what the hell am I doing? Have I no honor? No control? Haven't I caused enough pain?" He couldn't look at her as he knelt there, once again aware of the distant laughter and music floating across the grass. And then, like a man who'd had far too much to drink, he clumsily pulled her to her feet. As she stood, there was a tearing sound. One foot was still on the hem of her dress, and it ripped partially when she rose. "Oh hell!"

He assured himself that she was steady and then took one, two, three steps away.

Ignoring the lace which had detached from her gown, Lilly lifted her dress and fled as though the hounds of hell chased her. Barely able to comprehend his own actions, he watched her disappear.

This was madness!

Anybody could have come across them! Jilting his fiancée was not an option. An honorable man did not break off his engagement! There was far too much at stake!

For nearly a decade he had done all he could to uphold the honor and integrity of his father's and brother's legacy. Was it all to be for naught?

Furthermore, the political alliance he'd been so carefully building could fall apart. If the amendment failed, it was likely the current laws would remain and England would be that much closer to revolt.

He must get himself back into that ballroom by Lady Natalie's side, and he must not allow his baser instincts to get the better of him again. He could not think about Lilly now. They must set the past to rest once and for all.

It was the Duke of Cortland who smoothed the creases on his pants and brushed his hair back before turning to walk toward the ballroom. He would enter via the terrace. Alone.

Glancing at his hand, he realized it was shaking. A tremor ran through him.

What must Lilly have endured all those years, married to a man who resented her, or even worse, hated her and considered her unworthy of respect? Why had he not considered the possibility of this? The duke pushed these thoughts out of his mind.

It would be time for the supper dance. He strode purposefully back into the ballroom.

Chapter Sixteen
Michael's Evil Fiancée

Upon Michael's words, Lilly took one look at his face and an icy cold swept through her. He'd come to his senses and already regretted holding her. She did not want to hear him apologize again. She could not bear to hear it.

And so she fled.

Clutching her dress, lifting it so she wouldn't trip over the torn hem, she rushed to find the door they had used earlier.

But they had not been alone in the garden.

In her haste, she nearly collided with an older gentleman leaning against a column along the veranda, holding a lit cigar. In hopes that he hadn't been there long, she nodded hesitantly and skirted around him.

Thankfully, she managed to find her way to the ladies retiring room without encountering anyone else. Had that gentleman outside overheard her conversation with Michael? She refused to allow the thought to take up residence in her mind. She simply did not have room for it.

"Ma'am." A young maid jumped to attention as Lilly entered the retiring room. Thank God no other guests were present.

But glancing in the mirror, Lilly realized, besides her torn gown, her appearance was surprisingly normal.

Unless one examined her closely. The knot in her hair was loosened, and her lips were slightly swollen. She addressed the maid. "Do you have a needle and thread?"

"Aye, my lady, 'tis what I am employed for." She rummaged through a basket and pulled out a navy spool. The girl threaded the needle and then went straight to work on Lilly's dress. "Won't take me but a moment," she commented, weaving the needle through the muslin. "I can fix up your hair, too, if you'd like."

Lilly covered her face with her hands. What was wrong with her? She'd given in to him so easily, the same as before. She suffered a grave weakness where that man was concerned.

"Thank you, miss," Lilly said. After the maid tied off her thread, Lilly sat on a stool and allowed the maid to go to work on her hair.

What had she been thinking? She had not! That was the trouble.

If that gentleman had overheard their conversation or witnessed their embrace, all would be at risk. Michael's ambitions aside, a scandalous stepmother would ruin Glenda's prospects.

But that was not the worst of it.

She'd told Michael the horrible truth—the shameful secrets of her marriage.

Lilly nearly moaned at the thought. She'd not told a single soul of the humiliation or her torment. She didn't want pity. Especially from Michael. A soft wail of humiliation escaped her, and the maid paused. "Sorry, mum. I'll be more careful like. 'Tis a tender head ye have."

Lilly must bring her emotions under control. She

smiled at the servant in their reflection. "You are doing fine." She spoke encouragingly.

As the maid twisted her hair into a neat knot, another lady swept into the room. The golden-blond girl peered into the mirror before looking back at Lilly.

She was Lady Natalie Ravensdale.

She brightened immediately. "You are the Baroness Beauchamp, are you not? I became acquainted with your stepdaughter, Miss Beauchamp, earlier. She is so very cheerful and amusing to converse with. Silly of me, I know. We are supposed to wait to be introduced, but I am Natalie Spencer. My father is Ravensdale."

The girl spoke openly, Lilly could not help but return her friendliness. "I am Glenda's stepmother, and I am *so glad* she is meeting some young ladies her own age. We are just arrived to town, and this is her first season." Thank God she had not given in to tears. The young woman's exuberance helped Lilly to return to her normal cheerful self.

Lady Natalie sat down on another stool. "I think she is younger than I. I made my come out when I was twenty! Can you imagine that? Thank heavens, I managed a match my first season. Even if he is a bit *old*, and like my father, only talks of politics, he is quite handsome. I think he will make a pleasant husband."

Lilly smiled, amused that Michael's betrothed thought of him as old. She was surprised she could find amusement in anything just now. "I have heard talk of your wedding. To the Duke of Cortland, I believe. He cannot be *all that old*?"

Lady Natalie sighed deeply. "My father is *very pleased* with the match."

"Fathers have a way of getting their way in such matters." What an odd conversation to be having right now. About fathers and marriage…"My father pressed me to marry as well," Lilly admitted. "We love our papas so very much; it seems the most important thing in the world to make them happy." Lilly stared into the mirror as she spoke, remembering her father before he took to his sick bed. He'd been insensitive at times and a bit overbearing, but he had always made her feel safe. He'd loved Lilly and her mother almost too much.

"You do understand." Lady Natalie's eyes met hers once again.

Lilly swallowed hard, again, fighting tears. "Glenda spent all of last year mourning her father. It is time for her to dance. I am glad she is making new friends now."

Lady Natalie sat primly as the maid moved to work on her golden hair. Her expression, in the mirror, was all sympathy and concern. "Oh, how dreadful for her! And for you! I cannot imagine this world without my father. He spoils me horribly even though I can be a pestilence at times. I think I have been very lucky in both of my parents."

Lilly smiled at her.

Suddenly, Lady Natalie jumped to her feet, startling the maid. "They are announcing the supper dance! I best allow my fiancé to find me, or I will never hear the end of it. May I call on you tomorrow? I will bring my brother Joseph, if that is acceptable? *Will* you be receiving at Lady Sheffield's?" At Lilly's nod, she turned to go but stopped short and looked back. "I do believe my brother Joe is sweet on Miss Beauchamp. He never dances with anybody by choice, and he's reserved the supper dance with her! Oh, damn and blast, the supper dance!" With that, she fled the room leaving both Lilly and the maid with raised eyebrows.

Lilly wished Lady Natalie had been a hag with a large mole on her nose. Quite the contrary, however. Not only was she an extremely pretty lady, but she was the sort of person Lilly could befriend. As unlikely as it seemed, the younger woman's company had been comforting!

What a strange world this is, Lilly thought, returning to the foyer near the ballroom. More composed now, the weight of sadness from earlier had lifted…slightly. Not wishing to draw any notice, she crept around the edge of the ballroom until she was beside her aunt again.

Lady Eleanor examined her suspiciously. "And where have you been off to, Lilly? There have been two gentlemen looking to put their names on your dance card. That viscount, Danbury, and an old geezer."

Lilly didn't answer but shook her head and then allowed her gaze to search the dancing couples. Every now and then, she glimpsed a familiar face from her first season. Faces that were older than they had been before.

Two of them were Penelope Crone and Caroline Harris. Miss Crone looked much the same, although less bubbly than Lilly remembered. Lilly watched as Penelope nodded calmly at her dance partner and then stepped along the line. With serious eyes, she didn't seem to laugh as easily as she had before. Is that what growing up did to people?

Perhaps not everyone. Her other friend, Caroline Harris, seemed to be enjoying herself immensely but was less easily recognizable. Matronly and plump, she'd filled out considerably around her middle. Her face was round and full of laughter. She danced with a very friendly looking gentleman, only slightly taller than she. Lilly watched as he whispered something in Caroline's ear causing her to blush. Caroline smiled and then gave him a seductive look. The man must be her husband—two very satisfied halves of a love match.

As much as Lilly had anticipated catching up with old friends, she was in no mood to do so tonight. She caught her aunt's attention by placing her hand on the older woman's arm.

"One of my headaches is coming on, Aunt. Would you mind terribly if I took the carriage to the town house and then sent it back to collect you and Glenda later?"

Aunt Eleanor seemed disappointed but gave Lilly her permission. "Perhaps you should see a physician about them, Lilly. They seem to come on often." Her brow furrowed in concern.

Lilly felt guilty at the fabrication but needed to escape. It was not a complete untruth, anyhow. Pressure had built up behind her eyes in a most threatening manner.

"Go home, dear, and get some rest. I'll tell Glenda."

"I will, and thank you." Lilly affectionately squeezed her aunt's hand before maneuvering toward the exit. As she worked her way around the ballroom, she caught a glimpse of Michael dancing with the beautiful and, yes, likeable, Lady Natalie. They seemed comfortable in each other's arms, dancing in perfect harmony. As Michael's gaze found her, Lilly put her head down and slipped out of the room. An aching in her temples strengthened the excuse she'd given her aunt. These emotions needed to be put to rest.

Enough already.

****

Early the next morning, wearing an old morning dress and a large floppy bonnet, Lilly itched to begin work in the garden. She determined to free herself of the past with some satisfying manual labor, and the early hours were the best time to do this.

The hired man, Burt, had worked for her aunt for over five decades and had long since lost the enthusiasm to keep up with the area covered in a tangle of vines and weeds. Dear Aunt Eleanor hadn't the heart to replace him.

She found him leaning against the deteriorating gardener's shack, seemingly contemplating the day's duties, when she stepped outside. Concerned he might resent her interference, Lilly need not have worried. For before she could even ask, he located gloves, a rake, and a wagon for her use. Burt showed no reluctance whatsoever in handing over the gardening responsibilities.

Miss Fussy, who had followed her outside, took to exploring the perimeter.

Lilly did not contemplate tending the garden as a whole but took on a small area instead. It was easier this way, less overwhelming.

There, she allowed her concerns to work themselves out in the rich, cool soil as she pulled and cut and raked. As the sun rose higher, Lilly managed to clear a rather large area near the back gate. Under the long-dead dried brush, she was pleased to find several tender shoots which had survived the wintertime and were reaching upwards, eagerly looking forward to warmth again. She guessed them to be tulips. She also discovered some leafy clusters she thought to be lobelia. There was something spiritual about having one's hands in the dirt, turning the earth, and assisting the plants.

Seeing Michael again had overshadowed the fact that she was entering a new and peaceful time of her life. She loved her aunt, and her aunt seemed to enjoy her company as well. Lilly believed Aunt Eleanor had become somewhat lonely. Despite all her friends amongst the *ton*, there was something comforting, grounding rather, in one's own family. Lilly knew Aunt Eleanor had grieved deeply at Lilly's mother's funeral.

Yes, she was in a better place than she had been in years.

Her life at Beauchamp Manor had been depressing, demeaning, and just plain cold. Lord Beauchamp had sent Glenda away as often as possible, and when she had been home, he had controlled the amount of influence Lilly could have over the girl. Until his illness had nearly completely incapacitated him, the baron always had the final say about what was or was not good for his daughter.

Lord Beauchamp had forbade Lilly to work in the actual garden on the property, so Lilly had found isolated areas where she could cultivate flowers, herbs, vegetables, and shrubs of her own choosing. She shared cuttings with some of the neighbors, and when she managed a good harvest, she would take baskets of food around to some of the poorer people who lived nearby. She'd read every book she could find on botany and even written down techniques she'd discovered on her own for certain types of plants.

Stopping to stretch, Lilly considered the small garden area. This was healing, working in plain sight, not having to worry about drawing the baron's ire. Miss Fussy, tired of searching for unknown treasures, had found a sunny spot nearby and appeared to be sleeping soundly. Lilly smiled. How she loved the little imp.

Dragging the nearly full wagon, Lilly moved to the other side of this particular plot and discovered more lobelia. The pretty little blue plants made for delightful ground cover. They reminded her of Edgewater Heights. The plant had grown profusely along the driveway. Lilly leaned back on her heels and sighed. Although it was bittersweet to do so, she'd recalled the time she'd spent there hundreds, perhaps thousands of times.

Edgewater Heights was a delightful estate. Hopefully, the people Michael—no, she must try to think of him as the duke or His Grace. Yes, hopefully the people His Grace leased it to were keeping it in good repair. Thinking about Michael again, she touched her lips.

Lilly Beauchamp, the Baroness Beauchamp, had gone nearly nine whole years since last being kissed.

Nothing Lord Beauchamp had ever done could be considered a kiss.

The last true kiss she had been given had been very early in the morning, after returning from the waterfall when Michael kissed her goodnight, or more appropriately, good morning. They had both been tired and giddy from their lovemaking and love play in the water afterwards. It was amazing what two people could do underwater when there were no inhibitions to stifle their creativity.

Since that morning, throughout her entire marriage, Lilly had gone kiss-less.

Perhaps that was why she had become such a wanton under Michael's—no, *His Grace's,* no, Michael's—kisses the previous night. (She could not think of him as a duke while thinking of him in relation to kissing.) She'd become a wanton due to her kiss-lessness. She had been positively starved for kisses. That was a very logical explanation.

And now that she had experienced it again, she would not be nearly as starved should such an opportunity arise in the future. Lilly brushed her hands together to remove some mud and went back to work.

Both her mind and her heart relaxed as a mental picture formed of what the plot would look like in a few months. Her muscles were tired but not from tension, rather from healthy physical labor. This was much better. Finally, Lilly removed the muddied gloves, found Burt as he puttered about, and filled him in on what she thought ought to be allowed to stay and what must go. Tomorrow, she told him, she would cut back and then remove the old rosebush. It was gnarly, and the thorns made exiting the back gate a dicey endeavor.

Lilly *hated* roses!

"Lady Eleanor told me to let you make of it what you wish, ma'am. Just tell me what you'll be needing, and I can make arrangements to get it for you." The old man, rather than being put out by her interference, seemed pleased. Lilly's heart lightened upon hearing this. After all, she hadn't wanted to step on anybody's toes with her plans. She was so grateful to her aunt for allowing them to stay with her. Lady Eleanor extended more welcome to Lilly than she'd ever received at Beauchamp Manor. The feeling gave her a great sense of relief.

Lilly gathered Miss Fussy up and headed back into the house. The pup was covered in mud. "I think we both are in need of a bath, little one." She kissed the top of Miss Fussy's head. She would ask Betty about having water brought up. Catching sight of herself in the mirror, she grimaced. Dirt smudged her face, and several strands of hair had escaped the tight chignon she'd begun the day with.

Just as Lilly turned to climb the stairs, Glenda's voice cried out from behind her in alarm, "Lilly, you are going to dress properly today, aren't you? You must, Lilly! I am so nervous. What if he comes to call this afternoon? What if he *doesn't* come to call? I need you to be there because I know I will positively make a hash of things myself. He is *so handsome*! I believe I must be in love! He has the most beautiful eyes, and his smile is ever so charming…"

Feeling more than a little confused, Lilly's brows rose questioningly. "Whoever are you talking about?"

"You ninny! You must remember Mr. Joseph Spencer. He is the son of an earl, and he claimed two dances with me, Lilly! He told me I was the most beautiful girl at the ball! He promised to call upon me. I simply *adore* him." Ah, the young man who had been with Michael. Yes, Lady Natalie's brother. Good God, was this really happening? It would be laughable if it wasn't so ironically cruel.

"I am going to clean up as soon as I return to my chamber." Lilly smiled reassuringly. She *was* pleased for Glenda. She *did* want Glenda to be happy. She was her sister's daughter. Lilly had not been able to be a mother as she'd first thought, but if it was the last thing she did, she would make certain Rose's daughter had a promising future. "I met his sister, Lady Natalie, before leaving last night. I think they must be a very pleasant family, don't you?" At Glenda's enthusiastic nod, Lilly continued, "Now let me pass so I can be presentable for Aunt Eleanor's at-home."

Glenda laughed and then danced her way downstairs.

Lilly's own steps slowed as she considered this new development.

Very well then. Obviously, things would not be as simple as she'd hoped. It seemed Michael's fiancée and family were not going away. Lilly must find a way to endure them. No that was not fair. She *liked* Lady Natalie.

This was a good thing. It ought to be a very good thing.

Hopefully Michael—er, His Grace, that was—spent most of his time with an older set. Oh, blast, he was always going to be Michael to her.

Lilly could do this. Melancholy would not take hold of her again!

****

For a debutante newly introduced to society, the afternoon at home proved to be a rousing success. Several of the younger gentlemen arrived bearing bouquets of flowers and chocolates for Glenda. Most importantly, though, Mr. Joseph Spencer, with his sister in tow, kept his word and arrived as promised.

Lilly found him to be a rather pleasant gentleman.

She even allowed Glenda to accept an invitation to go out riding with him and his sister later in the afternoon. Lilly would come along as well in order to lend the outing more respectability.

Their visitors also included both Miss Penelope Crone and Mrs. John Tiddle (formerly Miss Caroline Harris). Lilly spent over an hour catching up on the events of both their lives.

Caroline, now the mother of four, yes *four* rambunctious boys ranging from age three to seven, confided she might be carrying again. Caroline and her husband resided in London year-round as he worked as a barrister and his office required he be at hand daily. The children were currently with a new governess, the former having recently married. Mrs. Tiddle gave Lilly considerable detail regarding each of her offspring, which although a bit tedious, was very sweet. Lilly was pleased to know her friend had made such an amiable match. She tried not to wonder how many children she and Michael might have had by now.

Miss Crone had turned down so many offers that her family now declared her quite firmly on the shelf. Penelope said she preferred it this way. Quietly, she told Lilly she would only marry if she could find the kind of love Lilly and Captain Redmond—the duke— had seemed to have found long ago. She said, although it had ended in heartache, for she knew Lilly must have been heartbroken, they had shown her true love existed. "And I cannot," she said, "quite literally, give myself, my very person, to a man unless he is passionately in love with me, and I feel the same in return."

Lilly listened as her friend told her how she had seen too many miserable matches amongst the *ton*, and she did not wish to become a member of such a hideous group. "If I cannot trust my husband to care for me more than for his own personal interests, why on earth should I give him ownership of my person?" Penelope was adamant about her position. Lilly agreed emphatically. She had been Lord Beauchamp's property.

It was a boon for Penelope to have been blessed with the financial freedom to eschew marriage if she so wished.

After the last of the guests left, Glenda glowed, and Aunt Eleanor declared her a dazzling success. Finally, Lilly thought, things were going smoothly.

For once.

Chapter Seventeen
A Second Season

Once the season began, there were events to attend nearly every day, sometimes two, even! Lilly, Glenda, and Lady Eleanor attended garden parties, musicales, and picnics and often went on shopping expeditions with Penelope, Caroline, and Natalie. (No more Miss or Mrs. or Lady this or that).

And of course, they attended balls. And the same as before, Aunt Eleanor managed to receive invitations to every single one—those that mattered anyhow. Each week, she and Lilly carefully considered which events would be the best to attend and which should *absolutely not* be attended. Lilly found that she could exist quite nicely in London without seeing Michael for days at a time.

She did find herself, however, spending a great deal of time with his fiancée.

A fiancée, she might add, who rarely mentioned him, and quite easily dismissed him from her life in favor of spiriting about with her more youthful friends. Natalie loved to shop and had made it her mission to persuade Lilly to shed many of her old and less than fashionable gowns. Unable to resist Natalie's tenacity, Lilly allowed herself to purchase a few evening dresses which enhanced her figure and coloring. Insisting it was completely acceptable for a widow, the modiste presented gowns which were inevitably cut low in the bodice and made up of reds and golds. Lilly would protest, but Natalie had a knack persuading Lilly that she *absolutely must* purchase this very one. "Besides," Natalie would say, "it is your duty to allow all of us debutantes to live vicariously through you. After I am married, I shall wear nothing but the boldest of colors! I'll never wear anything pink again!"

Lilly loved the idea of Michael's perfect duchess decked out in bright red and a daringly low bodice.

Having previously only worn her older clothing, Lilly chose the Mathison gala to debut the first of her new dresses. It was a deep gold color. "Just like your eyes," Natalie had said. It was designed to be worn without a corset or petticoats. Aunt Eleanor simply loved it and declared she wished she had worn something just like it when she had had the figure to carry it off.

The dress was enchanting! As though hibernating for a decade, the woman inside of Lilly blossomed upon donning it. Being a widow held some tantalizing possibilities. With little adornment, the dress draped Lilly in elegant sophistication. She was her own person, not the property of any man, including a father or husband.

Lilly's transformation did not go unnoticed. Whereas before, curious eyes would notice, inspect, and then dismiss, they now noticed, inspected, and then inspected some more. Lilly wished she had kept her shawl about her. The attention, as exciting as it was, also proved a little frightening. She had worn the dress because she liked it. She hadn't considered the fact that she would no longer blend in with the matrons and wallflowers. She'd not considered that she might, in fact, attract masculine notice. Upon finding a settee for Aunt Eleanor, Lilly took the space besides her. She *was* a chaperone, after all—and a companion.

Nonetheless, she found she did attract the attention of a few rather handsome gentlemen. (Not all of them were, in truth, handsome.) But Lilly pleased herself by finding a positive attribute in each one of her partners.

Oh, but the heat!

As the night wore on, the room, as was usually the case, grew warm. When a particularly lively country dance ended, Lilly and Penelope slipped into the ladies' retiring room to cool their temples with some tepid water. What with all the dancing and the candles, both admitted to feeling overheated. They took their time on the sofas provided.

"He's being a ninny," Penelope stated as she removed her slippers to massage her toes.

Lilly pretended not to know who Penelope meant by "he" but glanced around to be certain they were alone, nonetheless.

"I mean, Lady Natalie is a darling, of course! But she is so young! And now that you no longer have a husband—"

"Don't say it." Lilly jumped to her feet. Sometimes Penelope was far too outspoken. Why if anyone were to overhear—well, it didn't even bear considering. "Are you ready to return? My aunt will be wondering where I've run off to. I am her companion and Glenda's chaperone, after all." Lilly took her responsibilities seriously.

Penelope narrowed her eyes. "Very well." Resigned, she replaced her shoe and rose as well. "But in my opinion, both of you are being foolish. True love doesn't come along very often, and to allow it to pass you both by, a second time, is a travesty. Just my opinion, mind you."

Lilly shook her head but smiled. In spite of Penelope's outspokenness, it was difficult to be angry with her. "In this case, I'd appreciate you keeping your opinion to yourself."

Lilly had done well in not dwelling on Michael's presence. She did not need her friend reminding her. She smoothed her gown as they re-entered the ballroom and went their separate ways. Penelope returned to her mother, and Lilly, as always, found her aunt's side.

"Didn't know where you had gotten off to," Aunt Eleanor admonished her teasingly. "Wondered if you'd run away with one of these young bucks sniffing after you." Her aunt's laughter cut off abruptly. Lilly was surprised then to see the older woman's eyes narrow.

"Lady Sheffield, you must present me to your delightful niece. I have been unable to take my eyes off her all evening." A man, well past his middle years, with gray hair but thick black eyebrows, appeared as though out of thin air. Although he seemed somewhat familiar, Lilly could not place where she had seen him. Most likely at one of the seemingly endless events they'd been attending. The same people tended to appear over and over again at most of the *ton*'s affairs. Snatching her hand and raising it to his pouting lips, he bowed formally.

Her aunt was no more impressed than she. Sniffing into the air, Aunt Eleanor obviously did not approve of the man. But to deny him an introduction would be tantamount to giving him the cut.

"Lord Hawkborn, may I present to you my niece, Lady Beauchamp. Lilly, this is the Earl of Hawkborn." Lilly winced as her aunt's lip curled. She'd never seen her aunt be rude to anyone.

"Hawthorn. I am the Earl of Hawthorn," the gentleman said through clenched teeth. Then, in an effort to exert his manners in spite of the snub, he politely addressed Lilly. "Lady Beauchamp, it is my greatest pleasure to meet you. I daresay, the supper dance is next. Would you do me the honor of standing up with me?"

Lilly happened to be free for this particular dance. She'd left it, purposely so, in order to remain with her aunt for the meal. But she could not decline without good reason. Ah, well. It was only one set.

"It would be my pleasure, Lord Hawthorn." Turning to her aunt, she nodded and said, "Will you be dining with Lady Danbury, or would you like for me to find you in the supper room?"

Her aunt gave the earl a withering look. "Yes, come find me, dear." She paused, as though she had something else to say on the matter, but then turned away and began gossiping with another of her ubiquitous *very close* friends.

Lilly took the earl's arm and allowed him to lead her to the floor. He was very tall and gangly and hadn't yet begun to stoop with age. But there was something odd about him. He carried an unnatural tension. His arm felt thin and bony. She wondered if he wore padding in his shoulders. The dance was, Lilly realized too late, a waltz. As the earl placed his skeletal fingers at her waist, Lilly felt as though a spider had landed on her. She resisted the impulse to shudder. His other bony hand clasped hers firmly, and the dance began.

The last year at Beauchamp Mansion had been spent preparing Glenda to enter society. One of the lessons scheduled daily had been dance. Lilly had attended every lesson faithfully along with Glenda. If necessary, Lilly could waltz on her hands—blindfolded.

The earl was not as diligent and seemed somewhat distracted by the steps.

"I must admit, my lord," Lilly began, "I am surprised you would seek me out. I am a mere widow, a chaperone to my stepdaughter."

The earl looked up at her with pale and watery blue eyes. Suddenly no longer distracted by the steps of the dance, all of his attention focused upon her.

Again, she forced herself not to shudder. There was something very…off…about this man.

"You mean your…niece?" he managed to say without stepping on her toes.

Thinking there was a chance that he was simply mistaken, Lilly spoke coolly. "No, my lord, my stepdaughter." She would change the subject. "I understand your son, Lord Castleton, is in attendance tonight. It is always such a pleasure to have family nearby, wouldn't you agree?" she asked innocently.

The earl's face darkened. "Ah, yes…yes…He might be. I do not keep myself informed of his whereabouts." He glanced down at his feet for a moment before changing the subject to her once again. "No, I am not mistaken, my dear. I am referring to your niece, who also happens to be your stepdaughter." Lilly glanced into his eyes and then away from them just as quickly.

It was Lilly who nearly missed a step this time, as

she processed the fact that this man knew the truth of her marriage. "The distinction is of no importance." Perhaps it was not. Oh, please, let it not be!

The earl waited for her to expand on her words, but when she did not he continued in a threatening tone. "Oh, my lady, I think that it is. Am I not still in England? It is illegal, is it not? To marry one's dead sister's husband?" The earl leaned down so his mouth was very near her face. He smelled of an awful cigar smoke. She turned her head to avoid his breath. And suddenly remembered where she had seen him. He was the man she'd nearly collided with weeks ago, while fleeing Michael at the Willoughby Ball.

And then she realized where she'd heard the name before! Lord Hawthorn. The Earl of Hawthorn was the man who'd had hijacked Michael's carriage!

This was not about her at all.

Lord Hawthorn was Michael's political enemy. He would do anything to discredit him. He'd proven this already, earlier this spring. She'd found him familiar because he had been near the gazebo when Michael had kissed her. She'd nearly run headlong into him when she'd fled. What did he know? What was he up to?

Lilly's eyes darted around the ballroom. Michael was a mere ten feet away from her. But what could he do to help her? He danced with his betrothed. Unlike Lord Hawthorn he took long confident steps, steering his partner adeptly around the other couples. Lady Natalie, however, caught Lilly's eyes. There must have been something alarming in her expression for, after a moment of quick conversation with her partner, Michael looked over at her as well. His eyes narrowed.

And then the earl spoke to Lilly again. "You are a

211

more interesting lady than you would have people believe. A lady with a past always is."

This was not good. No, not good at all.

"Especially a past as incestuous as yours."

At these words, Lilly's head snapped back with a jerk. "I find your insinuations insulting, my lord. I'd advise you to change the subject now. You are being quite improper." She spoke sternly.

"Tsk, tsk, tsk." He shook his head in mock solemnity. "What would Mr. Joseph Spencer think if he were to discover the lady he courted was from a family who believed themselves above the law? Your marriage to your brother-in-law was illegal. Worse than that, sinfully incestuous!" That word again. Lilly held herself rigid and attempted to pull away from the earl's grasp, but those spiderlike fingers had suddenly become vicelike. He pulled her closer so that his face was very close. "I suggest you tell the Duke of Cortland, your lover, that if he does not desist with his amendment, I will make things very difficult for you. Very difficult indeed."

Whereupon, one booted foot stomped down upon her slippered toes. He released her at the same time. It was done easily, Lilly realized later. It merely looked like an embarrassing accident.

But in that instant, there was only pain.

Her slippers were satin, and the heel of a boot was hard, with sharp edges. As agonizing pain shot through her foot, she was also suddenly free of his constricting grasp. Lilly's own attempt to pull herself away from him added to her momentum, leading her to fall quite humiliatingly onto the unforgiving parquet floor. Wishing she could disappear to anywhere but there, she lay stunned, reeling from pain, embarrassment, and most of all, the earl's words. Other nearby dancers looked on in curiosity. The earl tsked and stood nearby, feigning concern. "Oh, my dear, I was under the impression you knew how to waltz!"

It took all of ten seconds before two other gentlemen, who had released their own partners, crouched down beside her. One of them was Viscount Danbury, whom she had come to know quite well that long-ago spring.

The other gentleman was Michael. They were joined by several others, and Hawthorn backed away slowly. "Oh, I say," twittered the bystanders surrounding her.

Stunned, Lilly's mind reeled as the earl's words replayed themselves over and over in her mind. *Incestuous. Above the law. The Duke of Cortland—your lover.*

It took a moment for her to recover her bearings enough to actually hear Michael and Danbury speaking to her. "Take deep breaths, Lilly." Michael's voice was closest. With one arm behind her back, he helped her sit up.

"Are you injured, my lady?" Danbury asked, looking around and then adding, "What the devil happened?" He spoke to nobody in particular.

"She fell, must have tripped," an unfamiliar voice offered.

Lilly tried to sit up on her own, but Michael refused to release her. "I've got you, love," he whispered in her ear, and then before she could move he had scooped her into his arms and was carrying her across the dance floor to the seating area where her aunt

Eleanor looked on in concern. Carefully placing Lilly on one of the sofas, he crouched down before her with a deep frown furrowing his brows.

Hawthorn had accused Michael of being her *lover*! Surely seeing him address her with such attentiveness would reinforce the man's claim. She needed Michael to be far away from her. He had called her *love*. He'd said those exact words to her once before, at the waterfall. He had been her lover once, but this was no longer true. She needed him to go away! Now!

The caring in his eyes was nearly her undoing.

She pushed his hands away and looked at him with as much disdain as she could muster. "I am fine, Your Grace. I need no further assistance," and then, "Thank you." The look in his eyes changed from concern to confusion. She wished he were not so close to her. She wished she could look anywhere else but at him. His presence overwhelmed her.

"Lilly?" he said softly.

"Thank you, Your Grace." She spoke harshly. And then she turned her head to the side so she would not see his eyes for even a second longer.

Lord Hawthorn stood across the room, leaning against a wall, appearing far too interested in the sight of Michael and Lilly together. *Incestuous, illegal, your lover...*She had known it could not become public knowledge that she'd married Rose's widower but had not considered the reality of what the ramifications would be if the truth were to be made public. Could it truly ruin Glenda's chances of making an advantageous match? She was not certain, but worried that ladies had, indeed, been ruined by lesser transgressions.

And she could never ask Michael to give up on his

amendment. She would not!

"Leave me be," she ground out. Hawthorn was watching!

Chapter Eighteen
An Enemy

Her eyes flashed such disdain, Michael nearly flinched. And she was telling him to leave her alone. She might just as well have slapped him across the face, so surprised he was by the venom she spewed in his direction. He had no choice but to rise to his feet and step back.

Taking in her stiff posture, he had to reconsider that perhaps she *did* blame him for everything. As she well should.

At the Willoughby ball, their parting had been wrenching. After what he'd learned, he would not—he could not—blame her for holding him in contempt. And yet…that was not her way.

He knew this about her. He would never forgive himself for the situation she'd been forced into—the mere thought of it stole his breath—but he'd believed in his heart she'd somehow forgiven him. He had not thought she hated him.

And when he'd carried her from the floor, she'd not resisted. It was the same as it always had been, when they touched, as though their hearts beat in unison—a coming home—of sorts. Had he imagined it?

And then he glanced in the direction of her gaze. Lord Hawthorn watched them intently, with a spiteful look in his eyes.

Lilly had been dancing with the blasted man when she'd suddenly *fallen down* in the middle of the ballroom floor. What had happened? What had Hawthorn said to her? What had he done?

Knowing he would not get any answers from Lilly right now, he bowed and then took his leave. She was under the watchful eye of her aunt now. She would be well cared for. But did she need protection as well?

Catching Danbury's eye, with a quick tilt of his head, he gestured for his friend to follow him so they could speak privately. Slipping into an empty room, just off the foyer, Michael made certain it was vacant and then shut the door firmly.

"What the devil was all that about?" Danbury asked him. "And why was she so out of sorts with you for assisting her? You realize who partnered her, don't you?"

At his friend's questions, Michael nodded. "Hawthorn." And then shoving his hands into his pockets, he turned his head in the direction from where they had come. After a moment or two of contemplation, he shook it, perplexed. "Hawthorn said something to upset Lilly. He frightened her somehow."

"*Lilly?*" Danbury asked with raised brows. "*Not Lady Beauchamp?* Are the two of you reconciled then? What of Lady Natalie?"

Brushing off the notion, Michael made an irritated grimace. "Have a care, Danbury. She is an old friend for whom I am concerned." Then changing the direction of Danbury's thoughts, said, "However, I need a favor, if you will."

Hugh Chesterton took a few steps toward the settee and dropped into it. Leaning back, he raised one leg up and rested his ankle upon his other knee. "I am at your disposal."

Michael rubbed his chin thoughtfully. "I am concerned for Lilly's safety. Unfortunately, she is intolerant of my company tonight. Will you attach yourself to her, and her aunt, for the remainder of the evening? And then see they arrive home safely? I realize this may pose something of an inconvenience. I would do it myself if I could, but..."

"Oh, I understand. Very unusual behavior for the lady, if I say so myself." Danbury placed both feet back on the floor and stood up. Brushing at his trousers to remove an imagined piece of lint, he looked back up at Michael. "Just an old friend, eh? A very beautiful widow, though." A gleam in Hugh's eyes disquieted Michael.

But Danbury knew how Michael had once felt about Lilly. Surely, he would not do anything to jeopardize their friendship, such as poaching on an old flame? "Perhaps you could encourage her to tell you all that Hawthorn said. Use some of that charm for which you are so famous."

"Absolutely." Danbury winked. Walking toward the door, his friend stopped a moment before turning to look back at Michael once again. "I'll see you in the morning then? Rotten Row at sunup?"

Michael nodded, and the viscount exited and closed the door. What the hell was Hawthorn up to now? The image of Lilly, fallen to the floor in pain came unwittingly to mind. Michael had been dancing with Lady Natalie, trying not to watch Lilly from across the room. He'd been doing a lot of that lately...trying not to watch Lilly.

Lady Natalie had been watching her too. And she had told him Lilly looked upset. Alarms had gone off inside of him for he'd known with whom she was dancing, but he'd thought himself paranoid. Lilly had seemed standoffish with the earl, but nothing more than that.

But when he'd glanced over at Lady Natalie's comment, there had been shock, revulsion, in Lilly's eyes. And then, yes, she had looked frightened just before she'd fallen. And the more he recollected the moment, the more certain he became that she had been attempting to pull away from the bastard. And then she'd fallen.

Wild horses could not have stopped him from rushing to her side. He was beginning to believe it would always be this way.

Ah, she had looked so beautiful this evening. She'd sparkled again just as she had that first season.

She had not dressed as a chaperone. She was dressed as a beautiful woman, one who had had every intention of enjoying herself.

Michael dropped wearily into the spot Danbury had vacated. Placing both feet firmly on the floor, he leaned forward and rested his elbows upon his knees. *What the hell was he going to do about her?*

****

With Lord Hawthorn's threats echoing in her thoughts, Lilly fought to keep panic from reducing her to tears.

Glenda wasn't an affectionate girl, or respectful even, but Lilly and Aunt Eleanor were the only family she had left. Glenda needed her.

And in a strange way, Lilly needed Glenda. And

219

she needed for Glenda to find the happiness that had eluded herself. Lilly must make certain Glenda found a good match, somebody kind.

Coming to London, Lilly had hoped Glenda might find somebody with a sweet temperament and a gentle spirit—a man who cared for her but also had the *wherewithal* to care for her. And Joseph Spencer seemed to fit this requirement to a T. If scandal were to attach itself to Glenda, merely by her association with Lilly, would Mr. Spencer remove his attentions? And if these unfortunate circumstances occurred, could that eliminate other opportunities her niece might be presented for making a good match? If so, it would be Lilly's fault!

Not because she'd married the baron in the first place. She would not berate herself for that. But rather that she had discussed her past in a very public place where any person might overhear. She ought to have protected such information dearly. Overcome by her emotions where Michael was concerned, she had been careless.

Having invested most of their funds on this season for Glenda, it could not all be for naught! She must prevent Lord Hawthorn from carrying out his threats. But how?

As the orchestra took a break and the murmuring of the guests broke into her consciousness, Lilly realized she had been watching the entrance to the ballroom where Michael and Lord Danbury had exited.

And now Lord Danbury was returning. Alone.

A roguish smile crossed his face when he caught her gaze, and he exaggerated his already confident swagger. Although known about town as something of a rake, he'd never said or done anything improper while in her company. He was similar to Michael in stature and coloring, but their likenesses ended there. Whereas Michael's eyes shimmered blue, Danbury's were nearly black. Lilly loved the creases she'd noticed recently around Michael's eyes. They hadn't been there before. They must have formed from smiling and spending time out of doors.

Danbury's dark eyes contrasted vividly against his paler skin. While Michael had been away at war, Danbury had been finishing his education at Oxford. Their differences, perhaps, were part of what strengthened their friendship.

Danbury was a very attractive man, but she'd never had any romantic interest in him whatsoever. She'd always thought Penelope carried a bit of a torch for him, however.

Smiling up at him, she would have chuckled at his wink, had she not been so upset by the evening's events. She'd developed a rather sisterly affection for the scamp.

Placing one foot forward, the viscount executed a courtly bow as though she were the queen herself.

"Sit down, my lord. Your charm has no power over me." Lilly gestured with a wave of her hand. Someone had fetched her a cushioned ottoman to rest her ankle upon, and her aunt had gone in search of something cold to put on the injury. Lilly hoped it wasn't a sprain, but she could see it swelling already. She was finally making progress in the garden and knew it would be neglected if she could not maintain it.

Danbury eyed the offending appendage with a wry smile. "Has someone gone after a cold compress?" His friendly demeanor was reassuring, considering she'd just ordered Michael away from her.

"Aunt Eleanor has," she said cautiously. Perusing the seats around her, she ascertained that Lord Hawthorn had abandoned his watch. Many of the guests were now milling toward the dining hall. "Thank you—for your assistance earlier." Looking down at her hands, she felt sheepish. She had been *very* rude to Michael. What must Lord Danbury think of her? But she'd had no choice!

"What did Hawthorn say to you?" He did not mince his words with trite conversation. "A vile creature. I can't imagine why you would dance with him."

Lilly stared thoughtfully at the handsome features of the man sitting beside her. She could not argue Lord Danbury's assessment of the Earl of Hawthorn. "A lady must accept unless she has already promised a set. If she wishes to stand up later in the evening, that is." And then, "Did His Grace send you to interrogate me? Because it's none of his business. And it's none of yours either." Why was she snapping at Danbury? What had *he* done to deserve this?

She felt frightened. That was why.

"Hawthorn *has* threatened you then. Cortland was right." Danbury suddenly didn't look harmless and good-natured anymore. "What exactly did he say?"

What had Michael told his friend? She could not take any chances. Especially not here. She'd voiced personal matters in a public setting before and look where that had gotten her. "I cannot discuss that with you, my lord." And then more softly, she added, "But I would speak with His Grace about it in a more private setting. If you would relay that to him."

Nodding slowly, Lord Danbury remained sitting beside her. "Of course." And then replacing his earlier mask of pleasant enjoyment, he smiled at her dazzlingly. "Tell me, lovely lady, what have you been up to this past decade?"

Lilly was to experience the effect of the full arsenal of Danbury charm.

And for the rest of the evening, it seemed, except to fetch her a plate of food, the viscount did not leave her side. He even followed her aunt's carriage on horseback, all the way back to the town house on Curzon Street. As one of her aunt's footmen let down the step, Danbury reined his horse to a quick stop, tipped his hat, and then finally left them to their own devices.

"Quite an admirer, you have." Aunt Eleanor spoke matter-of-factly as they handed their cloaks to Jarvis. "He didn't leave your side for a moment."

Lilly laughed, albeit uneasily, and then kissed her aunt good night. She was suddenly very, very tired. And as much as she loved her aunt, she did not wish to stay up and chat. "He was being chivalrous. The debutantes love that..." Then on her swollen and tender ankle, she hobbled up the stairs without further assistance. It did not seem to be sprained, thank the heavens. She could likely work in the garden tomorrow after all. She would most certainly need the peace it usually afforded her.

Chapter Nineteen
Between a Rock and a Very Hard Place

A fog hung low over Hyde Park early the next morning as Michael and Danbury simultaneously pulled back on their reins and slowed to a walk. They had given the horses a free head early on, and it was time to let them cool down. Both men had meetings scheduled around parliamentary duties most days and so had set aside one day a week to ride together while in the city. The early hours left the Row to themselves, and the air was usually crisp and fresh.

On this morning, however, they were to be joined by another.

Michael recognized the Earl of Ravensdale, his affianced's father, even from a distance, as the esteemed gentleman approached upon his own steed.

"Cortland, Danbury." Ravensdale nodded in both of their directions before glancing around. "A somewhat tolerable park, when it isn't swarming with dandies."

Danbury laughed, but Michael was in a less amiable mood. Although, as a duke, Michael held the loftier position in society, the earl was a powerful man—an enviable alliance to have—one who could also be a formidable enemy. "My lord," Michael returned.

The earl steered his horse so he could join their

conversation.

"I've obtained assurance from Riverton. We have his vote." He announced in a grim voice. "But it's tight, yet."

Danbury's eyes shifted toward Michael. Michael knew what Danbury was thinking.

He was concerned about Lilly's return and Hawthorn's interference. He would also be concerned that Michael's engagement was jeopardized. The timing was horrible, and Danbury, more than anybody, knew how Michael had felt about Lilly way back when.

There was a great deal at stake. His betrothal to Lady Natalie was more than a dynastic one. It had political ramifications as well. It solidified Ravensdale's support and improved Michael's reputation. A married man was always considered more responsible and worthy of respect than a bachelor. They needed all the help they could get if they were to have any luck at eroding the strength of the Corn Laws.

Yes, the timing of Lilly's return was regrettable indeed. And yet. Michael clenched his fists around the leather strap. And yet...

"I understand Hawthorn was involved in something of a mishap last night. With a friend of Natalie's, Lady Beauchamp." The earl spoke casually, but Michael knew better. He was not a man to waste his time with small talk. "Natalie told me she wasn't convinced it was an accident...She also told me the two of you assisted the lady afterwards."

Michael tightened his jaw. "Your daughter was concerned for her friend." He would say no more. He did not appreciate feeling coerced.

"Beautiful gel, Lady Beauchamp." Danbury

toggled his eyebrows. "I've had my eye on her all season." Danbury drew the earl's attention away from Michael. "Delightful. If anyone were to lure me out of bachelorhood…" Danbury's statement was tantalizing bait, indeed.

At this statement, the earl's brows rose. "Couldn't hurt, Danbury, couldn't hurt at all. The last thing we need now is even a hint of scandal." And then he nodded. Apparently, what he'd heard had satisfied his concerns. "Well, then, I'll leave you two to carry on." The earl spurred his horse and departed as quickly as he'd arrived.

Michael and Hugh rode in silence for a full two minutes before either of them spoke.

"How was she?" Michael swallowed hard.

"She was able to walk upon her ankle, without assistance"—his friend knew him too well, though— "when her aunt and stepdaughter were finally ready to return to home."

Michael nodded but continued looking straight ahead. "I appreciate your assistance last night. Did she tell you anything?"

"She was reticent but told me she would be willing to speak with you about the matter. *Privately*, she said. She will receive you if you call upon her at her aunt's home."

Relief swept through him upon hearing these words. If she were willing to see him, she did not hate him. But he remained stoic. "Hawthorn must have threatened her. She was downright hostile to me. But with what?" All sorts of things came to mind. Had Hawthorn gotten wind of their past? And then his horse shied a bit to the side, as though perplexed by the sudden tension in his rider's seat.

Danbury glanced over. "Despite your separation from Lady Beauchamp, I take it you are still affected by her."

Michael cleared his throat and then answered in a harsh voice, "It's madness, I know." He removed his hat and impatiently ran gloved fingers through his hair. "It seemed the entire world conspired against us that summer. We should be an old married couple by now with a full nursery and old established habits...These thoughts torment me because life *did not* conspire to let that happen. And now I am a betrothed man. It would be the height of dishonor to cry off. I will not jilt Lady Natalie." Not to mention the thousands who would be affected if the Corn Laws were not amended. "I have her father's blessing. Lady Natalie is a kind and sweet lady, and it would ruin her. It is not even something to consider."

"A scandal involving you would likely cost votes," Danbury pointed out unnecessarily. "Damned bad luck, Cortland. I wish things had gone differently. This sort of complication is only part of why I've avoided the leg shackle." But then he added, "You could set her up as your mistress. She's is a widow, after all...Except I know you, and you probably intend to be the faithful husband and all that."

Michael replaced his hat. He wouldn't acknowledge Danbury's words. Sometimes his friend went too far. "I must speak with Lilly," he said, instead, before leaning forward and urging his horse into a cantor. Hugh did not follow. He would let him alone. Michael would go to Lilly today. Ensure her safety from Hawthorn and then avoid her for the rest of the season.

****

Lilly was hard at work that morning in the garden house. Her ankle, although bruised and a little swollen, was well enough to limp outside.

Determined to keep her spirits up, she set to propagating some cuttings that had been a gift from Lady Ravensdale, Natalie's mother. After discovering Lilly's passion for horticulture, she had sent a basketful of various clippings over from her own garden. It was important Lilly treat them as quickly as possible for them to successfully root.

It was precious, that a friend could share something so lovely, which if nurtured properly, would grow stronger and more beautiful with the passage of time. It could then, in turn, be shared with another friend someday in the future. It allowed one to feel connected to other souls and to the earth somehow.

With a sharp knife, she sliced a few of the leaves off the vine cutting so it would have a better chance to root. Just as in new friendships, the plant could be weakened if too much was demanded in its early stages. She then dipped the stem in watered-down honey and positioned it in a prepared pot that sat in the sunlight. As she placed a clear glass bell over the cutting, the door to the work area swung open.

Jarvis peered in cautiously. He seemed perplexed at having to search for her out of doors.

"You have an early visitor, madam." He approached her and offered the guest's calling card. She read the engraved lettering and told Jarvis to escort the duke outside to the garden bench. "I will join him there shortly." She was not at all presentable, certainly not for a duke, but it would take her eons of time to clean up and he *was* Michael, after all.

Jarvis bowed, without offering his approval, and gladly removed himself from the dust and grime of the garden house. He'd probably soiled his white gloves when he'd turned the handle. Poor Jarvis.

Lilly covered the remaining cuttings with a wet cloth and then wiped her hands on her apron before hobbling outside.

Michael was just exiting through the servant's door to meet her. He greeted her with a tight smile and then a gentlemanly bow.

She addressed him through tight lips. "Your Grace." She already regretted not taking the time to make herself more presentable.

She felt awkward and a bit contrite. She had treated him poorly last night. "Thank you for coming. I didn't think I'd see you so quickly. It's early yet. I thought all members of the *ton* slept in the day after a ball."

Michael gestured for her to sit. "Not all of us lead such indolent lifestyles. My morning began at sunup, in fact." His expression was serious. And then exasperated. "Hell and damnation, Lilly, what happened last night? What did Hawthorn say to you?"

Lilly folded her hands together just below her chin. She had decided late last night what she would tell Michael. "The night you and I...spoke, at the Willoughby ball, he overheard some of our conversation. I am not certain how much, but he believes you to be my...lover. He has demanded that I use my...influence to persuade you to drop your amendment."

"Why would he think you would do that? Even if it

were true?"

Lilly flinched at the question. "Because I married Rose's widower! It was illegal! The earl has discovered this and is threatening to expose me to the *ton*. I have not made this information public, here in London. He must have investigated me somehow. I am not so concerned for my own reputation, but Glenda will be harmed if a scandal erupts. She would be harmed if such information became public. And, as I've told you already, she *must* make a decent match." Lilly kept her voice calm, but it broke as she continued. "He called my marriage incestuous!"

"And his threat was to expose this? Did he give you a timeline? Anything specific?"

Lilly composed herself and shook her head. "He did not."

They sat silently for a moment, and then Lilly began speaking again. "That's why I sent you away last night. I don't believe he could know for certain it was *you* who was with me that night. It was very dark, if you remember. There were no torches outside and very little moonlight. I wish to try to convince him that perhaps it was somebody else. Danbury, for instance."

"Danbury?" Michael asked.

"His threats only have power if he believes I can influence *you*. It is *your* amendment he wants dropped. If he can be convinced that you and I are nothing to each other, then it would do him no good to expose my marriage. Perhaps then he might leave me alone. It is a possibility, anyway." Lilly was not Michael's lover. He was engaged to Lady Natalie. This was not fair!

Nonetheless, here he sat, in her garden, and she was oh, so tempted to place her hand upon his, to bury her face in his chest. When he had carried her last night, the desire to stay in his arms forever felt so strong it alarmed her. She'd fought the urge to twine her arms around his neck and beg him to whisk her away forever.

And then his hand moved to sit atop hers.

His tanned fingers curled around hers protectively. "I am so sorry."

Chapter Twenty
Misdirection

Remorse flooded him.

Had he not already caused her enough pain? Was she now to be punished even further for her association with him? He turned and lifted her hand to his lips. Dirt clung to her nails, but her fingers felt tiny and fragile. "Whatever you need. Danbury will be more than happy to assist. In fact, I will make certain he is." It was more important now, than ever, for Michael to avoid her.

If not for his own good, then for hers, by God.

He needed to make damn sure her stepdaughter secured her match.

When he'd lifted their hands, Lilly turned slightly to face him, but her eyes were closed. "Will it never end?" she asked. And then she leaned forward, her head hitting him in the chest, just below his chin. He should not, but he placed one hand upon her back and held her closer. She turned her head and rested her cheek upon his jacket. When her arm wrapped around his waist, he could not stop himself from lifting his other hand to stroke her hair. She smelled of soap and dirt and honey. His Lilly.

His precious Lilly.

Would what never end? Her torment? Her unhappiness? Their love? Had it even really ended all those years ago? He had no answer for her. He was not free to follow his baser inclinations.

"Joseph Spencer is a good man, of a good family," Michael said instead, wishing to reassure her. "If he intends to make an offer to Miss Beauchamp, I do not believe he can be dissuaded. Even so, I won't let Hawthorn hurt you."

He should never have let Beauchamp hurt her. Or her father. Or himself, for God's sake. "Lilly, I am so sorry…so…For everything."

Lilly pulled away, and Michael's hands dropped to the bench. "I didn't tell you about Hawthorn so you would solve my problems, Michael. And I do not wish you to feel as though you are responsible for this." She looked at him earnestly now. "I simply wanted you to know what that evil man is up to. And I wanted you to understand why I sent you away from me last night. I do not want you to feel guilty. You have nothing to be sorry for."

Oh, but he did. He was sorry as hell they'd been separated. He was sorry he'd found her again. And he was sorrier than anybody could even know that he'd promised himself to Lady Natalie.

Sitting beside her now, he had an overwhelming urge to carry her to the soft grass. To lie beside her. To bury himself inside of her.

But she was as much an impossibility now as she had been nearly a decade ago, while he'd been trapped inside Summers Park, under a quarantine he'd ordered himself.

"I just wanted you to know…that's all…" She spoke in a whisper, unable to meet his eyes any longer.

Michael took a deep breath and then released it slowly. "I'll speak to Danbury. He will assist you. But

Lilly," he said seriously, "promise me if Hawthorn makes any further threats, you will send for me. If you need anything, and I mean anything at all, allow me to provide it. I have endless resources. There is no reason you should ever lack for anything."

Except for him.

****

Lilly wanted to protest. She would never, *ever* take anything from him. Doing so would tarnish what they had had. She couldn't bear his pity. She had endured much worse. She could live through this. "I will send word through Danbury if I am threatened again. But I will not need anything, Michael. Please do not ask me to promise that." She tilted her head and looked into his eyes. Oh Lord, they were mesmerizing. Even more so now that he had matured.

And then to signal the end of their meeting, she stood up. She could not sit here alone with him and deny herself any longer. She ought not to have leaned into him, embraced him, in her moment of weakness.

Michael, of course, rose to his feet as well. At his full height, so very near to her, she again fought the urge to step into his arms.

She took a step backward and then turned back toward the house. He followed silently. Once they reached the foyer, he turned and bowed deeply. "Take care, Lilly," he said, his voice a little gravelly. It seemed as though he were going to say more, but he pinched his lips together instead and then disappeared onto the street.

Lilly covered her mouth with one hand in order to hold back a gasp. A gasp of pain, for surely this was the end. Neither of them would seek the other out again.

****

Later that same day, Lilly received another visitor. This one none other than Viscount Danbury.

Her aunt and Glenda had both left a short while before for what promised to be an elaborate garden party hosted by Penelope's parents. Lilly had planned to attend, but after spending too much time on her injured ankle that morning, her aunt insisted she rest.

She felt decidedly depressed.

Which left her with mixed feelings when Jarvis announced the viscount's visit. A part of her had been happy to be alone, but another part was irritated with her feelings of self-pity and regret. A thousand times already that afternoon, she had berated herself for not taking just a few more moments to be alone with Michael. And another thousand times she'd berated herself for allowing herself to hold him.

Entering the room tentatively, Danbury took in her elevated foot and shook his head. "Oh, no, my lady. This simply will not do." He carried a bouquet of roses. Oh, how she hated roses. But he was smiling and bowed low before her. "I require any lady I squire about town to look merrier than this." His tone was teasing but also understanding.

She gestured for him to sit and then forced herself to appear cheerful...and welcoming. "Lord Danbury." She graciously accepted the bouquet. "You should not have. You most definitely should not have." She pulled upon the bellpull and quickly handed the aromatic flowers off when Jarvis entered. "I take it you have spoken with Mich—the duke?"

Danbury smiled wickedly. "I have. It seems you need a suitor, and I am most gratified to oblige." He

235

toggled his eyebrows at her and then leaned back indolently, crossing one leg over the other. "In the dark, it is very possible Hawthorn saw not you and Cortland, but you and myself. Although I am assisting Cortland with the amendment, I would not have the power to do anything to stop it, even if a lover of mine did wish it." He gave her a moment to consider his words. Michael had told him a great deal. "And," he added, "I do not have a fiancée."

She nodded in agreement. "I hope it is enough to discourage the earl. If he doubts any connection between Michael and me, I can only hope he will desist with this blackmail."

Danbury nodded sympathetically. "Cortland didn't relay many details, but I am more than willing to help." He took her hands and gave them a reassuring squeeze. "I shall find it most agreeable to play swain to your loveliness for the entirety of the season if necessary. Would that be so very difficult for you to endure, my lady?" He lowered his voice seductively and looked at her from beneath hooded eyes. This sultry look would have brought any other woman from the age of seventeen to seventy to her knees—but not Lilly.

Lilly merely rolled her eyes. "Well, I suppose if you are to be my *amore*, you should begin by addressing me less formally. I give you leave to call me Lilly."

"And you shall call me Hugh," he responded.

Once the decision was made, they agreed the fewer people aware of the scheme, the better. They didn't want Hawthorn to find any new opportunities to make trouble. With that matter settled, they then went over the upcoming *ton* events Lilly had planned on attending with her aunt and Glenda.

Danbury made notes to attend as well.

He would return later to escort the ladies to this evening's musicale.

****

It didn't take long before the possibility of a connection between the Baroness Beauchamp and the elusive Viscount Danbury created something of a stir.

By arriving together at the Shufflebottoms' musicale on one another's arm, they gave the gossips plenty of fodder. Many of the *ton*'s matronly gossips remarked upon the fact that the viscount had, in fact, paid court to the beautiful young widow quite attentively the previous evening. Throughout the entirety of the performance, Danbury only left her side for a few moments to procure her and the ladies refreshments during intermission. He also, quite scandalously, held her hand in his and raised her fingers to his lips more than once.

It would have all been vastly amusing, Lilly thought, had they not been sitting directly in front of Lady Natalie and her betrothed. It was as though Michael's gaze burned into her back. Each time Danbury place a kiss on her knuckles, it felt like a betrayal. Why, oh why, did life have to be so complicated?

Hawthorn was in attendance as well and appeared slightly perplexed as he watched Danbury's antics. More than once, Lilly caught the unnerving gentleman scowling in her direction. She had to admit having Danbury as an escort, as something of a protector, was soothing. Throughout her marriage, she had often been exposed to insult and injury. There was an ease in knowing she was not the only person watching out for her well-being.

Danbury entertained her and those around them by whispering very unlover-like things into her ear throughout the concert. He told her that her eyes were the color of a goldfish he'd had as a child. He told her he'd try to kiss her, but he'd be thinking of his goldfish while doing so and that would ruin his manhood for all others. He told her she probably would not enjoy him kissing her anyway, what with all of her fishiness and his feline charm.

It appeared to the world, however, that he was infatuated.

Hawthorn was not the only person present who was bothered by Danbury's display.

****

"Why on earth would Lilly enter into a liaison with Lord Danbury?" Lady Natalie leaned into Michael and whispered. "I know he's your friend, but he's not likely to have honest intentions! Oh, I do not wish to see Lady Beauchamp hurt. I think she has been sad for a long time."

Michael patted her on the arm but could not find the right words to respond. Did Danbury have to sit *so very close* to Lilly? Did he have to touch her *that often* and was that his hand *upon the lady's thigh*? And although he was charmed to see Lilly smothering laughter more than once, he could not help but feel annoyed that it was Danbury who incited it. Most likely he was murmuring romantic drivel into her ear.

The plan was most effective, nonetheless, for Hawthorn looked stymied indeed. Michael was coming to think that Lilly was right. Hawthorn could not have had a very good look at Lilly's companion in the gazebo. Perhaps he now doubted himself.

Even more encouraging, over the past few weeks, members of Parliament were coming to doubt Hawthorn. His ravings sounded increasingly like those of a madman, so much so even strong proponents of the Corn Laws had begun politically distancing themselves from him. Not that this meant they would change their vote, but it was likely, even if Hawthorn *did* expose Lilly, nobody would believe him. Michael hoped the situation would resolve itself soon enough. He was doing his best to leave the past in the past. Except was it the past anymore?

Chapter Twenty-One
Temptation

What with the work Michael was attempting to accomplish in Parliament, he had little time to visit his fiancée.

Furthermore, he lacked much desire to do so.

But it was expected of him. Her father expected it. Her mother expected it. Hell, all of society expected it.

And Lady Natalie was a lovely girl. She'd done nothing to put him off. In fact, he'd realized she wasn't nearly as empty-headed and frivolous as he'd feared.

No, it was nothing she'd done.

So, when she requested he attend a picnic she'd scheduled with her brother and Miss Glenda Beauchamp, he felt duty bound to accept. He set aside an entire day, rearranging meetings and appointments so he could participate.

She had failed to inform him, however, that Danbury and Lilly would be attending as well.

Seeing Lilly in society, even from a distance, had been difficult. She stirred a restlessness inside of him. And something else—something he was reluctant to identify.

But he was an engaged man. Contracts had been signed, and it went without saying he would dance attendance upon Lady Natalie. He was a grown man—a duke, for God's sake. He would be pleasant and sociable. He could control his urges for a few hours.

Nonetheless, upon arriving at Lady Eleanor's townhome in the Earl of Ravensdale's newest open carriage with Lady Natalie, her brother, and Danbury, Michael looked to the sky hoping for rain.

Not a cloud in sight. In fact, the morning air promised to turn unseasonably warm as the day progressed.

Planned to take place at one of Ravensdale's smaller properties, the picnic would be held a little over ten miles outside of London. The earl had told Michael he would be doing him a favor by inspecting the general condition of the estate. He also told him he was pleased to hear of the excursion.

Although modern and expensive, the carriage wasn't quite large enough to seat three gentlemen wide, which placed Michael snugly between Lady Natalie and Lilly. Facing him was Glenda, who had Mr. Joseph Ravensdale on one side of her and Danbury on the other. They were to ride thusly for over ten miles…good God!

His left side, cozily packed next to Lilly, sizzled with awareness. On his right side, where his fiancée pressed against him, he felt…nothing. Between the two ladies as he was, Michael sat buried in sweetly scented petticoats and skirts.

Danbury's eyes gleamed with laughter as he observed his friend's predicament, but Michael merely shook his head. And then nearly laughed himself.

For Miss Beauchamp chose that moment to open her parasol and nearly took out Danbury's left eye. Completely oblivious to the viscount, she placed it upon her shoulder and turned to address Mr. Spencer. "I daresay…" She paused. "Joseph…" A blush crept up her neck, turning her ivory skin a delicate pink. "This phaeton is marvelous! It was so thoughtful of your father to suggest it instead of a closed coach. It's such a beautiful day!"

"A bit cramped for six people," Danbury muttered.

The younger couple ignored him.

Joseph Spencer seemed to appreciate Miss Bridge's tantalizing blush when she'd spoken his name. "Simply beautiful." He returned her adoring gaze. Mr. Spencer then shifted nonchalantly and placed his arm possessively along the back of the bench, draping it casually on Miss Beauchamp's person, somewhat hidden by the parasol.

Danbury rolled his eyes.

Lilly failed to notice the untoward act. And as the official chaperone, she was the obvious person to demand Spencer remove his arm.

Nobody made any mention of it.

Lady Natalie then opened her parasol but rested it on the open side of the carriage. If she decided to place it upon her other shoulder, Cortland's eyes would be at risk as well.

"I think, perhaps, ladies carry stealthier weapons than our outriders, Cortland." Danbury mockingly glanced at the parasols. "They cover it in lace and pretend it is a part of their wardrobe, but at a moment's notice, they can whip it open and unhand the burliest of ruffians."

Lady Natalie smiled prettily at the viscount. "The ruffians are not nearly such a menace as the rakes who disguise themselves as gentleman."

"So a man must be either one or the other?"

Danbury asked, raising one eyebrow.

"But of course. Consider my fiancé, His Grace. He is always a gentleman." She placed her hand on Michael's arm. "I have never had any cause for concern because he has always acted, and always will act, with the most honorable intentions. For that, I am an extremely lucky lady."

Danbury laughed heartily at this, causing Lady Natalie to pout. "What is so funny?"

Michael glared at Danbury. "Nothing, nothing at all," he reassured her. "Lord Danbury simply has something of a questionable sense of humor."

But inside, Michael agreed with the irony of Lady Natalie's declaration, if not the humor of it. While his fiancée sat daintily on his right side, his left hand ached to hold the hand of the lady on his left. Lilly's tiny hands were folded politely in her lap. He felt her shiver slightly.

"Are you cold, my lady?" Michael asked her.

Lilly glanced around at the other passengers. "The wind is still a bit brisk. I imagine as the sun climbs higher I will be fine."

Michael leaned forward and removed his jacket with as much dignity as one could while smashed into a carriage, holding six, that likely was intended to hold only four.

Not giving Lilly a chance to protest, he draped it over her shoulders. At first hesitant, she touched the lapels as though uncertain as to whether she ought to accept his gesture. But then a cool gust of wind blew down the narrow street.

"Thank you, Your Grace."

Michael was satisfied to see her burrow into it

snugly.

"You see." Lady Natalie spoke pointedly to Danbury. "*Always* the gentleman!"

"Was he a gentleman when you knew him before, Lilly?" The young Miss Beauchamp had been paying attention to the conversation after all.

Upon her words, Michael felt Lilly sit up straight again.

But before she could speak, his fiancée turned to look at them both. "The two of you have a prior acquaintance?" Her eyebrows rose. She did not look angry, merely intrigued.

"Years ago." Lilly's answer was vague, obviously wishing to downplay the connection.

But Miss Beauchamp was not so cooperative…rather somewhat gauche, instead. "The duke was her beau."

"Glenda!" Lilly admonished her stepdaughter. And then to Lady Natalie. "His Grace and I were friends. It was a very long time ago. Heavens! I was barely Glenda's age."

Lady Natalie tilted her head to one side, and her eyes narrowed slightly. Most definitely not as empty-headed as he'd thought.

"He courted her before he was the duke," Miss Beauchamp supplied.

"I'd just returned from the war." Michael could not help but remember. It had been the most tumultuous year of his life.

"He was not a rake." Lilly surprised him with her statement. "He was a gentleman, even then." Upon her words, he felt a stabbing sensation somewhere near his heart. He'd acted most dishonorably.

He could not help but meet her eyes. She was being sincere. She was not mocking him, nor speaking sarcastically.

"I'll bet the viscount wasn't such a gentleman back then!" Lady Natalie laughed. Danbury took no issue with such a declaration.

"Of course I wasn't, my lady. Whyever would I want to be?"

****

Lilly did not participate in the remainder of the conversation, which mostly consisted of Danbury and Lady Natalie bantering between each other over who of the *ton* were and weren't either gentlemen or rakes. They both finally agreed that Viscount Castleton was worse than even Danbury. He must be! He was the Earl of Hawthorn's son and heir.

Lilly allowed their conversation to drift over her as she relished the warmth of Michael's jacket. Michael had never smelled strongly of any cologne, so a person could only know his scent if she was close to him. Feeling herself a pathetic fool, she inhaled the distinct scent that was him—cleanliness, sandalwood, and the outdoors. She savored it. She savored his closeness. Snuggling deeper into the jacked, Lilly closed her eyes. She would only rest for a moment. Lulled and relaxed, it felt as though hardly any time had passed at all when the carriage slowed. Lilly roused herself as the driver turned, taking them up a long and elegant drive. This must be London Hills, the Earl of Ravensdale's estate.

Glenda could not and did not contain herself from gasping charmingly as they passed the lake and home that came into view.

Encircled by lush greenery, tucked under an

assortment of lofty trees, the three-story house was fashioned of limestone the color of butter. The manor was built on a rise, surely providing magnificent views in all directions. Southerly facing, the perfectly placed windows and arbors reflected unfettered sunlight. Lilly caught glimpses of whimsical statues of various types of birds positioned between a few charmingly situated walking paths. One path led to a lily pond with the statue of a youthful boy with his hand aloft, a small bird perched upon his wrist.

The grounds appeared to be in pristine condition. "I thought your father said he hadn't done much with this estate and needed us to itemize maintenance issues." Michael spoke to Lady Natalie. "But at first glance, it looks to be in perfect repair. And it certainly isn't 'small.' "

Lady Natalie had a smug look on her face. "The property consists of just over eighteen acres. It passes through the women on my mother's side of the family. My mother's older sister did not have any girls. She passed away a few years ago, and it has been put in trust for me along with annual funds for upkeep." She turned to point out to Michael. "It's listed in the contracts."

Good heavens! Lilly thought, this property was part of Lady Natalie's dowry.

"It's a beautiful estate, my lady." Glenda looked to be in awe and perhaps a tad covetous.

The carriage pulled to a stop in front of the semicircular steps extending out and down from the grand entry. Barely waiting for it to halt, Michael climbed out to assist the ladies down from the vehicle. Lady Natalie then led them inside and directed Lilly and Glenda toward a retiring room so they could freshen up after the long ride.

When everyone met back in the front reception hall, Lady Natalie proudly offered them a tour. Leading the way, she took Lilly's arm while Cortland and Danbury followed. Glenda and Mr. Spencer dallied behind.

"Oh, Lilly, I am so very glad you came today. I especially wanted to show *you* one of my favorite places in the entire world!"

Lilly smiled and regarded her surroundings in admiration. "I can imagine! Do you think you and the duke will live here for part of the year after your marriage?"

"I don't know...I hope so." Lady Natalie sighed, and they both took several more steps before she spoke again. "Did you have many doubts before your marriage? You mentioned once that your father pressed you into accepting your husband's suit."

Lilly's breath caught. How did one answer such a question? Lady Natalie ought to be a lovely friend and confidante, but Lilly's previous relationship with Michael made this nearly impossible.

Perhaps she could speak with s*ome* honesty though. "I did not wish to marry the baron. I did so entirely to please my father."

"Did you not *like* the baron?"

This required some thought. She most definitely could *not* tell Lady Natalie about Rose—about the nature of her marriage to the baron. But she was sympathetic and also a little concerned at the girl's lack of enthusiasm to marry.

Which was ironic, indeed.

So, she would say what she could. "I respected him and accepted him as a member of our…of society. I did not know him very well."

Lady Natalie had more questions. Lilly suspected she was seeking some sort of encouragement. The younger woman would be looking for reassurance that arranged marriages could be comfortable and loving.

"Sometimes," Lady Natalie admitted, "I feel as though I do not really know Cortland. He is so distant…so formal with me. He is very pleasant and kind. I think he is a good man, but I am becoming less certain…about other things."

Oh, this wasn't fair!

Although it was a common notion, Lilly abhorred the notion of marrying for convenience's sake! Would she be wrong to relay her feelings to this young girl? Would she be even more wrong to withhold it? Lilly had escaped her own horrible marriage by sheer luck.

Of course, Lady Natalie was betrothed to a man who was the antithesis of the man Lilly had married.

But if Natalie did not think she could love him, should she not be given the idea that she ought to speak up now, rather than later?

"My lady, Natalie, I feel it is my place here to tell you, although I think you and the duke are a good match, if you have serious misgivings you ought to speak with your mother or father. You have told me they are good parents. Surely, they will take your opinion into close consideration." The women walked in silence as they neared the end of the corridor.

Lilly then felt compelled to extend a word of caution. "It is just…marriage is lifelong. It is forever— or until death, anyhow." Lilly grimaced to herself before continuing. "In time, I think you may very well come to love Cortland, but if you cannot fathom this…Well, are you prepared to live in a marriage that is platonic?" Upon these words, she forced herself to stop speaking. She must not allow her personal feelings for Michael to have any considerations in the advice she gave.

Lady Natalie sighed heavily. "I do *like* Cortland. The same, unfortunately, as I *like* all of my brothers. And sometimes…" She looked away. "Sometimes, I just want more."

"Ah…" This, Lilly understood all too well. "Romance."

Lady Natalie came to a halt and turned to face Lilly with an anguished look. "Yes, oh, botheration! And…and…I want passion! Is that asking too much? My father and my mother love one another. More than that; *they are in love with one another*! I know it exists. I often wonder, even, sometimes about…Well, there are other men in this world on whom I do not look as though they are like a brother to me." The girl's honesty was refreshingly forthright.

"It exists." That is all Lilly could say. Her own heart beat much too loudly. It was impossible. This discussion was all hypothetical. There was no way Lady Natalie would break her betrothal with Michael.

Lady Natalie looked skeptically over at Lilly and nodded. "I knew it," she said. "There is somebody in your past who was the love of your life. From the first moment I met you, I knew you were a woman with a past. There you sat, all buttoned up and quiet, but with a mysterious light in your eyes." At the look on Lilly's face, she quickly took Lilly's hands in hers. "Oh, don't be angry with me, Lilly. It's just, when I first met you, I knew you would be a special person to know. I thought, this lady seems like she would be a very good friend." And then she laughed at herself. "What must you think of me?"

Lilly swallowed hard.

"I think that you are a very special person to know as well. And," she added, "I think you are a very good friend to have." They both laughed, albeit self-consciously, and continued the tour.

Being such an enormous structure, the house required over an hour to view only some of the bedrooms, the drawing room, sitting rooms, ballroom, dining room, library, and kitchen. By the time they finished, the three couples were quite ready to return outside to the picnic which had been laid out by the quietly efficient staff.

Near the shore of the lake, blankets and pillows spread out on the ground with trays, plates, and glasses set for a meal which by no means resembled the basket of bread, cheese, and fruit Lilly had imagined. The ladies, quite picturesque as they delicately sat on the ground, doled out the delicacies provided. The bottles of wine ensured that conversation was lively and unstilted. And then finally, upon partaking of the culinary delights provided, Lilly rose to her feet.

"I've been dying to follow the walking path around the lake and see some of the gardens. Would anybody care to join me?" She addressed her invitation toward Danbury. He was charming. He could be quite diverting. He was safe.

He also appeared to be fast asleep.

Lady Natalie reclined upon the blanket and closed

her eyes lazily. "I'm not moving a muscle, Lilly. Cortland, you will escort her, will you not?" She gave him no choice, holding her hand over her eyes to protect them from the bright sun.

Glenda and Mr. Spencer had disappeared into the house to peruse the…library.

"I'd be honored." Michael rose to his feet. And to Natalie, "Are you sure you don't wish to join us? It may take a while to circle the entire lake."

Without opening her eyes, Natalie refused again. "I've been around it dozens of times. Take your time. I might enjoy another glass of wine."

Lilly knew she ought to sit right back down and announce she'd changed her mind, but the thought of exploring such a picturesque trail with him was too enticing to ignore. She would keep her distance, though. They would not speak of any personal matters.

Such were her resolutions.

Before he could offer his arm, she skipped ahead, away from the safety of Lady Natalie and Hugh.

She felt Michael following. Those long even strides of his would easily keep up with her.

Stopping frequently to examine flowers and shrubs along the way, she eventually forgot her misgivings and gave in to the enjoyment of the moment. And once she began talking, she could not help but tell him of the secret gardens she had maintained at Beauchamp Manor. She also enthusiastically described her plans to redesign the landscaping behind her aunt's town house.

Michael seemed intrigued and asked insightful questions about some of her grafting techniques. As a landowner, he said, he spent a great deal of his time thinking about planting and harvesting. He seemed to appreciate her opinions.

He also appreciated the smiles she flashed him. In fact, Michael enjoyed himself immensely. Despite his earlier discomfort, this picnic outing was proving to be a pleasant escape from the demands of the season. The gentlemen had discarded their waistcoats with the permission of the ladies, and there had been an unspoken agreement to allow some of society's rigid rules to be ignored. It had become a day to lower inhibitions and relax among friends.

And although bittersweet, he would accept this time alone with Lilly for the gift that it was.

"This outing reminds me of when we travelled to Edgewater Heights." Lilly spoke casually, seeming to read Michael's mind. And then her eyes grew wide. "Not exactly, though, mind you. Certainly not the— well, not all of it!" She blushed and looked away from him.

He smiled and finally was able to take hold of her arm. He would reassure her. She could speak freely with him today. "It was idyllic, wasn't it? Spending time with sympathetic companions, friends, not merely acquaintances of the *ton*."

Their steps fell in line with one another. They walked silently for a while, enjoying the beauty around them.

Being with her, he felt a sense of lightness. His worries distanced themselves. He was not the duke, but simply a man.

"Did you have a chance to speak with your father before he passed? Was he able? Did he recognize you?" She'd known he and his father had had something of a tumultuous relationship.

"Several times he spoke to me as though I were Edward," Michael answered her candidly. "But there were moments...I told him about you. I told him of my wish to marry."

Lilly glanced at him sharply upon hearing this. "What did he say?"

She might rather appreciate the irony. "He told me I was too young. He told me to wait."

She didn't say anything at all.

But then a bark of laughter escaped her. "Oh, Michael." And then she groaned a little and laughed some more. Her eyes glistened as she sobered. Michael wanted to touch the corner of her eye and catch the single tear that had escaped.

But Lilly turned serious once again. "Did he know about Edward? Did he know you had become the heir?"

"No." Michael remembered. "But I realized my resentment had been idiotic. I think as youths, we naturally rebel, at times imagining the worst in our parents."

"Oh, yes." She agreed readily. "And how did you learn this?"

He hadn't ever discussed this with anybody—not even Hugh. "He told me how proud he was of my military service. And he asked me about the war...he wanted to hear stories." In dawning appreciation, he realized he'd done his best to bury his memories of those weeks of what had seemed like unending death. But he had experienced some moments of contentment with his father.

Some peace.

Michael pushed a branch away from the path so she could pass in front of him. "In all my life, I'd never had my father's undivided attention as I did those last nights."

Lilly glanced at him sideways, smiling. "You brought him comfort, then."

Raising his brows, he considered her statement. "Perhaps I did."

And then he asked about her last days with *her* parents. He'd known her mother, but not her father at all. She told him of the last Christmas she'd spent with them both—and after—how she'd cared for her mother, read to her all of their favorite books. Lady Eleanor had travelled over for her mother's funeral and brought her Miss Fussy.

And then she told him of some of Miss Fussy's antics.

They laughed together and then fell into a relaxed silence.

A cool breeze rustled the leaves above them, and silver ripples appeared on the surface of the lake.

Lilly stopped to behold the view and inhaled deeply. "Being in the city, one forgets how perfumed country air can be."

But he had eyes for only her. "What perfume is in this air, Lilly?"

Stopping, she closed her eyes and inhaled again. "Pine, sage, grass, lavender, and…" She trailed off and then opened her eyes. For Michael had stepped within inches of her. He'd not done so consciously. But it didn't matter.

Nothing else mattered.

"No peach blossoms?"

At that moment, he was only aware of the fragrance of her, of Lilly. Memories and emotions assaulted him. Her closeness ignited a hunger he had hoped would fade away.

She held his gaze unwavering. Neither of them would speak. The sound of a few birds could be heard in the distance, and then the rustling of leaves again, as the cool wind tilted the tall grass.

And then, oh, so tentatively, Lilly's hand extended upwards, and she grazed her fingertips along his jaw. Michael grasped her hand, cradling it even. Turning his face and closing his eyes, he pressed a kiss inside her palm. If he didn't breathe, time would stand still.

She wrapped her other arm around his waist and tucked her face into his chest. This moment wasn't about passion or lust or wantonness. This was a moment to acknowledge love.

Michael embraced her fully.

Holding her was madness, insanity, but also the most natural thing in the world. Since the moment he'd heard her voice in that damned inn, his heart ought to have known it would come to this. Like the tides and the moon, they'd existed apart from one another, in different worlds. But also, like the tides and the moon, neither could escape the strength of their attraction. Michael dipped his head, not moving his hands, and kissed her temples, the corners of her eyes, her cheeks. She tipped her head back so he could find her mouth.

And once he tasted the sweetness of her lips, she parted them hungrily. Her hands were in his hair, clutching, exploring. His own boldly explored her softness.

Starved for one another, they both laid claim to what they desperately needed.

Chapter Twenty-Two
The Inevitable

It was heaven to feel his touch, his masculine hardness pressing into her. All along she'd wanted this; she'd hoped for this. And if she admitted it to herself, even before leaving Beauchamp manor, she'd dreamed of being with him again.

But she'd never thought it would come true.

Was she fool enough to give in to it now? Was she fool enough *not to*? His leg had managed to push through the material of her dress and petticoats so she straddled his unyielding thigh. These feelings were primitive, uncivilized...inconceivable. Heat blossomed in her center as she pressed closer into him. In mad desperation, she clutched at his hair. Teeth cut into flesh. She tasted blood. Was it her own? Was it his? She didn't care; perhaps it was both.

Letting out a gasp, she did not protest as Michael caught her up in his arms, carried her off the path and then lowered them both to the ground in a sheltered grassy cove. All of this, he managed, without moving his lips from her person. He was tasting her again, nipping, sucking, kissing.

"No love bites," Lilly said, suddenly remembering the red marks he had left on her after they had been together at Vauxhall Gardens.

Michael was in a haze. "What?" He looked at her

questioningly. He lay on top of her, his muscles straining as he protected her from his weight with his arms.

"Love bites," Lilly said with lips that felt tender and swollen from his kisses. "Those little red marks you left on me before. It took a week for them to go away, and my maid told me they were evidence of lovemaking."

The expression on Michael's face made him look like a child who'd raided the cookie bin. Suddenly, the years they'd been apart melted away. "I never meant to leave them, love. I've never been able to control myself around you." He bent down and kissed her neck tenderly, softly. "I never meant to hurt you, love. I promise I'll be careful." His kisses trailed lower as his hands pulled down her bodice. Exposing her breast, he feathered kisses all around the rosy tip. He lightly ran his tongue over the soft, sensitive skin along the underside before capturing the bud in his mouth. Arousal coursed through her core.

"Hurting you is the last thing in the world I ever wanted to do." He spoke between kisses. His voice was gravelly, choked with emotion.

Michael was greedy, and Lilly reveled in it. How many times had she dreamed this?

And then she realized he was trembling. Her Michael. Her love.

He lifted his face and searched her eyes. "I want you so badly, and yet I am tormented by the thought of hurting you again. You must know I love you. I never stopped loving you." His eyes glistened as he implored her to understand. "Even now, honor compels me to run. To run away from you." He took her hand, reached down with it, and placed it on the evidence of his arousal. "But you are the master of my heart, of my body. Tell me to stop and I will. God help me, but I will."

Lilly's hand pressed into him and wrapped around his thickness through the fabric of his falls. She would not deny him.

She would not deny herself.

Her thumb worked up and down, touching him from memory. Loving the knowledge that he needed her touch as much as she needed him. And then he pulled her hand away. "Not so fast, love. I'll make a fool of myself." The uncertainty she'd seen in his eyes before had transformed into wicked desire. "Let me love you first."

He had changed, and yet he had not. No one else ever saw this side of him. His passion, his insecurity, his sense of humor. His hand reached down to the hem of her skirts and his fingers gathered them into his fist. Tantalizingly, he exposed her ankles, her calves, her knees, and most of her thighs. Lilly wore no drawers. There were no barriers beyond her skirts.

Long ago, with just a hint of light from the moon, she'd undressed in his presence. She'd given him full access to her body as they'd frolicked in the spring-warmed waters. But he'd never seen her body in the daylight.

There had never been any daylight when Lord Beauchamp had taken her either.

She pushed thoughts of him from her mind. She did not want him intruding on this time with Michael. Michael slid down her body and began kissing the sensitive skin on the inside of her knee.

A tension grew inside her womb when she looked down and saw his dark head bent over her thigh. One of his hands had reached up and was touching her low on her abdomen. His other hand supported her leg. His mouth travelled along the tender skin of her inner thigh now. New whiskers scratched at her, and she jumped when she felt his breath upon her...

"Michael?" she asked, uncertain as to what he was doing. Well, she thought she had an idea as to what he was doing, but surely not!

His mouth was very close to the apex of her legs. He growled softly and then wolfishly looked up to smile at her. "Yes, love?" he said. "Is something the matter?"

"Um, are you quite certain you want to do...that?" It was difficult to speak, what with all the twitchy neediness he'd ignited. Her hips rose slightly, of their own accord, reaching for that elusive feeling she hadn't experienced in years.

She nearly cried out at the vibrations of his laughter. He paused for the briefest of moments and met her gaze. His lips were wet, and his eyes hooded. "Quite certain." And with that, he dipped his head and found her opening with his very devilish tongue. Lilly's hips jerked again as Michael licked and sucked and pulled at the swollen skin at her opening. Her knees were bent, and her heels pressed into the ground.

Lilly lost all coherent thought. She closed her eyes from the glare of the sun and gave in to this sinful delight.

Michael had moved his hands below her, tilting her up for better access, and then reached around to part her gently and slide one finger inside. And then another.

Her initial mortification forgotten, she now actively moved with him. Until she was falling, falling, falling. Waves of pleasure coursing through her.

She felt her womb pulsing, throbbing, around him when he finally paused his movements.

In her haze of bliss, she could not help but mourn the vanished promises of their youth. How had she lost him? Had the fates been against them all along? The warmth of his touch reminded her to remain in the present. She was here with him now. She would dwell neither on the past nor the future.

After placing a few kisses along her leg, Michael sat back upon his heels and stared down at her. His blue eyes looked darker, his pupils dilated, as he beheld her exposed body, flushed from his lovemaking.

He'd been the one, years before, who'd awakened her sensuality. She nodded slightly, and he reached to undo the fall of his breeches. She would have everything. If only for a day, if only for an hour. She'd learned the sweet bitterness of memories years ago. She welcomed new ones for the future.

She watched his bent head as he undid the buttons. And when he was free, she swallowed hard. He was larger than she remembered.

"See what you do to me." He leaned forward to cover her again.

This time he settled his arousal between her thighs. Her wet heat welcomed him as she opened wider for his entry.

Slowly, for this must last a lifetime, they joined their bodies together.

Her legs wrapped around him, inviting him further as he pressed his forehead between her breasts. They had come home to each other. There were no barriers. There was no awkwardness.

Together, they moved imploringly until finding the rhythm that was uniquely theirs.

When Lilly had first made love with Michael at seventeen, it had been enchanting, almost dreamlike as they'd tangled and touched like water nymphs in a cave. She had experienced joy but had also been looking beyond the moment, believing it merely a taste of the passion she would share with Michael in the years to come.

This time she was keenly aware of what her future could hold. This would be the last time she would allow herself to be with him thusly, and therefore, she was determined to take pleasure in every moment. Reaching through the dizzying passion, she forced herself to open her eyes and watch him as he moved above her. His hair fell forward, partially covering his closed eyes.

Sensing her attention, he opened his eyes and returned her searching gaze. It was as though they could see into one another's soul. Their two bodies became one, and for that twinkling of an eye, they shared one heart as well. Michael pulled back slowly and then firmly thrust again, burying himself to the hilt.

She welcomed the fullness.

They moved slowly at first, embracing each sensation until neither could hold back. But their passion had been denied for years, and a yearning hunger took over. Lilly clutched at him with her legs, her fingernails digging into the fabric of his shirt. And then the world tilted slightly, and Michael's movements quickened, faster and deeper still. The emptiness she'd felt for so long would finally be filled. Her legs gripped him tightly. She wanted this never to end, but as their tension built, she could not keep herself from falling into oblivious pleasure. Only then did she sense Michael's surrender. His movements quickened, faster and deeper, nearly violent in his excitement. But he had not lost all control. Before reaching his own satisfaction, he pulled himself free of her legs, breathing harshly.

Lilly nearly cried, although logically she knew it was for the best. Breathing heavily, she knew the sensation all too well.

His seed was warm and thick as it spilled along her thigh.

It was for the best, she told herself, searching for a handkerchief. She was not his wife, after all. She wiped at the liquid and turned away.

****

Afterwards, Michael rolled to one side of Lilly and pulled her into his arms. He wished to hold her forever. Not wanting reality to intrude, he rubbed his cheek upon her hair as they both relaxed into each other. "Are you all right, love?" She'd wiped away their mess and then settled comfortably back into his arms. Neither of them had spoken yet, and he wasn't ready to allow any distance between them.

She did not answer for so long, he thought she'd fallen asleep, but then she stretched her body and turned to face him. Her skirts and bodice were bunched around her waist, and Michael could not help but gaze at her skin, still flushed from their passion. He felt himself begin to harden again watching her move.

And then she spoke. "I know this, we, the two of us, for some reason is not to be. But I will cherish every moment with you, every touch." She paused and looked beyond him and into the sky. Sunlight reflecting off the leaves sparkled in her eyes. "I know there ought to be guilt, but in this moment, I feel none. So please, *please,* do not apologize."

Was he sorry? No. At least he'd been able to protect her somewhat. "I won't," he promised, one arm under her head, the other tucked between them. He'd not released his seed inside of her. When he'd tried to pull away, he'd had to free himself from her legs. He very nearly had not been successful. "My mind is in a turmoil, but right now the only thing I want to think about is how you feel. How you taste."

There would be plenty of thinking to do later. What to do. When to do it. But for now, he would see her smile.

He rolled onto his back, bringing her with him. Startled and now straddling him, she looked down into his face. Ah, there it was. That secret smile.

"You are a pagan goddess atop me."

She mesmerized him. Her hair had come undone and tumbled down her back. As she leaned forward, a strand swung down to caress his lips. The tips of her breasts rubbed tantalizingly over the fabric of his shirt.

"Lilly," Michael said.

"Yes," she whispered, finding his heat with her own.

"I won't apologize for this either." And with that statement, they both explored, touched, and joined again. And for all of these things, there was nary an apology spoken.

****

After what could have been hours or only minutes,

Michael led Lilly back to the lake where they tidied up as much as was possible having only two handkerchiefs and ice-cold water. Michael had managed to locate her hair pins, and together they'd somehow pulled her hair into a simple chignon. Her dress was wrinkled, however, and his breeches stained with grass. All Michael could do at this point was hope nobody noticed. He would not comment upon Lilly's disheveled state, though. She might not return to the others if he did so.

There really was no choice in the matter.

Relishing the time in one another's company, yet knowing it was nearly at an end, they walked arm in arm along the remainder of the path that circled the lake. Before emerging from the woods, Michael pulled her into his arms one last time. Forehead to forehead, they breathed each other in.

"I do love you, and I will never be sorry." Lilly spoke the words quietly, as though reciting a prayer.

"*I* love *you*, and *I* will never be sorry," Michael promised back.

Lilly dropped her arms and stepped away resolutely before twisting her face into a weak attempt at a smile. Michael placed his hand upon the side of her face.

And then it was over.

Unable to stop her, unable to offer her anything, he watched as she skipped ahead down the path toward the voices of their friends. She would emerge from the woods alone. Michael followed slowly.

He was beginning to see she was vital to his future happiness. And perhaps he was to hers, as well.

Chapter Twenty-Three
Awakening

The early morning sun barely peeked through the trees as Michael rode along Rotten Row in a peacefully deserted Hyde Park. He'd been so busy the past several weeks, he'd not ridden as often as he needed. The whirlwind of meetings and dinners and other social obligations had pulled him into a vortex of sorts, leaving him feeling somewhat out of control.

Enough.

Presently his state of affairs had been manipulating many of his actions and decisions. He needed to reexamine the forces involved in his situation.

What was important? What mattered most? Upon returning from London Hills, Michael had been a man pulled apart by his conscience and his sense of honor as a gentleman.

From the moment he became the Duke of Cortland, Michael had made a vow to himself. He would live up to the example both his father and older brother had shown him. Although he had not been included in much of the training Edward had been given, he understood the major principles upheld by the Cortland dukes for seven generations.

First and foremost, do nothing to bring shame upon the title while managing the land in a manner such that the tenants and their families prosper. Honor the pledge of loyalty to England. And lastly, provide for the succession of the title.

Somehow the responsibility of caring for his tenants and providing for a succession had become synonymous with marrying Lady Natalie. His promises involved his honor and his standing in society.

But long ago he had made another promise.

Not publicly, or even formally, but in act and deed he had promised himself to Lilly. He had made this commitment before he had become a duke, and his change in status had not nullified it.

He'd thought she'd abandoned him. Did her marriage relieve him of the promise? And then he learned something about himself.

It didn't matter.

None of it mattered.

The bigger issue was this: Could he extricate himself from his more recent promise without causing harm to the duchy, Lady Natalie, and for Christ's sake, England?

First, he considered his estates and his tenants. His obligation to help lower the price of food would be less crucial after the votes had all been cast. Ravensdale had been intentionally stalling to buy time to sway undecided members of the realm. They needed three more votes.

This could be accomplished without his marriage to Lady Natalie. However, it would have to be done before he cried off. That gave him a little less than six weeks.

If he could pass his amendment, then he would have done what he could for his country.

Which left Lady Natalie.

Lady Natalie was a beautiful, accomplished, and tenderhearted young woman, who, he was quite certain, *was not in love with him.* In fact, he believed ruefully, she was not even attracted to him. They treated each other almost as siblings. Assuming the vote could be presented in time, it was quite possible she might be convinced to jilt him. This was not completely impossible.

Then there was Lilly, the only woman he'd ever loved.

His dearest Lilly, a woman, essentially, alone in the world. Her deceased husband had not provided adequately for her nor for his own daughter. The only family they had left to depend upon was a quirky old woman.

Nearly a decade ago, he had made a promise. He'd promised Lilly his love, his name, and his heart. Years ago, he'd had every intention of honoring his promise.

But he had not.

He was being presented with a second chance.

Feeling invigorated by his decision, Michael leaned forward and urged his horse into a gallop in the direction of his offices. He had work to do.

****

Lilly sat back upon her heels and examined her work. With the sun barely peeking over the horizon, she had donned an old day dress and come outside to work in the garden. Sleep eluded her.

Over and over again, her mind returned to the moments she'd shared with Michael. Unable to help herself, she remembered what she'd felt when he'd touched her, when he'd laughed with her, when he'd looked into her eyes.

You must know I love you. I never stopped loving you.

She remembered the feel of his body pressing her into the soft grass beneath them.

You are the master of my heart, of my body.

Lying in bed, remembering how they had been together the previous day nearly stole her breath. She'd even been tempted to touch herself, closing her eyes, imagining his hands.

Continuing to rest on her heels, she placed her hand upon her stomach, over her womb.

In spite of society's expectations, in spite of her position with Glenda and Aunt Eleanor, an aching part of her soul wished Michael had released his seed into her body—that they could have made a child together.

During all her time with Lord Beauchamp, it was the one thing he could have given her which would have taken some of the sting out of being married to him—of living her life without Michael.

Carrying Michael's child would have involved numerous complications. She would become a fallen woman, shunned by all of society.

But she would have found a way.

She chastised herself for thinking thusly.

But she had remembered something. She had remembered when she'd wiped at her thigh, there had been some...some of it had seemed to be coming out of *her*.

Agitated at her own thoughts, she pulled at some weeds and broke up a large clump of dirt.

What if she were?

She would leave London—move to a small village far away. Her aunt and Glenda need never be exposed to her condition. Society need never know. As a widow, she could alter the date of her husband's death. People might suspect the truth, but she could live with that.

Upon which thought she threw the clump of dirt at a large tree.

What a fool to think such thoughts!

He'd protected her, and rightfully so. They'd made love twice, and on both occasions, he'd withdrawn. She needed to dismiss such fanciful and ridiculous thoughts from her mind forever.

She needed to move forward. Her future was going to be a pleasant one. As, it seemed, was Glenda's.

They were expecting a visit from Mr. Joseph Spencer soon. Of course, this was not something a person could depend upon, as Lilly knew all too well. But she was hopeful for her niece.

Furthermore, she'd received no further threats from Lord Hawthorn.

Glenda and Mr. Spencer seemed in love. It would be an excellent match for her niece, and then Lilly could relax, knowing her sister's daughter was cared for. Heavens, she sounded like her father now.

Hmm, Lilly thought. Negotiating the marriage contract was likely going to fall upon her. Perhaps she ought to obtain some legal aid. She had no experience with such and did not want to make a mistake that would come back and haunt either Glenda or their children years from now.

She tilted her head to the side as a thought occurred to her. Could she perhaps have a very small sum included to provide her with a minimal income so *she* could live independently? She most definitely was thinking like her father now.

Was that ethical? Was it even legal?

Not that she minded being beholden to Aunt Eleanor, but there would be relief in having some financial independence.

A woman had very few options.

She was either owned by her father or her husband.

Having neither, Lilly, finally, was in ownership of herself. And with that ownership came responsibility. She intended to honor that responsibility far better than her father or husband had.

As Lilly resumed her work, another thought loomed.

When—if—Glenda were to marry Mr. Joseph Spencer, there would always be the chance Lilly would encounter both Lady Natalie and Michael—as a married couple. They would be duke and duchess then. They would have children.

Lilly nearly gasped at the thought.

Lady Natalie was close to Aunt Eleanor. In fact, Lilly had learned Lady Natalie was Aunt Eleanor's goddaughter. Good Lord! She addressed Lilly's own aunt as *Aunt Eleanor!*

There would be no reprieve.

Lilly must make her own way. She loved her aunt, but she, herself, was going to need some time to get over all of this.

And *if,* by some miracle, she were carrying, she could never tell Michael. Even though it would be her deepest desire, she could not allow herself to do so. For if he knew, then either one of two things would happen.

Most likely, he would carry her off to Gretna Green for a hasty marriage to protect her and the child. Unfortunately, later he would realize he had ruined all of his political plans as well as relationships with the Earl of Ravensdale and other peers. He would come to realize he had shirked his responsibility to his tenants and dishonored his title, in his own eyes anyway.

He was a man of honor.

In the hours they'd traveled together on the way to London not so long ago, he had gone on at length about how exorbitant corn prices were harming people who had worked and lived on his land holdings for generations. He was deeply committed to this duty to them.

In the long term, if Michael shirked his duties as duke, he would ultimately come to resent her. And then their love, most certainly, would result in ashes.

She did not wish to find herself—ever again—tied to a man who resented her—a man who did not respect her.

And what of Lady Natalie? She would be jilted and heartbroken. Well, perhaps not heartbroken, but what would she think of Lilly? Would she believe Lilly had intentionally betrayed her?

The second course of action Michael could possibly take would be unendurable as well. Because it was possible he would go on to marry Lady Natalie anyway. He could perhaps offer to set Lilly up as his mistress.

Except she did not truly believe he would ever do that to Lady Natalie.

No, he would pay her a sum of money, not acknowledge his own child, and require her to disappear discreetly. But what had he said to her? *Hurting you is the last thing in the world I ever wanted to do.* In her heart, she did not believe Michael could *actually* do such a thing, but people had disappointed her in the past.

She did not care to give another person such an opportunity to fail her. No, Lilly decided adamantly, if she were *enceinte*, she would find a way to hide it until she could go away.

And grow her own damn garden, thank you!

All these thoughts were ludicrous at this point.

But what if she could go away on her own?

She would need an income that would provide for either the purchase or rent of a small cottage, enough for living, and perhaps enough to retain a housekeeper. It would not be an unheard-of amount.

She would not have to see Michael—on holidays, at family gatherings—with his wife…his children…She could avoid all that.

Hope rose inside her. Hope that she could take some control of her life and refuse to be manipulated by others again. Even though she could not possibly be with child, she began to form a plan. For regardless, she would not allow herself to wallow in self-pity while Michael married his bride.

She would be far away.

And eventually the pain would recede.

****

Later that afternoon, the first of Lilly's plan began to take shape.

Thick dark clouds had moved over London, and a heavy drizzle had fallen for several hours. What with the garden party they had planned upon attending cancelled, Lilly, Glenda, and her aunt spent the afternoon reading a novel they had begun earlier that week. Lilly read out loud as her aunt appeared to be dozing but would ask an occasional question disproving such, and Glenda worked furiously on a new design she was embroidering upon a handkerchief for Joseph.

The reading was interrupted when Jarvis entered the room and asked if Lady Sheffield and Lady Beauchamp would receive a call from Mr. Joseph Spencer. Lilly and her aunt glanced at one another with raised eyebrows. And then they both looked over at Glenda who was blushing profusely.

Lady Sheffield responded, "Glenda, make yourself scarce, gel. Jarvis, have him await us in the drawing room."

Embroidery forgotten, Glenda sprinted off to her room to change into a more flattering gown and repair her appearance. Lilly placed the book face down on a side table and addressed her aunt.

"Aunt, do you know anything of marriage contracts?"

Lady Eleanor considered the question for a moment and then answered surprisingly, "You've figured out that you ought to include a competence for your own future? I have been meaning to suggest this to you. The Spencers are one of the richest families in all of England. There is no reason you ought not to be included in the provisions.

"Ravensdale will, no doubt, have the contract drawn up by his man of business, but we can have my solicitor look it over as well. Knowing the family, I am reasonably certain an annuity will be included in the first draft, but if not, we will have it added. You ought never be concerned for your welfare again, my dear."

It couldn't possibly be that easy! Lilly nearly put her face into her hands and cried in relief.

She did not, however. Instead, after waiting quietly for several minutes, the two women eventually rose calmly and proceeded to the drawing room to meet with the prospective groom. They caught him pacing back and forth.

It was all, really, rather charming, Lilly thought, as Mr. Spencer very formally asked them permission to propose to dear, sweet Miss Beauchamp. He had not planned upon finding a wife this early in life, he stated, for he was only four-and-twenty, but love apparently had been unaware of his plans.

Lilly, acting as guardian to Glenda, put him out of his misery quickly, stating that the couple had her blessing.

"Assuming the marriage contracts are satisfactory," Lady Eleanor had added.

"Of course, of course," he agreed.

"And," Lilly added with a smile, "assuming the lady herself agrees." This important consideration ought not to be overlooked.

It was the most important one of all.

Rising to her feet, Lilly said, "I shall fetch Miss Beauchamp so you may ask her yourself."

Her aunt stood as well. "The door will remain open," Aunt Eleanor said, "and we shall, of course be eavesdropping from the other side."

Lilly rolled her eyes at Mr. Spencer, and they left him alone.

****

After Glenda had breathlessly accepted Mr. Spencer's marriage proposal, over the next couple of weeks, the mood in Lady Eleanor's household turned decidedly festive. Lady Eleanor had, in fact, invited her personal solicitor to explain the contracts to the two women. The Ravensdales *had* included a generous competence for Lilly of one thousand pounds per year! Lilly had been about to object, saying it was too much, but Lady Eleanor's scowl deterred her. Upon later consideration, Lilly decided, if she was carrying, it would be best to have additional funds to provide for her child. Lilly's heart jumped at the thought. She expected her courses any day now and awoke each morning with dread.

As of yet nothing had occurred.

A part of her was terrified at the thought of going through confinement, childbirth, and motherhood alone. Another part of her embraced the possibility wholeheartedly. Not knowing either way, at this point, was excruciating.

Despite the numerous events the ladies had been attending, Lilly had found no opportunity to see, let alone, speak with Michael. He'd made very short appearances socially, if at all.

But tonight, she knew, he would be present.

Tonight, the Earl of Ravensdale had insisted upon holding a ball so he could announce the betrothal of his youngest son to Miss Glenda Beauchamp. The family had been longtime friends with Aunt Eleanor and were quite pleased with the match. Glenda was, after all, the daughter of a baron. She was also a very pleasant young lady with whom their son had found love.

Michael would most certainly be in attendance. He was practically one of the family, after all.

****

Michael had been busy himself.

Throughout the fortnight, he'd successfully

275

obtained promises for two of the three votes needed. He'd also met with an American industrialist promoting machinery which could decrease the labor required for both planting and reaping. Interchangeable parts for the machinery allowed for the advancements to become more practical for common use. Michael was considering investing in factories which would build some of the tools. He could then provide for more productive harvests, more jobs for his tenants, and more income for the duchy to reinvest on other properties.

The idea required a great deal more examination, but upon initial review, serious consideration was merited.

Keeping busy during his waking hours had prevented him from dwelling upon his situation with Lilly.

They were yet short one vote.

The third vote, Danbury had surmised, might well be more difficult than all of the others before. For they had only two possibilities, lords Oliver and Newbold. Both of whom professed to be staunch supporters of the present language and requirements of the Corn Laws. If not for a conversation they had both had with Ravensdale over the wintertime where each had admitted to some reservations, Michael would not have considered them at all. As it was, they were holding their positions stubbornly.

Michael had, of course, been privy to the details of Joseph's betrothal to Miss Glenda Beauchamp. And at the last dinner he'd attended at the Ravensdales, Lady Natalie reminded him that he must be on hand for the engagement ball.

Following it, all preparations henceforth would be

focused upon Michael and Natalie's prewedding ball and the wedding ceremony which was to be held at St. George's Cathedral.

It had been ages since he'd spoken privately with Lilly.

She and Danforth had upheld the charade of a romance between the two of them, and it seemed as though they'd eliminated any threat from Hawthorn.

But Michael needed to see that she was well. He would not reveal his plans though. He would surprise her. He would promise himself to her only when he'd become free to do so.

But now that he been with her again, his entire being yearned for her. He wanted to be near her. At the younger couple's engagement ball, he could dance with her once. In fact, it would likely be expected of him. He would hold her in his arms for the duration of a set. He would be *certain* his dance with her was a waltz.

Chapter Twenty-Four
Last Dance

The Spencers were, indeed, a family of considerable wealth.

The mere fact that London Hills had been considered one of the family's smaller holdings should have demonstrated that fact to Lilly.

And their London home, Burtis Hall, provided further evidence of this fact. Located directly across the park behind tall iron gates, it was one of the largest in Mayfair.

It resembled a park in its own right.

The ballroom stole one's breath. Three giant chandeliers dangled from the ornate ceiling, each lit with literally hundreds of candles. No less than three stories tall, the walls boasted gilded molding divided by pillars holding up decorative archways. The parquet floor was polished to a high sheen, giving the incredibly large space a feeling of golden warmth. Heavy red drapes were pulled back from the numerous french doors leading outside to the decorated terrace, and spaced along the opposing wall were colorful tapestries.

The terrace doors had been thrown open, beckoning guests to view the fountain statues standing in circular pools spouting streams of water from various points. Within the fountains floated candles on wax lily pads.

At the far end of the room, a balcony perched level with the glistening chandeliers. It seated a full orchestra. Smaller balconies were spaced evenly around the room. It was the most impressive venue of any event Lilly had attended all season.

Lady Ravensdale had personally invited Lilly and Lady Eleanor to arrive early with Glenda so they could participate in the receiving line. Glenda's future mother-in-law, whom Lilly had planned on being in awe of, was warm, kind, and very handsome for a woman with five grown children. Lady Natalie had gotten her fine looks from her mother. She was slim and graceful, with blond hair that had a touch of white in it. Lilly felt she could have been a delightful friend.

The receiving line consisted of the earl and his countess, Lady Natalie and Lord Cortland, Glenda and her betrothed, and then Lilly and her aunt. As the very large entry doors swung open, Lilly felt out of place. It took over an hour to greet the arrivals before the majordomo signaled to enter the ballroom where the earl and his wife would commence the dancing.

The setting was majestic, the music divine, and champagne and wine flowed freely. Lilly stood next to her aunt and observed as Glenda's betrothed took her in his arms and waltzed with her alongside his parents.

Lilly had been limited in the amount of influence over her stepdaughter, but a lump of pride formed in her throat nonetheless. What must her sister have felt at this moment had she lived? Glenda held herself, beautiful and poised, following Mr. Spencer's lead gracefully.

"They make a charming couple." A familiar voice interrupted her musings. Michael had managed to slip behind her unnoticed. She wished she could lean back—into his arms.

"I am so happy for her." Lilly tamped down the emotions which had been threatening since the first moment she'd seen Glenda in the new gown they had purchased for the event.

Michael bent forward again. So close she felt his breath on her nape and behind her ear. "A place on your dance card, Lilly. A waltz, please."

Lilly turned then, to look into his eyes.

Did only she notice the fire behind the blue depths? She lifted her wrist upon which she wore her dance card and offered it to him. "I'd be honored, Your Grace." Lilly spoke formally, remembering how they had been overheard once before.

Pulling a pencil from one of his pockets, Michael took hold of her arm. His fingers covered her pulse, which she knew must be racing. He adjusted the card so he could read the names already upon it.

Lilly knew Danbury had already signed for both of the waltzes. Michael scratched out Danbury's name and wrote his own. Lilly expressed no complaint. She then glanced around at the spectacle surrounding them.

"The Spencers are an extraordinary family." She could find no fault in his choice of fiancée. "They ought to be the sort who consider themselves above everybody else, but they do not. In fact, they are pleasantly open and likeable people. I am very happy for Glenda. Have I said this already? Not for the magnificence of the family she is marrying into, but rather that they seem to love her already. I understand they have several family traditions. They are already making arrangements for the winter holidays. She will have warmth, and she will be able to raise her own children the same...I am rambling." By now, her eyes glistened with tears. "It is exactly what I would have wished for her."

"She is lucky to have you," Michael said.

Lilly smiled at him. It was a nice compliment. She wished she'd been able to be more of a mother for her. She wished she'd found a way to overcome Lord Beauchamp's insults and objections. If wishes were horses...and all that.

The music was loud. There was no one else nearby to overhear Michael's words. His brows drew together. "Have you...are you...?"

Lilly cut him off with a nod of her head. "I have, and I am not." She didn't trust herself to say anything more. She didn't trust herself to look at him again. She continued watching the couples dancing. She forced another polite smile.

Michael stood discreetly behind her.

"So, there is no..."

"There is no," Lilly repeated firmly.

Michael cleared his throat. "Very well, then."

His voice sounded husky, as though...he were...disappointed? She hadn't expected that.

And then the dancing came to a halt, and the earl and his wife and Glenda and Joseph all crossed the room to join them. Wherever was Lady Natalie? Joseph's parents were graciously thanking her and Aunt Eleanor for joining them in the reception line. The earl quite charmingly claimed a dance later on in the evening with Lilly. They were kind people.

Lady Ravensdale took Lilly by the arm and whisked her away to introduce her once again (because one simply cannot remember everyone one meets in a reception line) to her very best of friends. She hoped Lilly would work with her on some of her favorite charities.

Lilly considered inventing a dear friend of her own, one whom she could go visit for the rest of the summer somewhere south.

Her menses were seven days late. She had never been late before. Lilly did not feel any symptoms, however, as she remembered Rose had, so she continued to tamp down both her alternating terror and excitement. She had heard nerves could cause a woman to be late, and she had plenty of those.

After dancing the supper dance with Danbury, he escorted her into the dining room and seated them with the two engaged couples. Hawthorn had steered clear of them for nearly a month now, and they were hopeful they'd heard the last from him. Danbury graciously pulled out her seat and then excused himself to procure their plates. By this point, he knew all of her favorites and most of her aversions.

Lilly smiled at Lady Natalie. "You see," she said, "Lord Danbury isn't nearly the rake he is reputed to be. It's like we're an old married couple. He is an excellent escort on any excursion. He fetches me drinks, he carries my shopping bags, buys me ices, and lends me his coat."

Lady Natalie merely shook her head. For some reason, she had decided Danbury was a reprobate and that Lilly was a fool to allow him near her.

Lilly took a sip of her champagne and listened as Lady Natalie and Glenda discussed wedding arrangements. It seemed Glenda and Joseph were considering a July wedding at the earl's country seat near Bath. The Ravensdale children had spent most of their youth at Ravens Park, and Joseph considered it home. They would visit after Lady Natalie and the duke's nuptials and make a final decision then. Although Natalie's wedding was to be a grand affair, Glenda and Joseph were both in agreement on a simple ceremony followed by a tour of the continent during the fall. This suited Lilly perfectly, but it was difficult to hear about plans surrounding Michael's wedding to another. It was beginning to look as though she was not going to be able to avoid attending. Perhaps she might be ill…?

Watching Michael, Lilly found, was bittersweet.

He was so close and yet, so very far away. These days his features were grim and serious, as though he were working out a problem.

He had grown into and become a very fine duke.

She knew he doubted himself and compared his efforts to what his brother might have done. As they'd walked around the lake, he'd admitted as much to her. But watching him and knowing the lengths he'd go to for the good of his tenants, for the good of the country, for that matter, she was certain his older brother and father would have been proud.

He exuded energy and a quiet power.

Michael was a good man.

He'd lived an honorable life. He didn't live life on the edge as Danbury had. This was part of what she loved about him. He was kind to old ladies, wallflowers, and small animals. He would be a wonderful husband. He was going to make an excellent father someday. At this thought, she nearly gasped in pain. She experienced an urge to weep often these days. There would come a great relief after Glenda's wedding. Lilly would be more than ready for the peace and solitude of that small cottage in her imagination. She had already contacted a land agent who was researching some options for her.

The last waltz of the evening was the one Michael had reserved. None of the guests had left early, for a Ravensdale ball was likely to be one of the highlights of the season. Nobody wished to miss a moment of it.

Her eyes followed his dark and commanding figure as he made his way across the room. His stride was relaxed and confident. Their eyes held as he stood before her. "I believe this is my dance?" He winged his arm toward her. And then he added, "My lady."

"I told you—"

"You're nobody's lady, I remember. Humor me."

Shaking her head, Lilly reached her hand through the crook of his arm and allowed him to lead her to the dance floor. Once they stopped, he turned her to face him and placed one hand on her waist. He lifted her other hand to his lips before grasping it firmly. And then the music began.

The orchestra was one of the best in all of London, and the waltz they played was a slow and haunting tune. Michael led her confidently as the music rose and fell. She found it odd that it matched her emotions.

This dance would be her last.

It would be the last time he would hold her.

Staring into her eyes, he took long steps and guided her effortlessly around the other couples. She'd forgotten this feeling, of floating as he led her. His warm hand held hers with just the right amount of strength. Through the broadcloth of his jacket, his shoulders were firm.

Her eyes, in turn, drank him in. She watched his chin, his jaw, the way his hair was pushed behind his ears. Thick and straight, it had no tendency to curl, whatsoever. His valet attempted to control it with pomade, slicking it back while it was wet. But it would never stay that way. Like Michael, it had a will of its own.

When he dipped his head down, he inhaled deeply. She knew he was memorizing her scent—just as she was his.

And in his arms, she felt like a secret princess. She floated on air, feeling like an angel, as he twirled her around. They danced in perfect unison, as though two people could really become one. When she tilted her head back slightly, she remembered the sensation of his lips tracing the line of her throat.

They were in a world of their own. What a beautiful dance the waltz was. It must have been created for lovers. To be able to touch and move together, in public with no shame, was a gift.

The music continued, but the strings played more softly allowing the pianist to take the melody. It was as though the keys cried for the two of them. What should have been.

And then it ended.

Lilly curtsied, and Michael bowed.

He escorted her back to Lady Eleanor and walked away from Lilly, toward his fiancée. He leaned into the younger girl and whispered something near her ear. Lady Natalie nodded and then, taking Michael's arm, the two of them disappeared together onto the terrace.

****

Michael could wait no longer. The vote was scheduled for the day after tomorrow. He and his allies were not certain, but they had good reason to believe they would defeat their opponents.

"Is something the matter, Your Grace?" Lady Natalie took his arm and allowed him to lead her outside.

"You might say that."

She must have seen the determination on his face, for once outside, she led him along the french doors to a walkway he'd been unaware of.

"We can enter one of the drawing rooms through here," she whispered. "We will not be interrupted."

For a moment, he wondered if she thought he might be wanting to be alone with her for less than honorable reasons. But only for a moment. As soon as they entered the room, his fiancée released his arm, located a flint, and lit several candles. Once she'd turned around and faced him, he could hold back his words no longer.

"I cannot go through with this." He'd not meant to blurt it out like that, but the time was right. He already felt horrible for letting it go this long.

"Oh, thank God!"

Chapter Twenty-Five
Scandal (Also Known as Really Bad Gossip)

Scandals don't always begin in the drawing rooms of the *ton*. They don't always begin by ladies eager to share their rival's latest mishap. In London, the best of scandals became public knowledge on the society pages of the *London Gazette*. The ton, it was believed, had a mole. A person within its ranks who consistently shared all of the latest on-dits with K. Carmichael, gossip columnist at large.

The morning after the Ravensdale ball, the paper flaunted plenty of fodder. The most scandalous of which read as follows:

A young Mr. J—S—, who celebrated his betrothal just last evening, has aligned himself with a family who is hiding more than one skeleton. The prospective bride's stepmamma has acted both lawlessly and scandalously. The apparently sweet Lady B is not nearly as innocent and sweet as she has appeared all season. This reporter has discovered that the lady was not the first sister to marry Miss G—B—'s esteemed father. Not only is Lady B the stepmamma to the young miss, but she is her auntie as well, which makes the marriage not only illegal but practically incestuous! And if the marriage was illegal, then Lady B is not really Lady B at all, is she?

A very pleased Glenda Beauchamp arose for

breakfast the morning following the ball excitedly expecting to read about herself in the high-profile society pages of the exceedingly popular *London Gazette*. The grandest ball of the season had been thrown in her honor, after all. Would there be descriptions of her hair? Her betrothal gown? The grace with which she had waltzed with her handsome fiancé? She had shears beside her so she could cut out the article and save it in her memory book.

Within moments, however, the entire household knew something had gone amiss. For a piercing screaming horrifically disrupted the peace of the entire household. The newly betrothed lady screamed and ranted and raved in a hysterical fit, for what felt like hours to all of the servants. Glenda's lungs were powerful, indeed.

Lilly and Lady Eleanor rushed downstairs in their dressing gowns expecting to find no less than a bloodied corpse on the breakfast room floor.

The shears were not plunged into a dead body, though. No, they were standing straight up in the center of the table.

Upon seeing Lilly, Glenda's shrieks turned into ugly words. Holding the paper toward Lilly, gesturing toward the article, she shouted, "I hate you! You have ruined my life! He will cry off now, for certain! How could you? I hate you! I hate you! Who did you tell? You promised me you would tell no one! It was to remain a secret!" She went on and on and on.

Lilly grabbed the paper with a sick feeling in the pit of her stomach. She had thought Lord Hawthorn had given up on her. He hadn't spoken a word to her since that first evening. She read it through twice, fearing for the social standing of both her aunt and Glenda even more the second time. Collapsing, she sat down on one of the high-backed cushioned seats around the table. Surely the man was mad? What could Hawthorn accomplish with this?

What would it all mean?

"Damned jackals," Aunt Eleanor said. "They're all a bunch of jackals." Aunt Eleanor threw the paper on the table. "And you, girl, be quiet!" Aunt Eleanor never yelled.

Thank God, Glenda went silent.

Both Lilly and Glenda looked to Aunt Eleanor to say something, anything, which would explain the dreadful article and silence Glenda's awful fears.

"Lilly, expect visitors today, I imagine. We shall discover exactly what Mr. Joseph Spencer is made of. And Glenda, you had best put cucumbers on your eyes so they aren't bloodshot and swollen when your fiancé presents himself."

This statement drew a wail from Glenda.

"Don't start that again. If I know that family, and I do, an article such as this won't be cause for anything drastic. My guess is young Joseph will come to reassure you. So get yourself repaired." At that, Glenda dashed out of the room.

Turning to Lilly, Aunt Eleanor added, "That young Danbury needs to step up to the plate now as well. If his attentions were worth anything, it's a fine time for him to offer you his protection."

"Surely there is no need?" she asked her aunt helplessly.

"There is every need." Gesturing toward the article lying on the table, her aunt suddenly looked much older than she had the day before. "This sort of folderol can only be forgotten if you receive a very strong show of support." And then, rubbing her hand on her forehead, "Hopefully, Josephine and Broderick see past this."

Lilly dropped her head back hopelessly. Danbury would no more offer for her than Michael had. "What have I done?" she said again.

Aunt Eleanor shook her head. "I will send a note round to Danbury. It can only be hoped his attentions to you were in earnest."

"No!" Lilly said, her fist pressed against her mouth. She could not do it. Even if Danbury were to offer for her, she would not marry again.

She was so close to freedom.

How could she give her person over to a man for any reason other than love? Not everyone realized the magnitude of what a woman gave up when she married. If women knew what she knew, daresay there would be fewer marriages.

The viscount had been pleasant and friendly. He had acted the perfect gentleman, never once giving Lilly cause to doubt his motives or intentions. But she did not *know* him. She did not know his heart.

She could not do it.

She would not do it.

Just then Jarvis entered the room and addressed his mistress. "The Countess of Ravensdale is awaiting you in the drawing room. She says you are expecting her."

Lilly and Eleanor looked at each other forebodingly. This was not the visit of a young man wishing to reassure his intended.

They rose and smoothed their skirts.

Entering the drawing room, they found the

countess pacing back and forth. Her mouth pinched, worry clouding her eyes.

Lady Eleanor let out a loud sigh and then gestured toward the sofa. "I think we should have a seat, don't you, Josephine?"

Lady Ravensdale nodded graciously.

Lilly wanted to rush to speak, to deny the contents of the article. But she could not claim to be innocent. The information was true. Lady Eleanor spoke first.

"I suppose you are here to discuss that bedamned article."

"Oh, Eleanor," Lady Ravensdale said. "This is horrible, absolutely horrible." And then she paused. "Broderick and Joseph are in violent disagreement with each other. Joseph had intended to come over here at once, but that blasted stubborn husband of mine would not allow it. This business with the Corn Laws has him coiled like a snake."

She addressed her longtime friend, Lady Eleanor. Unshed tears glistened in her eyes. "He told Joseph, considering the circumstances, it would not be dishonorable for him to cry off. The vote on Cortland's amendment is to be held tomorrow morning, and Broderick is beside himself. They've worked on it for months now, and he insists we absent ourselves from any possible scandal." Dabbing at her eyes, she continued, "Joseph is enraged. His father has threatened to cut off his funds if he defies him on this." She sniffed. "I daresay, it has not been a pleasant morning."

Lady Eleanor squeezed her hand reassuringly.

Lilly felt herself being backed into a corner.

"I'll send a note round to Danbury. If he affords Lilly the protection of his name, I think we can ward off a great deal of fallout." Lady Eleanor could be very practical when matters called for it. "It's important we show a united front. The last thing we need now is a groom crying off. What's that damn fool of your husband thinking?"

Lady Ravensdale rose her eyebrows at the older woman's comments and then grimaced. "I'm afraid all he is thinking about right now is that amendment."

Lilly's chest tightened. She couldn't seem to get enough air. The walls were closing in on her. Surely Danbury would not make an offer. And if he did, there was no way she could accept.

Except that everyone would expect her to.

This could not be happening!

The blood in her veins turned ice cold. She had escaped marriage once. Most likely, she would not be so lucky a second time. Memories of her husband's hands clawing at her in the darkness roared through her mind. Vicious words rang in her ears.

She could not.

She could not do it again.

The memory of her father demanding she marry Lord Beauchamp taunted her. Guilt pressed in. He was dying! It was her duty as his daughter! Her mother quietly crying in the corner.

She would not consent to such a marriage again. She needed to escape. She needed to think. "Please excuse me." She burst to her feet.

Both women gaped at her.

But she could make no excuses. Lilly hastened from the room and, without retrieving her pelisse, fetching a chaperone, or even Miss Fussy, she exited the front door with no particular destination in mind.

The weather was spectacular that morning, the cloudless sky the color of lapis. Halfway through the month of May, flowers bloomed all around her. In a haze of anger and adrenaline, she walked aimlessly down Curzon Street and eventually found herself in the park. Not having any idea which paths led where, she disappeared into the greenery.

****

A very different scene played out in a masculine household that same morning. An occasional moan interrupted an abundance of quiet. The effects of downing large quantities of scotch the night before had the occupants reeling.

After speaking with Lady Natalie at the ball, Michael had made his excuses to the countess and then left with Danbury. Plans had been put into motion. All he could do at that point was wait.

And so, of course, the logical thing to do was open a twenty-year-old bottle of scotch and get rip-roaring, skunk-devilled drunk. Danbury happily participated.

But now that morning had come, Michael questioned his reasoning of the night before.

Especially with the thick green drink, promising to cure all, sitting before each of them at the table.

"Bloody hell!" Danbury rose from his seat. He'd been perusing the morning broadsheets.

Glaring at the offensive article, he dropped back into his chair and tossed it onto the table in front of Michael.

Michael read through the vicious ramblings and then chucked it onto the table himself.

He'd had enough. "Damn him to hell!" He grabbed his jacket and shoved his arms into the sleeves not caring whether his shirt wrinkled horribly beneath it or not.

Danbury met his gaze with his own bloodshot eyes. "Where are you going?"

Michael had no patience left. "Damn Hawthorn! He will pay for this!" Unwilling to waste even a moment longer, Michael ignored Hugh's halfhearted attempt to calm him down and slammed out of the house.

With anger seething inside him, Michael hadn't the patience to wait for the coachman to bring the vehicle around. Instead, he headed toward Hawthorn's London town house on foot. The bastard had done it! He'd hurt Lilly.

Hawthorn would pay.

Marching determinedly, adrenaline pushing him, Michael arrived at the earl's door in less than ten minutes. And when the door opened, he swept past the butler and demanded, "Hawthorn! I will see him now!"

The butler didn't answer but looked nervously over his shoulder at a closed door.

With murder on his mind, Michael pushed past the elderly retainer and threw open the door. There he discovered Hawthorne lounging on a loveseat with a pipe in one hand and a copy of the newspaper in the other.

The idiot ought to have wiped the smirk from his face. Michael crossed the room, grabbed the man's pristine cravat, and pulled the whey-faced miscreant off his chair.

Hawthorne laughed nervously, attempting to gain some control of the situation. "Ah, perhaps my initial assumption was correct after all. It was you, not the viscount, in the gazebo with her."

Michael pushed Hawthorn's rail-thin frame up higher, barely aware that the man's toes now dangled in the air. Making a choking sound, the earl began experiencing the effects of his cravat tightening about his windpipe.

"Hawthorn, do you know what it means to be a duke?"

The bastard gawked at him, eyes bugging out of his head, thin lips trembling.

"It means anything I say will be believed. It means I can kill you and walk away freely." Michael adjusted his grip menacingly. "It means I can buy off every damn one of your servants so no word is ever mentioned regarding my presence here this morning."

The earl's complexion had changed from pasty white to a reddish-purple color.

"I-I-I's s-s-sorry, Your Grace," he sputtered tightly.

Michael twisted the cravat and lifted the man even higher.

As the spineless earl struggled to breathe, Michael's fury diminished slightly. He could not, in fact, kill the man, as much as he was wont to do so. Some awareness returned, and the red haze that clouded his vision dimmed slightly. He released his grip suddenly, and Hawthorn collapsed back onto the chaise.

Michael *would not* put up with this man's antics any longer. And with his decision came an icy calmness. *He had had enough.* "You will leave England today, Hawthorn—that is, if you wish to live."

"You cannot make me do that!"

"Stealing horses is a hanging offence, you bastard. There are witnesses who will testify on my behalf. The treachery you have attempted will be exposed. Did you realize I assist the Regent with his investments, and he has experienced a great deal of success? I am quite within his favor these days. Did you realize it would take but a word from my dear friend to have your title, your lands, everything stripped from you?" Michael's voice was that of a duke—arrogant and confident. This troublemaker who'd plagued him all year would cease to be a problem today.

One way or another.

Hawthorn rubbed his neck fearfully.

"You will leave for the continent today. If you fail to do so, do not be mistaken. My threats aren't nearly as hellish as my actions will be."

Hawthorn's shoulders slumped, and his gaze dropped. He seemed to realize he'd lost. "I will have my carriage prepared immediately, Your Grace."

Michael nodded but then reached forward with one hand and pulled Hawthorn to his feet. With deadly intent, he pulled back his right arm, fisted his hand slowly…

And broke the man's nose. Blood streamed onto the ornate carpet covering the floor.

Locating his handkerchief, Michael wiped his hands on it and then tossed it at the earl. "Good day."

This hadn't solved the problems caused by the article, but Michael felt better, nonetheless. And he would no longer have to worry Hawthorn might harm Lilly.

Out on the earl's front step, he studied his fist and then rubbed his knuckles. He'd punched the man for hurting Lilly on the dance floor. It was about time he protected her.

Left alone, the Earl of Hawthorn reached for another handkerchief and shouted for his butler to attend him immediately. Cortland had been a thorn in his side for too long. Given half a chance, the young fool would be the downfall of the aristocracy.

Cortland, a duke no less, obviously didn't understand the working class were no better than animals. If allowed to prosper, they would turn against their betters and, as had happened in France, ignite an uprising.

"God damn it, that bloody hurts!" Hawthorn flinched as his valet dabbed at him with a wet cloth. He pushed the servant's hand away. "Pack my belongings. We're leaving for the country as soon as possible." *I'll be damned if I'm leaving England!* He snatched the cloth away from the servant and then tenderly dabbed at his nostril himself.

Damned idiot domestics, incapable of anything but the simplest of tasks.

He winced, and at the same time realized his nose now leaned slightly to the left. Damn Duke of Cortland had broken it! Hawthorn didn't know how, or when, but he vowed Cortland would pay for this!

Chapter Twenty-Six
Finally, a Bit of Truth

By the time the viscount arrived at Lady Sheffield's town house, Lady Ravensdale had been joined by her youngest son, her daughter, and her husband. Lord Ravensdale and Lady Natalie sat on the sofa with the countess. Mr. Joseph Spencer, on a loveseat beside his betrothed. He held her hand affectionately in his.

In a large cushioned chair, Lady Eleanor presided over them all.

Jarvis announced the new arrival and backed slowly into the foyer, closing the double doors as he did so.

In what appeared to be a gallant effort at cheerfulness, Lord Danbury stepped inside and greeted them all with his usual charm.

And then, never a man to beat around the bushes, he proudly announced, "I have come to offer for Lady Beauchamp." He glanced around the room, a perplexed frown marring his forehead. "Is the lady at home?"

Lady Eleanor pinched her lips before answering. "My niece, overset by the article, has gone out for a walk. We are awaiting her return." She glanced at a small timepiece and then added, "She has been gone a worrisome amount of time already."

Danbury located another chair. Pulling it closer to

the group, he spoke matter-of-factly. "Then I shall wait with you." Before sitting, he made his bow to the ladies present and raised both eyebrows. "That is, as long as no one objects?"

As Lady Eleanor assented with a nod, Lady Natalie chose that moment to speak up. "I have been telling Papa this morning that Lady Beauchamp did not wish to marry the baron, her first husband. She told me she did so only to please her father. It's all a dreadful mistake, Papa." Her eyes implored the earl to see reason where her brother was concerned. And something else flickered in her gaze as well.

Broderick Spencer, the Earl of Ravensdale, cleared his throat and then responded with his usual authority. "Be that as it may, if Danbury offers for her, she will be spared censure."

"No, Papa." Lady Natalie spoke firmly to her father. The flicker in her eyes began to burn brightly. "Lady Beauchamp does not *wish* to marry Lord Danbury. And, truth be told, Lord Danbury does not wish to marry Lilly."

But she did not stop there.

"Just as His Grace *does not wish* to marry me—and I have no wish to marry him! It is not Danbury, but Cortland who is in love with Lady Beauchamp."

"Be quiet, girl! This is hardly the time to be spewing such nonsense!" He bolted out of his seat.

Lady Natalie and her mother rose to calm him. Reaching for her husband, the countess pulled him back to the settee until he was again seated beside her. Lady Natalie, however, paced the room.

"And..." Joseph Ravensdale spoke up as though his father had not made any comment at all. "The only two people in this room who *do* wish to marry are myself and Glenda. And you, *you*, are impeding *our* match. I won't have it, Father, I won't! And If Natalie does not wish to marry Cortland, I will stand by her as well!"

Ravensdale was a proud and stubborn man, both as a barrister and then later in life, as a high-ranking member of the aristocracy.

He was also, however, a father. Who, as unlikely as it might be…loved his children. He looked at his two youngest with hurt in his eyes.

His wife lovingly placed her hand upon his. "We must listen to them, Broderick. It is *their* lives, *their* marriages."

He closed his eyes and rubbed his forehead. Taking a deep breath, he opened his eyes and looked over at his daughter. "Why, allow me to ask, Daughter, have you waited until now to inform me you do not wish to marry Cortland? And what makes you believe he does not wish to marry you? Has he said something? Done anything? I will kill him!"

Lady Eleanor sat up straight upon hearing his words. "I had thought the couple's feelings were in the past, but it is possible…Perhaps they never stopped loving one another. They were nearly betrothed years ago…" She then went on to tell him of the season of 1815 and the circumstances which had ended the young romance.

"I knew it!" Lady Natalie said out loud. Danbury glanced sideways at her, cocking one eyebrow and putting his finger to his lips as though to shush her.

The room fell silent for a moment as they all absorbed this new information.

Finally, shaking his head from side to side, the earl made a decision. "That is neither here nor there. We have a betrothal. Contracts are signed. We have one scandal on our hands, and we don't need another. The viscount can marry Lady Beauchamp, and everybody will just damn well have to learn to get on together. Where is that gel anyway? Shouldn't she be back by now?"

Lady Eleanor asked the maid to check in Lilly's room and for Jarvis to check the garden. When both returned and reported her still absent, an aura of concern descended upon the room.

The issues which had come into the open would be set aside so the gentlemen could go in search of Lady Beauchamp. Most likely, she was simply wandering in the park. But be that as it may, it would be best to locate her and assure themselves of her safety. Lady Eleanor appeared very tense as they discussed where they would search.

Danbury and the earl told her not to worry and then both disappeared onto the streets of Mayfair themselves.

Chapter Twenty-Seven
Missing

Michael strode toward his London town house, satisfied that he was finally taking matters into his own hands. Lilly would not face this alone. He broke into a run.

His town house was a mile or so away, and he was suddenly overcome with an unwavering need to see Lilly. To hold her.

To claim her.

They'd wasted too much time already.

Vendors and pedestrians looked at him curiously as he sprinted past. It was not every day a gentleman of the aristocracy was seen dashing headlong through the streets of Mayfair. One old woman selling flowers shook her head and rolled her eyes. "Don't those nobs have horses and whatnot to get them about town? Never did understand the quality."

When Michael arrived home, he called for Duncan, took a quick bath, and stood fidgeting as his valet finished tying his cravat.

Both his and Lilly's futures were at stake.

He knew he could make her happy, but would she allow it?

After a glance in the mirror, Michael made a quick stop in his study, going directly to his safe. Behind several documents and a stack of pound notes sat a box containing his mother's most valuable jewels.

Michael hastily opened the velvet-lined case and searched around until locating what he wanted. The stone in the ring was a princess-cut, three-carat yellow diamond in a setting made of twisted platinum. It was the ring he'd always planned on giving her. The night they met, he'd instantly recalled it. The diamond shone like her eyes, and the metal was the color of her hair. He'd never even considered giving it to Lady Natalie. It would have reminded him of what never was…

Shoving it into his pocket, he carefully returned the case to the safe and turned the knob, resetting the lock. He'd ordered his carriage brought around earlier, so it was ready and waiting as he exited.

Lumbering through the cobbled streets toward Curzon Street, he breathed deeply. He was ready for this. He'd been ready for nearly a decade.

There would be no more delay.

The driver covered the short distance quickly, and as the carriage came to a halt, Michael pushed the door open and jumped down to the sidewalk. Skipping every other step, he dashed up to the all-too-familiar doorway and rang the bell.

Jarvis answered quickly, as though waiting for somebody. He looked behind Michael, and upon seeing no one, asked, "She isn't with you, Your Grace?"

A sense of unease swept over him. "Who, Jarvis?"

Jarvis's thick black eyebrow lowered in concern. "Lady Beauchamp. She left on foot, hours ago, and has not returned." The man's hands gripped one another. He poked his head outside again, looking both up and down the street. "My lady was hoping she had gone to you."

Just then Miss Beauchamp stepped into the foyer. She had obviously been crying. Her eyes were swollen and her nose, quite red. "Oh, Your Grace. She has been gone for hours! I didn't mean it when I told her I hated her," she wailed. "I was so dreadful, and now nobody knows where she has gone."

Beginning to comprehend the situation, Michael took the distressed young woman's hands in his and looked her in the eyes. "Did she take a maid or a footman with her? Did she take Miss Fussy?"

Lady Eleanor stepped out of the room behind Glenda. "She did not. Come inside, Your Grace. We have been awaiting her return for quite some time now." The previously unshakeable lady looked around the room anxiously. "We thought she had merely gone for a walk. She was deeply troubled by that dreadful article." Pulling the drape aside, she peered out the window, frowning in concern. "After waiting for her for quite some time, Ravensdale and Danbury went searching. She left nearly three hours ago."

A woman, a lady, walking around London alone was vulnerable to any manner of vile attacks. She'd been gone for almost three hours.

Three hours!

Was it possible she was merely meandering in the park? Making a quick decision, Michael turned back toward the door. "I am going to the park to find her. If she was upset, she would have headed for the gardens. I have two outriders and my driver to come with me. I'll leave one of them here to fetch me if Danbury and Ravensdale are successful. If—when—I find her, I will return immediately as well." With that, he left as abruptly as he'd arrived.

Instead of climbing into the carriage this time, he jumped onto the driver's seat. As they pulled into traffic, Michael described the situation to John, and they devised a plan for an efficient search. Lilly was distraught and alone. Michael ran his hand through his hair trying not to imagine the worst.

****

By the time Lilly's panic subsided, she had wandered unthinkingly to her favorite garden in Hyde Park. The statues and fountains reminded her of the beautiful grounds at London Hills Manor. No, she mustn't allow herself to think of London Hills Manor. There would be plenty of time to dwell on that later.

The shadows were long on the ground, and the sun no longer high in the sky. She must have been walking for hours. She sat down, ruefully. Her aunt must be terribly worried. She had no idea how much time had passed since she'd left so abruptly, with no word of where she was going or when she would return. At first, she had been so angry, she had been completely unaware of her surroundings. Words had repeated themselves over and over in her mind. Words from her father. Words from Lord Beauchamp. Words even from Michael.

She had made a decision; she would no longer be manipulated by guilt. She was not going to be forced into another marriage—to anybody. She was not going to live in shame either.

Upon signing the marriage contracts for Glenda, she had been given a nonreturnable installment on her annuity. She would take it and leave if she must. She was more than sorry for causing her aunt and niece scandal and pain, but neither knew what it was like to be an unwanted wife.

If Joseph Spencer would not fight for Glenda, then perhaps they ought not to marry anyway.

Lilly would not do it again. She'd endured enough for a lifetime. It was time to inform her family and the Spencers of her resolution.

Having come to terms with what must be done, she suddenly felt exhausted. She would cut over to Kensington Road and hail a hack to take her back to her aunt's home. But before she could flag one down, as she stepped off the path onto the sidewalk, an unfamiliar crested carriage came to a halt beside her.

"Is that you, Lady Beauchamp?"

It was the Earl of Hawthorn—a rather bruised and bloodied Hawthorn, but the earl nonetheless. Looking around nervously, she tentatively approached the carriage. "It is, my lord."

Hawthorn smiled at her and indicated the cloth he held up to his nose. "Don't mind this, my lady. I have just come from your aunt's home. I stopped to offer my apology, as demanded by His Grace, and was informed she has had some sort of attack. I told them I would help find you and return you there as soon as possible."

"No!" Lilly gasped. "She is unwell?" This was too much!

Dear, dear Aunt Eleanor had only ever offered her kindness. And now she suffered due to Lilly's own stupid stubbornness. It was nearly enough to shatter her resolution.

The earl and one of his riders assisted her into the carriage. Settling in, she did her best to refrain from panicking. "Please, oh please, hurry," she begged. She sat in the carriage and looked down at her hands as the earl gave instructions to his driver outside. The footman handed him something and then climbed into the carriage behind the earl.

A footman inside of a carriage was highly unusual. Seeing the earl's expression, she suddenly had second thoughts about accepting this man's assistance.

"Oh, we will, my lady. We will." And then, raising one hand, he pointed a gun directly at her.

Her instincts had kicked in thirty seconds too late.

Just as she began screaming, the footman placed a scarf into her mouth and tied another behind her head. The earl leaned forward and pressed the gun between her breasts.

"Best not to struggle, my lady. I have nothing to lose by ending your life today. I won't hesitate to do so if you give me too much trouble."

The mad look in his eyes lent truth to his promise.

Lilly stilled. Staring back at the earl, she attempted to calm herself and analyze her situation. As she did so, the footman tied her hands uncomfortably behind her.

The footman then crouched on the floor to tie her feet. As he did so he pushed her dress up to her knees. When he was done, the earl turned the gun on his own employee. "Hand me your other pistol," he ordered.

With an uncertain look in his eyes, the servant obeyed and turned over the weapon.

"You ought to know better than to touch a lady that way," he said. "Damned animals—every one of you." He spat at the man and then shot him right between the eyes.

****

Michael found himself running past pedestrians for the second time that day but did not stop until he reached the gardens he knew Lilly loved. Breathing heavily, he looked around frantically. She wasn't here!

But she must be!

He'd been so certain he knew where she had gone!

Bang!

A loud cracking sound echoed off the nearby marbled gazebo. Recognizing a gunshot, Michael leapt over a concrete bench and raced toward the street. It sounded as though it had come from Kensington Road.

He didn't want to believe it had anything to do with Lilly, but an ominous foreboding filled him at the sound. Guns were not often fired in Hyde Park.

As Michael drew nearer to the road, a flurry of venders and park goers were ogling a carriage racing away at a dangerously high speed.

Accosting a sweeper who stood on the curb with his broom, Michael demanded, "What did you see? What happened here?"

The sweeper wiped his mouth before speaking. "I think the bloke 'at took off with the lady were a nobleman. She seemed willing enough but let out a scream once she were inside wit' 'im."

Fear coursed through him. "What did she look like?" Michael demanded.

"Pretty li'l thing. She 'ad the most unusual 'air, not silver, but not yellow like, either."

"And the carriage, what did it look like?"

"Oh, it was fine, sir. That's 'ow I guessed it was one o' you lords. 'Ad one o' them fancy designs on it."

A crest. The Earl of Hawthorn.

It had to be. It was the only possible explanation. The man was insane and today, in a fit of temper, Michael had pushed him over the edge!

Michael hailed a hackney and returned to where he'd left his driver. He would need help if he were to save her from the earl.

And then the horrible, unthinkable truth hit him.

It was possible she was already injured, or worse. Where had the pistol been aimed when the shot was fired? He forced the thought from his mind. He could not, would not allow his thoughts to go in that direction.

He arrived back at the Sheffield town house to find Ravensdale and Danbury had returned ten minutes earlier. Michael was ushered into the drawing room where a number of concerned faces turned to look at him hopefully.

Mr. Joseph Spencer stood behind his fiancée who was sitting on the loveseat holding lady Eleanor's hand tightly. Lady Natalie sat beside her mother. Danbury stood by the window. Lord Ravensdale was pacing the room like a caged tiger. They all looked at him expectantly.

"She has been kidnapped," he told them. "She may be injured."

****

After Hawthorn shot the footman, Lilly'd taken one look at the dead man's lifeless eyes and fainted.

Now, gradually regaining her lucidity, she realized the danger of her predicament. Not wishing to attract the earl's attention, she carefully peeked from under her eyelashes. Hawthorn was slumped in his seat, watching out the window. The carriage jostled and bounced uncomfortably. They were travelling at such a high rate of speed, Lilly feared they might tip over at the slightest turn. She worried for the horses. They wouldn't last long at this pace. Even as she contemplated the animals, the coach lurched with the crack of the driver's whip.

A man as wicked as Hawthorn ought not be allowed to own animals.

Lilly was ever so grateful she had not taken Miss Fussy with her when she'd left the house. Thinking about Miss Fussy, she nearly began crying.

She hadn't shed a single tear all day, but the thought of dying and leaving her pet alone horrified her.

Hawthorn looked up and caught her watching him. "My apologies for the footman's disrespectful handling of you, my lady." He seemed oddly regretfully but still held one of the guns loosely between his hands. Another weapon lay on the floor by his feet. "No lady ought to suffer the touch of the working class."

Lilly wasn't sure how to respond to his statement. The man was not of sound mind. The look in his eyes was dispassionate, void.

She tried to speak but could not. She'd forgotten about the gag tied around her mouth. Once aware of it, though, it was all she could focus on. Suddenly, she could not get enough air into her lungs. She took deep breaths through her nose attempting not to panic.

The earl reached forward and tugged the handkerchief out of her mouth and below her chin. Lilly gasped gratefully.

"Please, don't scream," he said tiredly. His shoulders were slumped. He looked tired.

"I won't." She wanted only to keep him calm.

"It's not that I wish to harm you, but I've run out of options."

"Options?" she pressed.

"If Cortland changes the Corn Laws, England will cease to exist as we know it. The duke is misguided in his attempt to ease up on the masses. The peasants, the crofters, the lower classes must be kept in their place. They have begun revolting against their betters, and we cannot allow this."

"But what have I to do with any of this?"

"The duke is in love with you. He thinks he has beaten me, but he will learn…Yes, he ought to have listened to me all along. A man in love will do nearly anything."

"How do you know?"

"I was in love once. Hard to believe, isn't it? Loved my wife." He dropped his eyes to stare at the gun. "She's dead now, though. Died during childbirth. Killed by my heir." Lilly briefly remembered what her aunt had said about Hawthorn's son, Lord Castleton. No wonder the man was something of a hellion. He had a lunatic for a father who blamed him for his mother's death.

Lilly didn't ask any more questions, allowing Hawthorn to remain lost in his thoughts. Better for him to focus on anything but her. She'd been silently attempting to loosen the length of rope around her wrists. Since they were tied behind her back, the earl was unaware of her movements.

Coming out of his reverie, he eyed her once again. "The duke will come after you. And when he does, I will have to kill him." He shook his head. "I didn't think it would come to this…But you see, I cannot let him win. If he wins, all of England loses. Generations of noble families over hundreds of years have been procreating to establish a civilized human race. It is inconceivable that it could all be for naught."

Lilly weighed her words carefully before

responding to this. "The duke will not come for me. You are wrong. Even if he loves me, as you say, he will not come. What you do not understand is I am not a priority in the duke's life." She spoke the words fervently. Were they true? A duke's honor was not to be compromised for anything—even love. "His Grace would not dishonor himself by breaking his word to Lady Natalie. The duke will stay in London until the vote is taken, and afterwards he will wed his fiancée."

The earl's face contorted in rage. "Shut up!" He lifted the gun and pointed it directly at her again. His hands shook. Lilly closed her eyes and prayed. Was this to be her last moment on earth? She waited to hear the shot of the gun. When nothing happened, she opened her eyes again.

The earl seemed to be having difficulty breathing. Dropping the gun to the floor, he clutched at his left shoulder and winced in pain. "Don't speak of such things. You don't know what you are talking about. The amendment will fail." He closed his eyes, and his skin began turning white.

Lilly thought to assist him by untying his cravat, but her hands were still bound. She had been unable to make much progress, if any, at loosening the ropes.

Chapter Twenty-Eight
Rescue

Michael stood in the doorway and scanned the faces in Lady Sheffield's drawing room. "It's Hawthorn. I'm certain of it. I visited his home this morning and demanded he leave London, leave the country for that matter. But I'm afraid I pushed him too far. And now…And now he's taken Lilly…"

Michael dropped heavily into an empty chair and put his head in his hands. "All I managed to do was enrage the man. When he saw Lilly leaving the park, he saw a way to get back at me."

Sitting now, fatigue pulled at Michael's body. His earlier adrenaline was giving way to hopeless exhaustion.

Where had they gone? Where would Hawthorn take her? He pictured her as she'd been that afternoon at London Hills Manor. Her hair spread around her on the ground as he'd gazed into her golden eyes. Her lips tilted up, smiling seductively at him.

He recalled the moment at the inn when he'd first heard her voice. He'd been unable to believe it was her. His mind had convinced him their love was dead, but his heart had known all along.

In fact, she'd possessed it since the moment he'd seen her standing in the foyer of the Willoughby ballroom. And she'd kept it all these years.

She'd been through so much already. Somehow, Lilly had survived an intolerable marriage for the sake of her family. Out of respect for Glenda, she had observed the mourning period, pretending grief for a man who'd treated her abominably. Her spirit had kept hope alive. She'd returned to London determined to do for her stepdaughter what everyone else had failed to do for her. Assure her happiness and peace.

He pictured her as she'd danced with him. Had it just been last evening? It hadn't even been twenty-four hours since he'd held her, guided her, and twirled her around in the Ravensdale's ridiculously ornate ballroom.

Was she alive even? She had to be! Surely his heart would know if she'd left this earth.

He rubbed his hands over his eyes before facing the room's inhabitants.

Lady Natalie looked meaningfully at Michael and then her father. Her father looked enraged.

Michael spoke softly, his voice sounding guttural. "I'm going after her."

These were apparently not the words the earl had been expecting. "You bastard!" Ravensdale was on his feet in an instant, fists clenched at his sides. "I trusted you with my *daughter*, my *only daughter*!"

Lady Natalie jumped out of her chair and placed herself in front of her father. "No, Papa! Please. I am the one who does not wish to marry Lord Cortland! Please, Father, please, let him go!" she begged. Michael was surprised to see tears spilling down her face. "Father, please understand, I cannot marry Cortland. I do not love him. Lilly needs him! Let him go!" Lady Ravensdale rose and wrapped her arms around her weeping daughter. Natalie would have collapsed had her father not taken hold of her and guided her back to her seat. She wept softly.

"Enough, Broderick." The countess spoke firmly to her husband. "Our children are not to be used as chattel in a business deal, or politics, or anything else." She gently stroked her daughter's hair and looked him in the eyes. "Enough."

The earl knelt before of his daughter. At that moment, he was something of a broken man. Michael knew Ravensdale's greatest priority in life had always been his wife and children. With a fatherly tenderness not normally exhibited, the earl gently brushed Natalie's hair from in front of her eyes. "Sweeting? I thought this was what you wanted. I thought you were happy with the match."

Lady Natalie brushed her hands at her eyes like a child. "That's because *you* were happy with it, Papa. I *so wanted* to make *you* happy, but…I do not love Cortland and he does not love me, and I want what you and Mama have. I have come to realize that marriage ought to be undertaken with much more than a daughter's desire to please her father." She tucked her head onto her father's shoulder and quietly wept some more.

Ravensdale looked over at Michael and gave him a helpless look. "My girl doesn't wish to marry you, Cortland. Can we agree to destroy the betrothal contacts?" There was a hint of a threat in his voice as both men knew Michael deserved the blame for the dissolution of the betrothal.

But a gentleman could never cry off.

"We can," Michael said, lifting his head up from

315

his hands. "Please, Lady Natalie, accept my heartfelt apologies…"

Lady Natalie peeked out from her father's arms to look over at him. The only two who could see her face were Cortland and Danbury. Her tears had magically vanished.

And then—the little minx—she winked at him! "I'm the one who is sorry, Your Grace."

It was what they'd planned, but not this way. Had she deliberately become hysterical for her father's benefit? He'd have to thank her later but was more restless than ever to be on his way to Maple Hall, Hawthorn's estate. It was where Michael had discovered his stolen carriage and team. It made sense that Hawthorn would take Lilly there as well.

When he'd arrived at Lady Eleanor's town house, he'd sent John to retrieve mounts for them to go after Hawthorn. They could travel faster that way.

John and Arty would both be riding with him.

He gave Natalie what he hoped looked like a grateful nod and then, unable to wait a moment longer, stood and moved toward the door.

"I'm leaving for Hawthorn's estate as soon as John returns with the horses. My apologies, Ravensdale, Danbury, for missing the vote tomorrow."

Lady Eleanor had pulled a bell to call for a maid. When the maid arrived, she directed her to pack some food and drinks in bags that would fit on a saddle. She must have been terrified, but the look she bestowed upon Michael said she trusted him to save her niece.

He hoped he was worthy of such faith.

Ravensdale went into the foyer with Michael. Putting one hand on his shoulder, he held out his other for Michael to shake.

Michael grasped it firmly.

"Don't worry about the vote." Ravensdale glanced back at Danbury with a grim determination. "We'll take care of matters here."

Danbury turned to Michael before responding. "Not if Cortland requires my assistance." His eyes were sincere.

Michael shook his head. "I've got John and Arty traveling with me. You stay with Ravensdale and see what can be done when the call is made." Just then, Jarvis appeared to inform them John had arrived. The maid ran in, curtsied, and handed him three saddlebags. He took them gratefully.

He would find her.

She would be alive. He had to believe this as he and his two servants, who had turned out to be as loyal as any of his friends, rode hell-bent for leather, to find and save his Lilly.

Just as he ought to have done years ago.

****

Lilly had thought the earl dying before her eyes, but as quickly as the chest pains came, they seemed to cease. Although his hand remained upon his chest, his color returned, and he leaned back in his seat again.

"No more talking," he ordered.

Lilly closed her eyes and continued picking at the knot the footman had tied. The sun had set, and the driver was forced to slow the carriage as darkness overtook them. She was glad for the horses, they had been pushed too hard.

As happy as she would have been to see Michael, she did not think he would come after her in truth. Not for the reasons she had told the earl. But because no one knew she had been taken—let alone that she was even with the earl.

Aunt Eleanor must be beside herself. Perhaps they assumed she'd simply decided to leave town and never return. Perhaps they believed she had childishly run away, for that's what she'd wanted to do initially.

"Is my aunt truly ill? You were lying, were you not, when you told me she had fallen ill?" She ignored his instructions to remain silent.

The earl leaned his head back against the bench and observed the ceiling of the coach. "She is an old woman. She will die soon. We all die."

"Oh, please! She is not truly ill though, is she?"

"For God's sake, no, girl. Leave me in peace."

That was something, anyway. Relieved by this knowledge, she again focused upon her current predicament. After so adamantly deciding she didn't need a man in her life, she was already being tested. She must escape on her own. It was possible she had more reason to live than for herself.

Her courses were still absent. She'd never been late. Not after her father's death, her mother's death, or even when Michael had failed to return to England. Oh, yes, she had something to live for.

If she was going to become a mother, her duties began now. She must protect her life and that of the child she might be carrying. She needed to escape.

Ignoring the pain of the rope digging into her, she pulled relentlessly at the knot until it finally loosened, and she could wriggle her hands. Relief swam through her as she loosened the knot further.

But she kept her arms behind her back. She needed

to be smart about this. The earl still possessed a gun, and she had nowhere to go. She could not throw herself from a moving carriage as that could harm the baby. *If there was a baby.*

She watched the earl from under her eyelashes. It was dark enough that he must believe her to be asleep. He winced occasionally and rubbed his chest with his right hand. He'd retrieved the pistol he'd dropped earlier and now held in loosely in his left.

His nose had stopped bleeding, but there were black crusts of blood dried on his upper lip. If he hadn't been holding her captive, she might have felt sorry for him. Even so, she thought, the man was sick of the mind and probably deserved her pity.

But he was also a murderer. A dead man lay on the floor, blocking the door. Lilly couldn't bring herself to look at him. Nausea threatened each time she remembered a corpse lay only inches from her feet. She could not dwell on that.

The carriage slowed and turned onto a bumpier road. Noting a few familiar landmarks outside the windows, she realized they had passed through Reading and must be headed toward his estate. The carriage jostled and tipped, the roads rutted from recent rain.

Lilly wrapped the ropes so they would still appear knotted and clenched them tightly in her fists.

After what felt like hours, the carriage slowed to a halt in front of a long brick stable and then bounced slightly as the driver jumped off. When he opened the door, allowing the light from his lantern to shine in, his own eyes opened in horror when the gaze of the dead footman reflected back at him.

The earl scoffed dismissively and took command

of the situation. His authority gave the driver no leeway to express his concerns.

"Take care of this mess." Hawthorn ordered him.

Pausing only a few seconds, the driver removed the lantern and then pulled the dead man out the door. His attempts to prevent the body from hitting the ground failed, and there were several cracking and thumping sounds until it was dragged away.

The earl spoke politely. "My dearest Lady Beauchamp, welcome to Maple Hall, my humble country estate." He climbed out of the carriage and then reached back in to assist her. Lilly slid across the bench and poked her bound feet out the door. Leaning forward, she allowed the earl to pull her weight forward and catch her as she hopped to the ground. She gripped the rope tightly behind her, not wanting to be discovered.

The dead footman lay a few feet away from the carriage. It was too sad. Did he have a family? Children? She closed her eyes for a moment of respect and then turned away.

"My lord." She spoke in refined tones, looking down. "If you would be so kind as to unbind my feet, I give you my word, as a lady, I will not attempt to run away. I wish to arrive upon your doorstep with more dignity than these ropes allow. You have my word"— she repeated solemnly—"as a lady."

Honor, be damned.

This deluded man believed her gentility would prevent her from lying to him. Bending down, he unwound the ropes from around her ankles. Moving stiffly, Lilly followed him across the drive and over to a large, somewhat dilapidated manor.

After stepping inside, the earl guided Lily up the staircase and down a long corridor. Thick layers of dust covered the furnishings, and the musty scent of neglect filled her nostrils. When they arrived at the end, he opened the door to a very large bedroom with a raised bed, dark green velvet drapes, and a canopy. Again, dust had settled everywhere. The room must have gone unused for decades. Where were the earl's servants? He pointed to a high-backed wooden chair and told her to sit. Not wishing to draw his attention to her unbound feet, she did as he said.

"This will be your chamber for the duration of your visit. If you will excuse me, I have a missive to send. We shall see, my lady, if the duke has any honor after all." With that, he backed out of the room, closed it, and from the clanking sounds of metal, turned some sort of heavy lock. Lilly waited for his footsteps to recede before pulling the ropes off her hands and freeing herself.

Unexpected pain shot through her arms.

She'd not considered that having them in such an unnatural position would cause her muscles to cramp. Massaging her hands and wrists, she set her blood to circulating once again. She then stretched and twisted to relieve the kinks she had developed over the long, uncomfortable drive.

Feeling somewhat better, she went to the door and tested the knob. It was locked, as she had suspected. Next, she tiptoed over to the window, quietly managed to push it upwards, and looked down.

A considerable distance stretched between the window and the ground, but a branch from a nearby tree beckoned, just within reach. In a pinch, she thought she could reach it and climb down the tree to safety. She chuckled. If this wasn't a pinch, she didn't know quite what was.

But it would be near impossible in her gown.

She pulled her head back into the room. The earl had left the lantern, and she used it to illuminate the shelves inside the large wardrobe. Just what she needed!

She'd located a pair of men's breeches and a large shirt. Knowing she would never make it down the tree in her skirts and corset, with somewhat of a struggle, she managed to undress herself and slip into the less cumbersome clothes. The pants hung loosely, so she tied the waist with the rope that had bound her hands and rolled the bottom of the legs up. Grabbing a sharp letter knife from the top of the desk, she tucked it into her waistband and then went back to the window.

This aspect of her escape was going to require more than a little courage.

Setting the lantern down on a small table by the window, she tentatively slid her bum onto the ledge and then reached one foot through the window so she straddled it. Clutching the building between her thighs, she reached her arms out as far as they could go.

The branch was just out of reach.

Damn, damn, and double damn!

She leaned back inside but stilled at the grinding of the lock on the heavy door once again. Triple damn!

She didn't have a choice.

No longer tentative, she pulled both feet up to the base of the window and crouched on the sill.

One, two, three!

Using all of her strength and sending up a quick

prayer, she launched herself toward the branch awkwardly. As her feet pushed away from the sill, one of them inadvertently caught the edge of the lantern and knocked it off the table. As she grasped at the branch, she was vaguely aware of the sound of shattering glass.

But she had made it to the tree.

Grasping the branch for dear life, she reached around with her feet until she could steady herself on a few of the lower branches. She'd done it. As she analyzed where she ought to climb next, a few crackling pops sounded from the window and an odd sensation warmed her back.

She looked over her shoulder in dawning horror.

Flames climbed the counterpane of the bed and had spread across the floor. The fuel from the lantern must have saturated the carpet! Even the leaves and the trunk were now illuminated by golden light flickering through the window.

She'd set the manor on fire!

In the next instant, the earl lurched into the room. Indecision contorted his features. Should he stop Lilly or attempt to douse the blaze?

Not waiting for his decision, Lilly swung herself around the branch and pulled herself closer to the trunk. Once there, she slipped and clawed her way down. She was terrified if she took too much time, she'd find the earl waiting at the bottom. After what seemed like forever, she finally deemed herself close enough to the ground to jump. Letting go of the rough bark, she pushed herself away from the trunk and once again launched herself into the unknown.

The ground was hard, but she rolled as she landed. As she caught her breath, her gaze was pulled back to the window.

Flames greedily reached toward the branches of the tree where she had just been. Screaming, tortured wails sounded from the open window. He was still upstairs in the bedroom.

Was he trapped in the inferno?

If the earl stayed in that room any longer, he would likely not make it out alive.

Surely he would come after her any moment.

She jumped to her feet and took off for the stables. There did not seem to be any household servants about, and the stable employees ignored her to gawk at the fire.

Not one of them seemed to care that their employer was inside. Lilly shivered. They were going to let him die. It was no wonder. Why would they have any loyalty for such a villain as he?

But would any of them come after her? She needed off this estate! She would ride!

Running into the stable, Lilly located a mare who appeared to be calm and gentle, and yet strong enough to carry her. Good Lord, how was she going to do this? When she'd ridden before, there had been a mounting platform! And she'd had Michael and a groom to assist her.

She was going to have to get herself onto that horse.

One of the adjacent horses whinnied. And the others sounded restless. The nearest of them stared at her with a vulnerable look reminiscent of Miss Fussy.

She could not abandon them.

Unwilling to leave the animals trapped in the barn, Lilly rushed about, opening stalls and encouraging them to escape. They too, would have their liberty.

Fearing she'd wasted too much time already, she frantically returned to the enclosure holding her chosen mount and unlatched the stall door. Stepping on the slats, she climbed to the top of the wall, took hold of the mane, and then swung one leg over the horse's back.

She did this as calmly as possible. It had been nearly a decade since she'd ridden. She didn't wish to spook the horse, for already chaos abounded outside and she was a strange rider.

"It's all right, sweetheart. You and I are going for a ride, that's all. I'll take you far away from that bad man." Lilly spoke in a soothing voice and gently allowed her weight to settle on the horse's back.

Instinctively, she gripped the mare's flowing mane and urged the horse forward and toward the door. As soon as they exited the barn, Lilly headed down the long drive.

Afraid of being thrown, but even more fearful of someone stopping her, she urged the horse from a canter into a full-out gallop. "Good girl," she said, squeezing the mare's girth with her legs. She continued talking to the horse. "Let's get out of here, but please, please, please don't throw me!" She hadn't ridden since Edgewater Heights those many years ago—and that had been with a sidesaddle.

She only knew she must travel as far as possible, *as quickly as possible*. But to where? She hoped they were headed in the right direction.

Not really knowing what she was doing, she allowed the horse to run freely for what seemed like a very long time. When they finally slowed to a walk, every bone in her body felt as though it had been jarred loose.

But she'd kept her seat. She'd not fallen off!

When a thunderous roar echoed behind her, Lilly glanced back and saw the entire manor engulfed in flames. But that was not all. The tree she had used for her escape had caught fire. It had fallen onto the stables.

Thank God she'd left the barn doors open. The horses inside had fled in all directions.

As the roof collapsed onto the manor, Lilly patted her horse's neck. "Well done, my lady. Now let's get out of here."

Chapter Twenty-Nine
Rescue?

After changing their horses in Reading, Michael
and his men found the going slower after turning onto
the less-travelled route to Maple Hall. Muddy and full
of ruts, the condition of the road required the mounts to
pick their steps carefully. Slowed but not deterred,
Michael tamped down his frustration until something
unusual caught his eye.

Off in the distance, an orange glow lit the horizon.

"Lilly." Michael mouthed her name.

A shiver ran down his neck as he realized the
pungent scent hanging in the air was smoke.

And then, like a mirage, he spied a lone rider in the
distance approaching. He remembered the young
grooms who had assisted him and John the last time
they had been there and hoped they were safe. The fire
appeared to have engulfed several of the estate's
buildings.

"Oh, God, Lilly…" he whispered raggedly into the
darkness.

Rightly suspicious of the rider up ahead, John and
Arty both pulled out their pistols.

"Ho, there!" Michael called out roughly. "Hold
up!"

The rider seemed to consider them for just a
moment before turning off the road and racing into the

woods.

"Oh, hell, he'll kill himself *and* his horse running in this mud." Arty put his pistol back into his waistband.

Michael wasn't sure, but he'd thought he'd seen a flash of silver-white hair in the moonlight as the rider turned. Pulling his reins to the right, he spurred his own horse into the darkness in desperate pursuit. *It had to be her.* He couldn't bear the thought of a world without her ever again.

"Lilly!" he hollered. "Lilly!"

At first, he thought the rider would try to elude him, but then the horse abruptly halted and the rider slid to the ground.

"Lilly!" he called out again and then nearly cried when she turned in his direction.

"Michael!"

It was her. His heart raced. With his eyes locked on the glint of her hair, he urged his horse forward until her shadow took shape.

The clouds moved in just that moment, and the moon lit the field. Beside the horse, on the ground and covered in mud, sat Lilly.

She lifted her arms toward him. "Michael."

He dismounted his horse in one easy motion.

Not quite believing he'd found her, he forgot about the mud, lost his footing, and fell headlong in the darkness.

Breaking his fall with one arm, he caught hold of her with the other and together they lay in the mud. "Thank God! It is you! Are you hurt?"

She was covered in mud, laughing at him and crying at the same time. Michael ran his hands along her arms and waist, assuring himself she was all in one piece.

She touched his face in wonderment as though assuring herself that he was real. "I'm fine. Oh, Michael! You are here!"

With a surge of intense relief, Michael took her face in his hands and pressed his lips to hers almost violently. His tongue pushed through her lips hungrily as though she were an oasis to a dying man.

She was alive. She was safe!

Lilly grasped the back of his head in her muddied hands and pulled his face closer still. Their teeth gnashed, and she explored his mouth with equal longing.

Abruptly, Michael leaned back and looked into her eyes. "Did he hurt you, my love? I should have killed the bastard!" His eyes burned. He fought back tears of anger and relief.

Lilly, somewhat clumsily, sat up in the mud. "No, I am f-f-fine. When I saw you, I tr-tr-ied to get off my h-h-horse and fell instead!" She began trembling. And then a sob shook her.

Michael wrapped his arms around her, holding her tight. Rising to one knee and planting one foot firmly on the ground, he put one arm under her knees and pushed himself to his feet. Careful not to slip again, he placed Lilly upon his horse, in front of the saddle and then pulled himself up behind her. All the while murmuring soothing words.

The other horse didn't have a halter, so it was impossible to pull along. Luckily, the mare followed of her own accord. Michael allowed his mount to carefully find his footing as they headed back to the road. Arty met them halfway.

"It is Lady Beauchamp?" he asked in surprise when he realized the duke wasn't alone.

Michael nodded and indicated they head back toward Reading. "Ride ahead and reserve some rooms at the inn. Then hire a carriage for the trip back to London tomorrow morning."

"Right," Arty said, looking stunned that the baroness had managed to get away with no assistance from them whatsoever.

John jumped from his mount and placed a makeshift lead on Lilly's mare so he could pull her safely behind. But then his eyes lit up as if a thought occurred to him. "If we traveled back by carriage tonight, Your Grace, you could make it to Westminster Palace in time to vote."

"No," Michael said, "Lady Beauchamp needs rest. She's in shock, I think."

Michael kept tight hold of Lilly, aching each time he felt a tremor run through her body. "You're safe now, love," he murmured, leaning down to whisper in her ear. "We've a short ride ahead of us, but we'll get you cleaned up and tucked into a soft bed as soon as we get to Reading." He pressed his lips into her hair. "Lean into me, sweetheart. I've got you." He couldn't believe they had found her. Or that she had found them, rather.

Lilly stirred. "Your vote? Your vote is tomorrow?"

"It's no matter." Michael dismissed her concern. "You aren't up to traveling tonight, and I'm not about to let you out of my sight." He chuckled ruefully. "This day has taken ten years off my life."

"Arty!" She sat up so quickly her head knocked him in the chin as she yelled after his driver. "Get the carriage for tonight. Let's get the duke to London in time for the vote."

Arty, having turned back when he'd heard her call, merely tipped his hat before resuming his errand.

Aware of the man's propensity to carry out Lilly's orders, Michael knew exactly what he'd find when they pulled into Reading. Arty would be awaiting them with a carriage and fresh horses. Night travel was difficult but not impossible. The moon was high and full. With some luck, it just *might* be possible to make the vote.

"Are you certain you're up to it?" he asked her. It seemed impossible to still make the vote. And yet, with Lilly in his arms, he was beginning to believe anything was possible.

"Absolutely! We can rest in the carriage." She snuggled back into him. "Now, tally ho and all that nonsense. Let's get a move on."

Michael laughed and spurred his horse forward. After only a few steps, Lilly perked up again and began telling him everything that had happened.

"I didn't mean to leave for so long!" she explained. "But they wanted me to marry Danbury! Danbury! Can you imagine? But I was planning to return, and then Hawthorn told me Aunt Eleanor had suffered an attack! She did not really, did she?" At Michael's reassurance, she continued. When she informed him the earl had shot the footman and then pointed the gun at her, Michael tightened his grip around her. "It was horrible, Michael, but I couldn't dwell upon it. He's crazy, the earl, but I got him to untie my legs, and then…" She told him of the tree, and the fire, and the horses. "And then I found you, and now we are going to get back to London so you can make your vote!" She'd turned into a bundle of energy, and by the time they arrived in Reading, she seemed, once again, her normal self.

Every time he imagined what the outcome could have been, he had to force the scenario out of his mind. This day could have ended in a very different way!

But it did not.

It had not.

As Lilly slid off the horse into Michael's waiting arms in Reading, he noticed for the first time her unusual attire. She wore a man's britches! And they hugged her firm behind in a way no dress ever would.

Being with her, touching her, was almost unreal. She was safe. She was alive. And now he was certain, she would be his.

Adjusting his own trousers, Michael climbed into the rented carriage and closed the door behind him. The cabin lurched a bit as the coach began to move. Reminded of the bags Lady Eleanor had sent along, sitting on the floor, he reached for one and tossed it on the bench next to Lilly.

"Are you hungry, love?"

Lilly returned his gaze with a devious grin. She was a seductress, this mud-covered urchin of his.

He laughed softly. "For food, my love. In the bag."

And then her stomach chose that moment to make a growling sound.

They both laughed this time. "Don't make fun." She blushed as she opened the pack. "I haven't eaten all day!" When she pulled out some bread and cheese and a flask of wine, Michael realized he too, was famished.

Handing the wine back and forth, together, Lilly and Michael finished off the crusty bread and pungent cheese in a comfortable silence. By some crazy chance of fate, she was given one more night alone with her love. They were both exhausted, however, and filthy.

Michael stuffed the leftover bread back into the bag and then moved across the carriage to sit beside her. Wrapping one arm around her shoulder, he reclined them both against the side of the carriage while keeping one foot on the floor for support.

His hands covered hers, which rested upon her stomach.

If she told him she thought she might be carrying, he would never let her go. She had to force herself to remember the reasons this wasn't a good idea. What were those reasons? His honor, a duke's honor, to his people, to his betrothed. She could have him for herself, but in choosing her, he would sacrifice that which he lived to uphold, in the name of his father and all those other dukes before him.

She mustn't take that from him.

Instead, she moved her own hands to cover his…so his now rested on her still flat tummy.

This was most likely the closest he would come to touching their child—if one existed. She smoothed her palms over his strong long fingers. Oh, to be like this with him forever. Lilly did her best to stay awake. She didn't want to miss even a minute wrapped in his arms.

She drifted off moments after he did.

****

Michael awoke when the sounds of street venders and other carriages rumbling along intruded on his dreams. They were pulling into London just as the sun was rising. John and Arty had made incredible time. Michael's hands were under Lilly's shirt, and he couldn't resist tenderly caressing her warm skin. As she stretched like a cat, Michael allowed his fingers to drift downwards until he was threading his fingers through tight curls.

Her breathing hitched. Oh, yes, she was awake now.

She was his. She would always be his.

He teased and massaged her warmth, feeling his own breaths quicken as he did so.

"Good morning," he whispered, nipping at her tiny ears. She made a soft mewling sound as his fingers moved slowly, in and out of her most tender of openings. He knew exactly what she liked, what she needed. How had they gone so long without one another?

Moving more purposefully with him, she turned her head and searched for his lips with hers. Aroused, but intent upon her satisfaction, he kissed her languidly, thoroughly. Their breath, tasting of the wine they'd drunk the night before, mingled. As he continued his motions with his hand, Lilly wound one arm around his neck. She clung to him but also arched beneath his touch. Her tongue mimicked the motion his fingers made as she thrust it in and explored his mouth.

She held back nothing of herself from him. It had always been this way.

Although aroused and hard, Michael pleasured her enthusiastically until she broke down, shaking, and pushing herself into his hand. And then, gasping, she let her head fall onto his shoulder.

Ah, yes, ah yes. So beautiful, his Lilly. Michael kissed the side of her face, her neck.

He never wanted to move.

Until, that was, he realized they were heading

down Whitehall directly for the palace.

Good God, the vote! As he tensed, Lilly's eyes flew open, and she too apparently realized they were travelling along a very public route in the center of London. Scampering off him at the same time the carriage hit a rut, Lilly landed in an ungainly heap on the floor. Looking up at him, she appeared startled and then burst into laughter.

And Michael laughed with her.

How could one not laugh? She was alive. They were together. And he planned on righting the wrong he'd done nearly a decade ago.

Lilly tightened the rope around her breeches, climbed back onto the bench, and with the napkins left over from the packet they'd devoured the night before, brushed at the mud on his face, in his hair, on his shirt...

Michael stilled her busy little hands.

"I have a change of clothing in my office," he assured her when she tried to swipe at another chunk of mud. And then he stared into her eyes. "Whatever happens today, will happen."

"You've worked so hard for this..."

But he shushed her. "The most important thing in the world to me, right now, is in my arms."

She looked all of seventeen again wearing a shirt several sizes too large, with tangled hair about her flushed face. Her lips were full and lush though. Ah, yes, he could believe they had just made love.

The carriage had sat, unmoving, now for several moments. Michael knew John must be standing outside. "I'll come to you as soon as the vote's over. You're not to worry about anything." He reassured her one last time before kissing her hastily on the lips. He'd not leave her right now for anything, but it was at her insistence they were even here, in London. "Wish me luck?"

Lilly took hold of his face and pulled him into her desperately. "You won't need it." She said against his lips. And then with one last kiss, she released him. "Now, go!" Her eyes were bright, but her smile encouraging. Feeling alive again for the first time in years, Michael leapt out of the carriage and rushed into Parliament.

Chapter Thirty
Déja Vu

Lilly felt disoriented. She knew, since the vote was being held that very morning, that some issues had been resolved, but others had not. Nobody pressed her with the necessity of meeting with Danbury, nor did they mention Glenda's endangered betrothal.

Instead, she'd arrived at her aunt's home to an abundance of hugs and kisses and profuse apologies from her niece. She had barely mentioned that she would appreciate a quick bath before Glenda had run to the kitchen and ordered one made up in Lilly's room. Her aunt had wrapped her in a blanket to cover her scandalous attire from the servants, and then lovingly escorted her upstairs.

"Oh, darling, I am so happy you are not harmed! When we heard Hawthorn had taken you and there had been gunshots, we were hard pressed not to imagine the worst. But you are safe, and everything is going to be fine! I am so happy." And then her very stoic and enduring aunt burst into tears. "Ignore these, my dear. I am just so happy you are not harmed!"

It was Lilly's turn to embrace her aunt. She was the one person in the world who'd never failed her. "I love you, Aunt. I am so sorry to cause you worry." Sitting on Lilly's bed, they held each other and cried softly. Miss Fussy was not to be left out. Frantically wagging her tail, she jumped at Lilly and attempted to lick away every tear. And she would not be dissuaded. Lilly finally hugged her little dog tightly, settling her down. Both women were laughing as Glenda came marching in ahead of the maids and footmen to fill the tub.

"Enough of that," Glenda said.

The women dabbed at their eyes and smiled ruefully at each other.

"Aunt Eleanor, how can you sit by her? Lilly, you smell as if you have been rolling in manure. Come along, Aunt." She dragged Aunt Eleanor toward the door. "Let's leave Lilly to her bath and the soap—plenty of soap!" Holding her fingers as though to plug her nose, she peeked around the door and smiled at Lilly. "I am so very glad you are back, Lilly, even if you do smell like something dragged in from the stables!" And then she left.

Lilly undressed, and Betty slipped into the room just as Lilly slid into the steaming hot water. It felt heavenly as the maid massaged Lilly's favorite hyacinth soap into her hair and then poured more warm water to rinse it out.

When she finally climbed out of the tub, the maid wrapped her in a warm towel and led her to sit by the grate. Any remaining tension left her body as Betty brushed out her hair, using the heat of the fire to dry it.

A nightgown came down over her head, and like a child Lilly raised her arms to slip on the garment. Her wrists were bruised, and there were a few other places where she had managed to acquire some violet-purple marks. Perhaps they were from throwing herself out of a window, climbing down a tree, or sliding off a horse. She couldn't quite remember it all, and that was fine.

She was home.

Before Betty pulled the covers to Lilly's chin, she had drifted off soundly.

****

After accepting many handshakes and backslaps of congratulations, Michael made a quick stop at his town house and then went directly to Lilly's aunt. Jarvis opened the door and graciously allowed him to enter.

Lady Eleanor greeted him with enthusiasm, so much so that she embraced him. She was oh, so grateful to him for returning her niece to her safely. Michael shook his head and declined any credit. "She saved herself, Lady Eleanor. I merely gave her a ride home."

Lady Sheffield tsked admonishingly and then invited him in, ordered a tea tray, and asked him to tell her all the details. Leaving out some of the more alarming parts, Michael relayed what Lilly had told him. It was astonishing, really, how she'd managed to escape down the tree and flee from both Hawthorn and the fire. He knew she was going to feel guilty when learning of the man's demise. News had arrived in town this afternoon that the earl had, in fact, perished in the fire. She would not be insensitive to a man's death—any man's death. Michael remembered how he'd felt when he had first realized he'd killed another human being while in combat. The man he'd shot had been an enemy. If Michael hadn't killed him, he would have been killed instead. It didn't do much to tell oneself this. The guilt remained forever.

Lady Eleanor explained to him Lilly was fast asleep and had been for four hours now. Glancing at his watch, he figured he could use a bath himself. He wasn't tired. He felt energized. He had an idea and was eager to follow it through.

"I'd like to return this evening, Lady Eleanor," Michael said seriously. "I would like to ask for Lilly's hand."

Lady Eleanor nodded and said, "I will tell her you are coming and that she should be prepared to receive you."

****

Awakening and lying in her bed, Lilly took a few moments to remember all that had happened over the last twenty-four hours.

He had come for her.

But what did it mean?

Sighing loudly, she sat up and stretched her aching limbs. No matter what, she would not allow any further self-pity. She had made it through the previous day's events alive!

Nothing—no scandal, no guilt—was ever going to steal her peace again. If, and she was more certain each day, she was carrying Michael's child, she would claim it as a gift.

There was a light knock on the door, and Lilly bid the maid to enter. Betty relayed that her aunt had declared this evening's meal to be a celebration and requested that Lilly dress formally for dinner. After putting her aunt through so much worry the day before, Lilly was more than happy to comply. Rested, but slightly bruised, Lilly allowed Betty to pull her hair up and curl the loose tendrils that fell softly on her neck. Lilly donned the golden dress she had purchased with Lady Natalie. In dainty silk slippers, she descended to the drawing room where her aunt awaited her.

Lady Eleanor was not alone.

Michael rose from the sofa when she entered. He wore black and white evening attire, a perfectly tied cravat, and shoes buffed to a high sheen. It looked as though his butler had attempted to force Michael's hair away from his face with pomade, but a few straight, heavy black locks had already escaped and fell along the side of his face.

A bouquet of peach blossoms lay on the small table beside him.

He strode forward and then bowed deeply over her hand.

Lilly didn't move. She thought she ought to pinch herself in case she was still sleeping and this was a dream.

Aunt Eleanor had risen as well and was standing at the doorway. "I shall leave the two of you alone for a few moments. However," she added, "I will leave the door open, and I will be eavesdropping, of course." She smiled lovingly at Lilly and winked as she left the room.

For despite her words, the door clicked softly behind her.

Lilly rolled her eyes and laughed a little self-consciously. She certainly hoped her aunt was not expecting an announcement from the two of them. Michael was still engaged to Lady Natalie!

How she loved him, though.

He reached into one of his pockets and, still holding her left hand in his, dropped to one knee.

What was he doing? Surely not! Tears stung her eyes. "Oh." Lilly covered her mouth with her free hand.

"Lilly," he began, gazing deeply into her eyes. "I know I am late. I know you waited for me—nine long years ago—only to be disappointed."

She was shaking her head though. No, she didn't want him to blame himself for not coming. He'd had no choice.

"I made the biggest mistake of my life when I let your father take you away from me. I was an idiot, a young fool...but," he continued, "I realize, now, there is nothing more important in my life than you. Making you happy is the only thing in the world that will make my life worthwhile.

"I love you, Lilly Bridge, Lilly Beauchamp. I love the person you were nine years ago, and even more, I love the woman you have become. Will you do me the greatest of honors and become my duchess, my wife?" He lifted a ring to her as his eyes waited for her answer.

"You are free to give yourself to me?" she asked, thinking he would never ask if Lady Natalie would be hurt by his doing so.

"I am," he said, "I am free to love. Free to live." And then, "Will you be mine?"

Lilly nodded as tears flowed down her cheeks. "Yes," she said softly. She didn't know how this had become possible, but she believed in him. If he said he was free, then it was so.

Michael slipped the spectacular ring onto her third finger and then rose. As he wrapped his arms around her, she slid her hands over his chest and around his neck. With his face buried in her neck, his words were slightly muffled. "You needed a hero, and I wasn't there. I was a goddamned duke and didn't do a thing to help you. And then yesterday, again, you needed saving, and I wasn't there to save you. I couldn't even be your hero then."

But Lilly had tilted her head back so she could look into his eyes. Swallowing hard, she placed a finger on his lips. "I don't need a hero." She spoke earnestly, for she would never have him feel guilty for this again. "I don't need a knight in shining armor. I don't even need a duke. I just need the man I love. I just need you, my love." She placed her lips against his. "My Michael."

They held onto each other in wonder. Before they could get into too much trouble, though, the door was flung open, and a group of revelers came bounding in.

Lady Eleanor, Glenda and Joseph, Viscount Danbury, and even Penelope Crone must have all been eavesdropping. Congratulations were in order.

Epilogue

It was a night for celebration. Amazingly, the vote had passed, and Lord Ravensdale had removed his objections to Joseph and Glenda's upcoming nuptials! There was a perfect sweetness to it all; Michael and Lilly were finally reunited.

As they dined in Lady Eleanor's rather large formal dining hall, champagne glasses clinked and toasts were made for Michael and Lilly's engagement and then again for Glenda and Joseph's. For practical purposes, the younger couple were going to make use of Michael and Natalie's wedding plans and take their vows in the grand cathedral on the same day. Natalie had sent a missive to Lilly and assured her *adamantly* that she was most definitely *not* heartbroken. It had been Natalie who had broken the engagement.

I am so happy for you, Lilly! the young woman had written. *I hope someday I shall marry for love too.*

Throughout the meal, everyone asked Lilly and Michael when they might set a date. Lilly secretly smiled inside at this thought. For if she was correct, a hasty marriage would most likely be in store for them. But it wasn't because she had to.

It was because she wanted to. She hugged the thought to herself as Michael—her Michael—laughed at something Danbury said. Catching her watching him, Michael returned her look with tenderness and love.

344

Neither of them had any reason to hide their emotions tonight.

He was hers. She was his. Together, at last, they would have their happy ever after.

At last.

Watch for Lady Natalie's story,
A Lady's Prerogative,
coming Summer 2018.

A word from the author…

Married to the same man for over twenty-five years, I am a mother to three children and two miniature wiener dogs. After owning a business and experiencing considerable success, my husband and I got caught in the financial crisis and lost everything—our business, our home, even our car.

At this point, I put my BA in poly sci to use and took work as a waitress and bartender.

Unwilling to give up on a professional life, I simultaneously went back to college and obtained a degree in energy management.

And then the energy market dropped off.

And then my dog died.

I can only be grateful for this series of unfortunate events, for, with nothing to lose and completely demoralized, I sat down and began to write the romance novels which had until then existed only in my imagination.

I am happy to have found my place in life.

Finally.

Follow me on Facebook at
https://www.facebook.com/HappyWritingGirl
and
sign up for my newsletter at www.annabelleanders.com